Water Signs

Praise for the Mysteries of Janet Dawson

"Rail enthusiasts will welcome this light mystery full of information about train travel of an earlier era."

—*Publishers Weekly* [on *Death Deals a Hand*]

"Jill is a charming and intelligent heroine... atmospheric descriptions of this chapter in the 21-year reign of the *Zephyr*, whose famous Vista-Dome cars delighted passengers with unparalleled views."

—*Kirkus Reviews*

"Dawson provides rich detail about the many different passengers... I found it interesting and enjoyable. So take a trip back to 1953 and travel the *California Zephyr* at a time when the porters were subject to blatant racism, people still remembered Prohibition, and riding the train was still considered romantic, in part because it was."

—*Reviewing the Evidence*

"Dawson knows how to blend real history and real crime into an intriguing mystery about a missing man and the people, and the land, he loves."

—*Mystery Scene* [on *Cold Trail*]

"Exciting... Dawson keeps the suspense high as Jeri seeks to find her brother before it's too late."

—*Publishers Weekly*

Mystery fiction by Janet Dawson

THE JERI HOWARD MYSTERY SERIES
Kindred Crimes
Till the Old Men Die
Take a Number
Don't Turn Your Back on the Ocean
Nobody's Child
A Credible Threat
Witness to Evil
Where the Bodies Are Buried
A Killing at the Track
Bit Player
Cold Trail
Water Signs

SHORT STORIES
Scam and Eggs

SUSPENSE FICTION
What You Wish For

CALIFORNIA ZEPHYR SERIES
Death Rides the Zephyr
Death Deals a Hand

Water Signs

A JERI HOWARD MYSTERY

Janet Dawson

Perseverance Press / John Daniel & Company
Palo Alto / McKinleyville, California, 2017

A Perseverance Press Book
Published by John Daniel & Company
A division of Daniel & Daniel, Publishers, Inc.
Post Office Box 2790
McKinleyville, California 95519
www.danielpublishing.com ce

Distributed by SCB Distributors (800) 729-6423

Book design by Eric Larson, Studio E Books
www.studio-e-books.com

Cover photo: William Fawcett/fotoVoyager/iStockphoto

10 9 8 7 6 5 4 3 2 1

LIBRARY OF CONGRESS CATALOGING-IN-PUBLICATION DATA
Names: Dawson, Janet, author.
Title: Water signs : a Jeri Howard mystery / by Janet Dawson.
Description: McKinleyville, California : John Daniel & Company, 2017.
Identifiers: LCCN 2016046130 | ISBN 9781564745866 (paperback : alk. paper)
Subjects: LCSH: Howard, Jeri (Fictitious character)—Fiction. | Women private investigators—California, Northern—Fiction. | Murder—Investigation—Fiction. | GSAFD: Mystery fiction.
Classification: LCC PS3554.A949 W38 2017 | DDC 813/.54—dc23
LC record available at https://lccn.loc.gov/2016046130

To those who work to preserve
San Francisco Bay and the California coastline

I am grateful for the assistance of Roger Cunningham, who graciously took me out on the Estuary in his boat *Selkie*, so I could look at the waterfront from the water. I also appreciate the input of Heather Hood, my former coworker at UC Berkeley's Institute of Urban and Regional Development, for information on how developments are approved and built.

I also wish to thank John and Susan Daniel of Perseverance Press, for publishing my books; Meredith Phillips, editor extraordinaire; and Eric Larson of Studio E Books for his excellent book design.

Water Signs

Chapter One

IT WAS a season for funerals.

I don't like funerals. They make me sad.

I'd been to three of them in the past six weeks. Uncle Dom was the first. He was my great-uncle, on my mother's side of the family. Dominic Ravella was a salty old fisherman who spent his whole life in Monterey, fishing the waters of the beautiful bay and the restless Pacific Ocean. After he retired, he spent his days playing bocce at the courts near the old Customs House. He was well into his nineties when age and a life well lived caught up with him in late September.

The funeral was at St. Angela Merici Catholic Church on Lighthouse Avenue in Pacific Grove. The church was crowded, standing room only. A lot of those people were related to Uncle Dom, by blood or marriage. After the funeral, we went back to the house he'd shared with Aunt Teresa, who had been his high school sweetheart. People filled the house and the backyard. We ate, drank wine, and told stories as the sun descended, turning Monterey Bay into shimmering gold.

Norm Gerrity was the second. Norm was a fellow private investigator who'd started his working life as a cop in Boston, putting in thirty years on the force. He had moved to San Jose after his wife died, to be closer to his daughter and her family. Wrangling grandkids only went so far, though. "Once a cop, always a cop," he told me in that Boston accent. So he had obtained his California PI's license and worked out of his home.

Norm and I had connected during a case several years earlier and friendship grew out of that. I knew I could count on Norm and his insight. I also knew he was getting on in years. At some point he'd mentioned that his daughter had surprised him with a seventy-fifth birthday party. In early October, I thought about him, realizing I hadn't heard from him in a while. I called and got his voice mail. I left a message, hoping he'd check in with me. The next day, his daughter returned my call, telling me Norm had just died, due to a bout with pneumonia. She told me when and where the services would be held. I was there to pay my respects.

The third funeral, which took place in the second week of October, was the hardest of all.

Errol Seville was my mentor. He was the private investigator who'd zeroed in on me when I was working at a law firm in Oakland. He thought I'd make a good operative, so he'd brought me into his own agency. I worked for Errol for several years after I'd obtained my own PI's license. He was a superb investigator, an excellent teacher, a man with a mordant sense of humor.

Then Errol had a heart attack, his second. He closed his agency and retired. He and his wife Minna went to Carmel, where they had a house. I visited him when I could. He was enjoying his retirement. The last time I saw him, he had just celebrated his eighty-third birthday. Errol being Errol, he joked about the odds of making it to ninety.

With his ticker, the odds were against him. The third heart attack was fatal. And once again I went to a funeral.

As October moved inexorably toward November, I wasn't in the mood to hear that anyone else I knew was dead.

That's when Madison Brady showed up in my Oakland office. Best laid plans, right?

Chapter Two

MADISON BRADY had the same intense blue eyes as her father, piercing me now with her gaze as she leaned forward and put her hands on my desk.
I was surprised to learn that Calvin Brady had a daughter in her twenties, and even more surprised when she showed up in my office on Tuesday morning. Cal was an acquaintance, a former colleague, back in the day when I worked for Errol.

Cal had told his daughter something different.

"He said you were a friend." Madison tugged at the collar of her shirt, a black-and-red checked flannel worn over a pair of tight black jeans. "That's why I'm here. I don't know who else to turn to. The cops don't seem to be interested in the truth. Dad was murdered. I just know it. I want you to find out who killed him."

I was still processing the news that Cal had died. Truth be told, I didn't know much about his personal life. We had worked together for less than a year. As coworkers, we'd kept our private lives separate from our work lives.

Saying Cal Brady and I were friends was a stretch.

I didn't correct Madison's assumption. Instead I leaned back in my office chair. "I didn't know Cal was dead. I saw him last week, at Errol Seville's memorial service in Carmel. Tell me what happened. And why the police aren't interested."

She frowned and fingered one of the gold hoops she wore in

her earlobes. "Dad's body was found in the Estuary on Sunday morning. People are saying Dad was drinking on the job and he must have fallen into the water and drowned. That's total nonsense. But I'm afraid the police might believe it." She stopped and took a deep breath, then let it out with a frustrated sigh. "It can't be true. Dad wasn't drinking anymore. He was sober. He hadn't had a drink in over three years. Believe me when I say that."

I didn't say anything. I considered what she was telling me now, and what Cal had told me the week before. I spoke with him after the memorial service, when those of us who had attended gathered at the Sunset Center in Carmel, raising glasses and sharing anecdotes about Errol. I was drinking Chardonnay. Cal sipped from a bottle of sparkling water. He made a point of telling me he was sober now. That was a good thing. Because Cal's alcoholism was the reason he had been fired from the Seville Agency.

"Where was your father working?" I asked.

"Dad was a security guard. He worked for a company here in Oakland, called Manville Security. He'd been with them three years or more. Since last spring he had been working at a construction site for a development that's being built on the waterfront. His schedule varied between days and nights. Saturday he was on the night shift, eleven at night till seven in the morning."

"Which development? Brooklyn Basin?"

Madison shook her head. "Brooklyn's the big one. Dad was working on a smaller site nearby. It's called the Cardoza project."

I nodded. Both projects were in the process of transforming stretches of the Oakland waterfront south of Jack London Square.

A security guard. Cal hadn't mentioned any details about his employment when I'd seen him at Errol's funeral. All he said was that he was living and working in Oakland. We hadn't actually talked that much. The focus of what conversation we did have was Errol, our late boss.

Alcoholics do go off the wagon from time to time, I thought. Maybe Madison Brady was closing her eyes to reality.

But…Cal had been quite sincere and even proud when he told me he was sober. I believed him then. I believed him now.

"He would have gone to work just before eleven on Saturday night," Madison said now. "To relieve the guard who was working the shift from three in the afternoon. Dad was alive at one-thirty in the morning. He sent me a text message."

She took an iPhone from her pocket and swiped her fingers across the screen. Then she put in a four-digit code and pressed the Text Message icon in the upper left corner. She shoved the phone across my desk. I picked it up and read the message she referred to—a quick "Luv U, Dad" sent at 1:30 A.M. She had texted back, "Luv U 2." There were no further texts from Cal.

"We texted a lot," she said. "He usually sent me a text to let me know he was home from work. And he would have that day. We were planning to have brunch Sunday, around noon. But I didn't hear from him. Then I got the call—"

She stopped. Tears spilled from her eyes. She brushed them away, fighting down her emotions.

I passed the iPhone back to her and she put it into her pocket. "Has an autopsy been done?"

Cal's body had been found on Sunday morning. It was Tuesday. It might be too early for the postmortem. It would depend on how busy the coroner's office was. The autopsy would reveal whether Cal had a blood alcohol content, or anything else in his system.

"I don't know," Madison said. "It's only been two days. I haven't heard about any results. But the cops seem to buy the story that Dad was drunk. At least the man did. The woman was more open-minded. I was over at the Oakland Police Department earlier today. The cops told me the people working at the construction site found liquor bottles several times after Dad had worked the night shift. Then two weeks ago, the week before Dad went to that funeral, he was coming off the night shift and somebody there at the site said he was drunk and threatened to fire him. That's totally bogus. Dad wouldn't do that. It meant so much to him to have a good steady job after going through treatment and all those AA meetings. I'm telling you, he was sober."

She leaned closer, an anxious look in her eyes. "Will you help me?"

"I'll look into it," I said. "Who are the officers involved?"

Madison bent down, reaching for the blue backpack at her feet. She unzipped the top, rummaged through the contents and produced a wallet. She opened it and took out a business card. "The woman is Detective Portillo."

"I know her. I'll call and see what I can find out."

"I'll pay you," Madison said, determination written on her face. She had told me she was a graduate student at the University of California. I figured she couldn't afford my usual retainer.

I waved my hand. "Let's just say for now I'm looking into it, informally. Because…your dad was a friend."

Chapter Three

I SHOULD HAVE called him back.
After Madison Brady left my office, I turned to the coffee-maker on the credenza near my desk and poured myself a mug of strong dark coffee. Then I sat back in my chair, both hands circling the mug as I stared at nothing in particular.

I should have called him back. But I hadn't.

When we'd talked the day of the memorial service, Cal said, "I'll call you. There's something I'd like to discuss with you. Maybe we can get together for coffee."

"Sure." I gave him my card and told him to call me any time.

A few days after the service in Carmel, Cal Brady left a voice mail message on my office phone. He didn't say why he had phoned, just that he'd like to talk.

I didn't return the call. Now I wished I had.

To be fair to myself, I was quite busy the week after the service, juggling several investigations. The day that Cal left the message, I was at the Alameda County Courthouse, giving testimony in a superior court civil case. Returning Cal's phone call had slipped through the cracks. The slip of paper on which I'd written his number got buried on my desk.

I hadn't given Cal's message another thought. Until now.

Why had Cal phoned me? Was it just to propose a coffee date? But he'd said there was something he wanted to discuss with me.

What? Was that something work-related? Had this information gotten him killed?

Sipping coffee, I took time out from my guilt trip and replayed that last conversation with Cal, in Carmel, where we'd all raised our glasses to Errol's memory.

When Cal walked up to me and said hello, I didn't recognize him. He was six or seven years older than I was, and in the years since I'd seen him, he had visibly aged. His hair, once light brown, was liberally salted with gray. His face was mapped with wrinkles that spoke of hard times in the past. But his eyes were clear, the same piercing blue, and that day they'd held a glint of good spirits and self-deprecating humor.

Our connection was Errol Seville, the man whose life we were celebrating. After graduating from the University of California in Berkeley with my history degree, I didn't want to teach. I'd worked a variety of jobs to pay the bills and keep a roof over my head while I figured out what I wanted to do with my life. I wound up working as a legal secretary for several years, at law firms in San Francisco and Oakland. Then I took classes and got a paralegal certificate.

I was working at a law firm in Oakland when I met Errol, the private investigator who was involved in one of the firm's cases. With a twinkle in his eye and his considerable charm, Errol lured me away from the world of legal briefs and depositions, promising a more challenging and satisfying career, a way to use my skills.

Errol had an office on Broadway in Oakland, a couple of blocks below Grand Avenue. The neighborhood was called Uptown, and its boundaries were hazy. Uptown was trendy now, with all sorts of restaurants and bars, but at the time I'd worked for the Seville Agency, our stretch of Broadway was decidedly down-at-heels. That made for a less-expensive rent, Errol once told me, with his usual wry smile. I was one of several operatives at the agency. Errol had mentored a lot of people in his long career as a private investigator, and in the years I worked for the Seville Agency, I saw coworkers come and go. Some left because they weren't suited to the work, others to go on to other jobs, other fields. Some, like Cal, had been fired.

Before coming to work for Errol, Cal had been an officer in the Navy. But he hadn't stayed in the service for the whole twenty-year career. Instead he'd left the Navy and moved to the Bay Area. In addition to working for Errol, Cal took classes at California State University in Hayward, where my father taught history. He, too, was trying to figure out what he wanted to do with the rest of his life.

Cal was tall and lanky, good-looking in a rakish way. He was pleasant enough and sometimes showed a quirky sense of humor. Along with the other operatives at the agency, we would sometimes go out for a beer after work.

That's when I realized Cal had a drinking problem. I usually went home after one beer. He didn't. According to some of my coworkers, Cal had a habit of closing down the bar before he headed home. More than once I'd heard that he was weaving as he walked down the sidewalk. Fortunately his apartment was somewhere near the office.

Cal was a high-functioning alcoholic, good about hiding his consumption while he was working. But he was on a downhill slide and he couldn't hide it forever. Then came the day when he botched a surveillance operation because he was drinking, the vodka hidden in a water bottle. Errol fired him. He also told Cal to get help.

Evidently Cal had. I didn't know the particulars of his climb out of the bottle. Until I ran into him at the memorial service, I hadn't seen him since the day he lost his job with the Seville Agency.

What had Cal told me, beyond assuring me that he was now sober? I went back over our conversation, brief as it was. He said he was working in Oakland. But he hadn't told me where, or what sort of job. He congratulated me on my success as a private investigator, saying he'd read about me in the paper, in conjunction with a case I'd worked on earlier this year.

Then he took a swig from his sparkling water and added, "I always enjoyed investigative work. One of these days I'll get back to it."

I hadn't called him back, telling myself I might phone him

later. Now I wondered if he'd had a more urgent reason for contacting me. According to his daughter, Cal had misgivings about something that had been going on at his job site. He had seemed troubled a week or so before Errol's memorial service, she added. Something was going on, he said, and he was looking into it. He hadn't shared the particulars with her.

What if Cal had been trying to share that information with me? Was that what he had wanted to discuss?

He'd indicated that he'd like to get back into investigative work. What if he had? I pondered that for a moment. If something was off-kilter at Cal's job site, would he have investigated, digging into it the way he would have as an operative of the agency? What if his unofficial probing got him killed?

What if he had started drinking again, and his daughter was understandably unable to accept the fact?

A lot of "what ifs." These scenarios were pure speculation on my part. That wouldn't get me very far. I needed facts.

I set my coffee mug on the desk and picked up the phone, calling the Oakland Police Department's Homicide Section. Detective Portillo was not in the office. I left a message asking her to call me.

I reached for the paperweight on my desk. It was shaped like a cresting ocean wave, made of deep blue glass curling over on itself, topped with a froth of white glass. Affixed to the bottom was an engraved brass plate reading SCORPIO—WATER SIGN. I was born in late October, so that makes me a Scorpio, one of the three astrological signs—the others are Cancer and Pisces—associated with the element of water. According to the words on the plate, those born under water signs are perceptive and good at spotting clues.

Scorpio is the perfect sign for a private investigator. That's what my friend Cassie told me when she'd presented me with the paperweight, last year on my birthday.

The paperweight was beautiful and I often found myself touching the curved wave at the top, a talisman while I thought. Now I stroked the blue glass and moved the weight to one side, picking up the letter I'd received several weeks earlier.

I leased a small office in a building on Franklin Street in

downtown Oakland, near Chinatown. The term of my lease was up at the end of January and the building owner was taking that opportunity to offer a new lease at a higher price. The increased sum made me wince. Paying more for my office would make considerable inroads into my profit margin, which was narrow to begin with. To add to my financial worries, the nearby lot where I paid a monthly fee to park my car had also slapped me with an increase.

I had been contemplating my alternatives, which included finding a place that cost less. One of my colleagues, a private investigator named Rita Lydecker, had recently given up her office in downtown San Rafael, over in Marin County. Now she operated out of a spare bedroom in her house.

I could do that. Not out of a spare room, but there was an apartment over my garage, a studio that I'd rented out for the past few years. My tenant, a young woman named Darcy Stefano, had graduated from the university last spring. She was currently working at an internship in San Francisco. Darcy was leaving, though. After the first of the year, she was starting a graduate program at the Massachusetts Institute of Technology. She had already given notice that she was planning to move out of the apartment at the end of November. She would stay with her grandmother in San Francisco through the holidays, then head for Massachusetts in January.

Come December, my studio apartment would be empty. I could easily rent it out again. My Rockridge neighborhood was near the border between Oakland and Berkeley. There were plenty of students looking for places to live. My house on Chabot Avenue was just a few blocks from College Avenue and the AC Transit bus that ran from Oakland to Berkeley, with several stops at the south side of campus.

Or I could use the apartment as an office.

But there were drawbacks to working out of my home, even if it was the garage apartment. I needed to check and see if there were any zoning issues that would factor into such a decision. Besides, given a choice, I'd rather keep my personal life—and space—separate from my work. Did I really want clients parked at the curb in front of my house in a residential neighborhood? There were good reasons I'd chosen to locate my business in downtown Oakland, including the building's close proximity to the police department and the Alameda County Courthouse.

I wondered what Cassie planned to do. My friend's law firm—Alwin, Taylor and Chao—was located in this building, just down the hall from my office. Cassie was still on maternity leave after the birth of her son in late August. She hadn't decided when she was coming back to the office but I knew she was working from home in addition to bonding with her new baby. I knew from talking with her partner Mike Chao that the firm had received a similar letter to mine, as had the other tenants in the building.

I had plans to visit Cassie on Saturday. I would talk with her then, to find out what she and her partners planned to do.

In the meantime, I had other matters demanding my attention. I returned phone calls, answered emails and set up appointments, with existing clients and potential clients. I had recently been hired to track down several witnesses to a serious car accident that took place here in Oakland. My search for the witnesses had taken me all over the Bay Area, up to Richmond in Contra Costa County, across the Carquinez Bridge to Vallejo in Solano County, then out to Livermore in the eastern part of Alameda County. I had eventually talked with all the witnesses, taking statements. Now I wrote a report for my client, who worked with the insurance company representing the person who was injured in the accident.

Around noon I looked at the clock. My stomach told me I needed lunch. I shut down my computer and locked the office, heading downstairs.

Chapter Four

~~~~~~~~~~

THE OCTOBER DAY was sunny and clear, with a slight breeze in the cloudless blue sky. It was shirtsleeve weather, the temperature in the seventies. After several years of drought, we needed rain, and I hoped we'd have a rainy winter. A gust of wind blew leaves and litter over the pavement.

I strolled down the sidewalk. At the corner of Franklin and Eleventh Streets, I stepped off the curb into the crosswalk. As I did so, I felt an annoying twinge in my left knee. I had twisted it a couple of weeks ago while hiking in the coast redwoods with my friend Dan Westbrook, up at Redwood Regional Park in the hills to the east of Oakland. Ice and ibuprofen had helped, but the knee still gave me some pain now and then, particularly if I stepped wrong.

The knee, and my approaching birthday, reminded me that I wasn't getting any younger. It's the nature of my job that I spend a lot of my time at my desk, or sitting in meetings. That's why I walked to a lot of places. Hiking with Dan, and the t'ai chi class I attended a couple of times a week, kept me moving, which was all to the good.

Midway down Eleventh Street, I entered a deli I liked. I debated getting my usual, pastrami on rye, and opted instead for bacon, lettuce, tomato and avocado on whole wheat. After paying for lunch, I turned to leave and came face-to-face with a customer who had just walked into the deli. The woman in gray slacks and blue jacket had short dark hair combed back from her face, falling just below her ears. We had something in common, an Oakland police detective named Sid Vernon. Sid was my ex-husband and the woman, Detective Grace Portillo, now lived with him.

"Hi, Grace," I said.

She looked as startled to see me as I did her. Whenever we met, it felt a bit awkward.

"Hello, Jeri."

"How's Sid?"

"Better. He's going back to work in a few weeks, in Robbery."

She didn't say "Thank goodness," but I was willing to bet she was thinking it. Sid was still recuperating from the knee replacement surgery he'd had last summer. He wasn't the best patient and the last time I'd visited him, he was grumpy and growling about his physical therapy appointments and his hiatus from work. I think he was concerned about being put out to pasture.

Grace studied the menu board above the counter, then spoke to the woman behind the deli counter. "I'll have turkey on whole wheat. Mayo and mustard, but no onions, please."

I'd met Grace several years ago, while working on an investigation that involved one of Sid's cases. Sid had worked Homicide for many years. He was in his fifties, more than a decade older than me. I was in my late thirties and I figured Grace was about the same age. She had a teenage son by her first marriage. She, the boy and Sid now shared his house in the Temescal section of Oakland. I'd heard rumors that they were getting married, eventually.

I knew Sid was itching to get back to work, no matter what assignment. Grace had recently transferred to Homicide.

"I left a message at your office."

"Haven't been back there yet." She paid for her sandwich and stepped away from the counter, paper bag in hand. "What's up? Why did you call?"

"Calvin Brady. His body was found at Clinton Basin on Sunday morning."

Her eyes narrowed. "How did you know that?"

"His daughter came to see me. She claims he was murdered."

"That's what she told me and my partner. Those were the first words out of her mouth. Seems like she's quick off the mark to bring in a private eye."

"I knew Cal Brady. That's why she came to see me."

She took a step toward the door. "I've got to get back to the office."

"I'll walk with you."

Grace looked as though she was deciding whether to play this one close to the chest or give me some information. She nodded. "Okay."

We left the deli and headed up Eleventh Street toward Broadway. The Oakland Police Department was four blocks away, on Seventh Street.

"How did you know Brady?" Grace asked.

"We worked together at the Seville Agency."

"He was a private eye? What was he doing working as a security guard on a construction site down on the waterfront?"

"He had a drinking problem. It got him fired. That was a long time ago. I saw him a week ago, at Errol Seville's memorial service. Cal told me he was sober."

"Maybe he fell off the wagon," Grace said.

We stopped and waited for a walk signal at the corner. "Maybe he did. Or not. For what it's worth, I think he was telling me the truth."

"All it takes is one slip." She frowned when she said it. I wondered if she was speaking from personal experience, whether someone in her life had been an alcoholic.

The light turned green. We stepped into the crosswalk. "What can you tell me?"

"We'll know more after the autopsy," she said. "The coroner's backed up so it could be a few days. The body was found about nine o'clock Sunday morning, washed up on shore at Clinton Basin, which is south of the Fifth Avenue Marina. A guy who has a boat at the marina was walking his dog. He says the dog ran ahead to investigate and the guy followed. He spotted the body and called nine-one-one. My partner and I responded, and so did the department boat, which is tied up at Jack London Square. The body was tangled up in line—that's what the boating types call rope—and caught on a fence that extends into the water. When the body was out of the water, we looked it over and then it was transported to the medical examiner's office."

"Was there any trauma?"

The fact that Grace didn't answer my question right away told me there was. Finally she nodded. "Some, around the head and upper torso. Which could be explained by the body being hit by a boat or bumping against pilings. We'll find out when we get the coroner's report."

Trauma to the head could mean Cal Brady had been struck before going into the water.

"Which security company was Cal working for?" I asked.

"Manville. It's a small company here in Oakland. Brady was wearing a shirt with a logo, so we called the agency. It was Sunday, but they have someone on the phones twenty-four/seven. The operator got hold of Gary Manville, Brady's boss. As it turns out, the daytime guard, the one who was supposed to relieve Brady Sunday morning, had already called Manville to tell him Brady was missing. Brady's car was still at the construction site. But no keys. They were probably on him. When we called Manville, he was already at the work site, with the guard. My partner and I went down there, talked with them. Manville gave us the contact information for Madison Brady. We went back to the site again on Monday, when there were more people there."

"What did they tell you?"

Grace looked at me as we stopped for another red light. "Several employees told us that Brady had been reprimanded a couple of weeks ago, because he appeared to be intoxicated."

"Was Manville one of those people?"

"No," she said as the light turned green. "Manville avoided the question. I got the impression he really didn't want to talk about it. It was the site manager, the guy who works for the construction company, who was really vocal about it. He said Brady had been stumbling around on the day in question, either drunk or hung over. He's the one who reamed out Brady and threatened to have him fired."

"What construction company? And what's the site manager's name?"

"Hasseltine Construction. The manager's name is Brice—" She stopped as her cell phone rang. She reached in her pocket and punched a button, holding the phone to her ear. "Portillo. Yeah, I'm right outside." She ended the call and quickened her pace. "I've got to go, Jeri."

She waved at me as she jogged across Seventh Street and entered the Oakland Police Department headquarters building at the corner of Broadway and Seventh Street.

I turned and retraced my steps, back to my office near Eleventh and Franklin. I wanted to talk with Gary Manville as soon as possible. I also wanted to interview the site manager from Hasseltine Construction, Brice something-or-other. I should be able to find his name.

I ate my lunch at my desk while I returned several phone calls and set up an appointment with a prospective client. After I finished my sandwich, I went to my Internet browser.

The Bureau of Security and Investigative Services is part of the California Department of Consumer Affairs. The bureau is responsible for registering guards who are employed by licensed private patrol operators or security employers.

To become a security guard in California, the applicant must go through an initial eight hours of training and pass an exam. Only then can he, or she, get a job. To be registered, and obtain what's called a "guard card," requires an additional thirty-two hours of training, as well as a criminal history background check by the Federal Bureau of Investigation and the Department of Justice. The guard must also complete eight hours of continuing training each year and carry the "guard card" while on duty. Carrying firearms, tear gas or a baton require additional permits. The guard's registration must be renewed every two years.

The bureau's website has a search function, allowing me to

check registrations. I typed in Calvin Brady's first and last names and clicked on Alameda County. When Cal's name popped up, I saw that he had a valid guard/patrolperson registration, issued three years ago in Oakland. He had a baton permit, but no others. I did a search for Gary Manville and discovered that he also had a "guard card," issued five years ago, with all three permits.

The Manville Security website told me the company provided security for a variety of customers, focusing on commercial rather than residential services, guarding office buildings, warehouses and construction sites. The website had a contact form for job quotes, but it also listed an office with an address on Telegraph Avenue near Twenty-fifth Street, north of the downtown area. I did a search on the company and found it was registered as a corporation in the state of California five years ago, with one principal, Gary Manville. Judging from the testimonials on the website, Manville had done a good job of building his clientele in that short time period.

Manville was at the top of my list of people to talk with. When I called the firm's office, I was told he was out, visiting a job site. I had a hunch which one.

I closed and locked my office. Downstairs I exited the building and walked to the nearby lot where I parked my Toyota. I drove out of the lot, heading for Broadway and the Oakland waterfront.

Chapter Five

≈≈≈≈≈≈≈≈≈≈

OAKLAND IS a place shaped by water. The city was incorporated in 1852. That same year, large shipping wharves were built along the Estuary, the strait that separates Oakland from Alameda, the island city where I grew up. Alameda used to be a peninsula. In 1901, a shipping channel was cut through the narrow strip of land connecting Oakland and Alameda, creating the Tidal Canal that connected the Estuary with San Leandro Bay to the south.

The transcontinental railroad was completed in 1869, with Oakland as its terminus, providing the important link between water and rail transportation. The Estuary, originally two feet deep at low tide, was dredged and deepened many times over the years to accommodate larger ships.

In the early days, shipbuilding and ship repair facilities proliferated along the waterfront, providing jobs for Oakland's workers. Fishermen from Alaska wintered in Alameda and the shore was lined with cargo wharves. Oakland was the first major port on the Pacific Coast to build terminals for container ships. Now it's the fifth busiest container port in the United States. The waterfront is lined with container terminals and huge cranes that look like weird creatures rising against the sky. The cranes loom over the enormous container ships that sometimes block the view as they move slowly on the Estuary, dwarfing sailboats and ferries.

The Outer Harbor was at the foot of the Bay Bridge, near the now-closed Oakland Army Base. The Middle Harbor was the location of the Oakland Mole, the big train shed where ferries from San Francisco landed passengers to board long distance trains like the *California Zephyr.* The Mole is gone now, razed to the ground, memorialized by markers in what is now a wildlife preserve for shore and water birds and a park with picnic tables and walking paths.

The Inner Harbor was on the Estuary itself. Jack London Square, named after the writer who had once plied the waterfront as an oyster pirate, was built in the area of the old waterfront and produce district, where wharves once stood. Now shops and restaurants mix with the Port of Oakland's offices on Water Street. The railroad tracks along Third Street had been removed, the street repaved.

There were still railroad tracks along the Embarcadero. This was one of California's busiest rail corridors. The Amtrak station was located at the foot of Alice Street, between Second and the Embarcadero, and the vast Union Pacific rail yard was just north of here, feeding into the port. Constant rail traffic, both passenger and freight, was the reason two pedestrian bridges had been built over the tracks. In years past, before the bridges had been built, passing trains could tie up foot traffic, and I'd seen a few foolhardy souls climb through stopped trains, a recipe for death or serious injury should the train start again. A train was a huge piece of machinery and should be treated with caution.

At the corner of Broadway and the Embarcadero, I turned left, driving parallel to the tracks. As I neared the station, a *Capitol Corridor* train stood at the platform. The whistle blew and bells clanged as the crossing arms went down, barricading the tracks on Oak Street, where it intersected with the Embarcadero. The train moved out of the station, heading south.

I drove along the Embarcadero, past apartments, office buildings, and a restaurant. To my left, on the other side of the tracks, was a storage facility. Beyond this was a multi-story tower used by the Oakland Fire Department for firefighter training. I passed the entrance to Estuary Park, site of the Oakland Aquatic Center, and approached the two-lane bridge that spanned the Lake Merritt Channel, which led to the tidal Lake Merritt near downtown Oakland.

Plans were in the works to reinvigorate Lake Merritt and the channel. The lake had been a slough before nineteenth-century modifications made it the body of water it was today. One of the proposals I'd read about was turning the channel into a park where people could walk on either side of the waterway, all the way from the lake to the Estuary. Small boats would also be able to move between the waterways.

It would be great if that happened, because the current state of the channel was, frankly, a mess. The south shore of the channel had turned into a large homeless encampment. I counted seven tents and a couple of makeshift cabins that had been cobbled together from plywood and discarded lumber, all of these surrounded by shopping carts and cardboard boxes, even a few bicycles. Trash dumping was a problem all over Oakland. People left furniture and appliance discards in places like this. Or some fly-by-night hauler would get paid to dispose of an old sofa or television set, and simply dump it out the back of a truck onto a street.

Whether the trash had been discarded by the homeless or the homed, the channel shore was an eyesore, a dump, with junk stretching all the way from the road to the railroad tracks, where a railway bridge crossed the channel.

On the other side of the bridge, the elevated portion of Interstate 880 loomed high above. There was a stop sign at the intersection of the Embarcadero and Fifth Avenue. I heard clanging bells and glanced to my left in time to see the crossing arms come down on either side of the railroad tracks that crossed Fifth under the freeway. A train horn blew its warning signal. A northbound Union Pacific freight, its cars covered with graffiti, lumbered by, heading for the Port of Oakland terminals on the other side of Jack London Square.

To my right, the street was narrow, crowded with buildings that were home to small businesses and artists' studios. Fifth Avenue dead-ended a block away, with a marina on the water.

I continued through the intersection, heading down the Embarcadero. The waterfront in this area was for the most part an expanse of industrial acreage that had once been used for the maritime industry—piers, warehouses, and shipyards. All the shipyards were gone, and so were most of the warehouses. The piers remained, in varying states of disrepair. In some cases, the ground was dirt, gravel, weeds or deteriorating pavement.

South of Fifth Avenue, construction had started on the high-profile Brooklyn Basin development. Through the chain-link fence surrounding the property, I saw earthmovers digging up concrete. The project encompassed some seventy acres that had once been the property of the Port of Oakland, signed over a few years ago to the developers. Most of them were local, but recently a Chinese investment firm had joined the scheme.

Brooklyn Basin would be a high-density development, with high-rise and mid-rise apartment blocks providing 3,100 condos and apartments, as well as office and retail space, marinas and parks. There were supposed to be open spaces and trails, as well, with access to the Estuary. This venture would bring major change to the city's waterfront.

The developers promised all of this construction would benefit the city, providing jobs as well as improving the neighborhood. As a longtime Oakland resident, I was enough of a cynic to have my doubts.

The buildings would dwarf the structures on the privately owned land at Fifth Avenue. I knew from past news stories that the residents were concerned about the changes.

Change seemed to be the constant in Oakland these days.

The names of Clinton Basin, a small inlet south of Fifth Avenue, and Brooklyn Basin, the large section of the Inner Harbor, were echoes of the past. For a few years in the nineteenth century, much of what was now East Oakland had been a town called Brooklyn. There was another town called Clinton. Both communities had been annexed by Oakland but their names lived on in maps and navigational charts.

The current Brooklyn Basin development had been proposed

a number of years ago. At that time it had been called the Oak to Ninth Project, because the land involved stretched between Oak Street, at the south end of Jack London Square, all the way to the old Ninth Avenue Terminal. From what I'd read about the project, it had gone through the usual fits and starts, from conception through the design and approval stages.

The controversy surrounding Brooklyn Basin had not abated, though. According to another article I'd found on the Internet, the developers were also supposed to restore some marsh habitat but somehow that had gone by the wayside. The waterfront activists who had opposed the project, favoring open space instead, were not happy about this latest problem.

The Cardoza project was much smaller in size and scope, and the land was privately owned. Construction had started in the spring of this year, and the project was farther along than Brooklyn Basin.

I drove past Tenth Avenue, where a hotel had been built, one of several along this stretch of the Embarcadero, catering to travelers who don't care that their accommodations front on a busy, noisy freeway. To be fair, the place backed up to the water, with a view of the Estuary. Behind the hotel and other businesses was a public access shoreline path. Here and there on the Embarcadero, travelers of another sort had parked down-at-heels campers and RVs, living in them, one step above the homeless people who had pitched their tents near the Lake Merritt Channel.

South of the hotel was a rectangular building with a strip of businesses, retail on the first floor and offices on the second. At the south end a familiar green-and-white sign signaled the location of a Starbucks. At the side of the building, a path led back to several marina docks on the water. The Cardoza property was another twenty or thirty yards down the Embarcadero, a long strip of land. It looked across the Estuary to Coast Guard Island, a hundred-acre island in the middle of Brooklyn Basin, constructed from dredging spoils back in 1916. Both Oakland and Alameda had claimed the island, which a court awarded to Alameda. In 1934, Alameda deeded the island to the Coast Guard, for a base and a customs station.

The construction site was roughly rectangular, somewhat larger than a football field, perhaps an acre and a half to two acres. I knew from years of driving along the Embarcadero that this site, or part of it, had once contained several warehouses. If memory served, a few years ago, there had been a marine supply retailer located here, selling all sorts of gear for boats, from boat parts to outboard motors to oars, trailers to haul boats, even clothing and shoes.

The warehouses and the store were gone, the ground leveled. In back of the former store site, two docks remained, stretching like fingers into the Estuary. The building that would be constructed on the site was slated to be retail space on the ground floor, with apartments on the upper levels. Construction was in the early stages.

A high chain-link fence with a wide gate fronted on the Embarcadero, about twenty feet from where I parked. A sign on the fence told me construction was being done by the Cardoza Development Corporation. A security guard stood near the gate. On the site itself, I counted eighteen workers, all men, wearing yellow hard hats, most of them clustered just this side of a large rectangular excavation. They were getting ready to pour walls, judging from the network of braced wooden forms lining the perimeter of the foundation, and the two cement mixer trucks parked on the long side of the rectangle that faced the Embarcadero.

A white pickup truck with HASSELTINE CONSTRUCTION painted in green on the passenger-side door passed my Toyota. The driver was broad-shouldered, with shaggy light brown hair. The truck pulled up to the gate and the security guard waved the driver on. The truck pulled onto the site and headed toward a trailer near a row of portable toilets. The truck parked on the other side of the trailer, next to several other vehicles. The driver got out and entered the trailer.

I got out of my car and walked toward the gate. The guard, an African American man of medium height, wore a uniform of brown pants and a khaki shirt with MANVILLE SECURITY embroidered in orange above the left breast pocket. His ball cap was dark brown and had the company name on the front above the bill. Around his waist was a leather belt with a holder containing a radio. I didn't see a gun or a Taser. Perhaps being a security guard on a construction site didn't require a lot of weaponry.

He held up his hand. "Sorry, this is a restricted area. Better keep clear."

"I'm looking for Gary Manville," I told him. "Is he on site?"

The guard nodded. "Yes, he is. I'll call him. Can I have your name, please?"

"Jeri Howard."

"Can I tell him what this is about?"

"I'd rather tell him myself."

The guard smiled, as though amused at my reply. He took the radio from his belt and punched a couple of buttons, then spoke into the mouthpiece, turning away so I couldn't hear his end of the conversation. A moment later, he turned back toward me. "Mr. Manville will be with you in a few minutes."

It was more like ten minutes. I waited by the fence, the entrance gate to my left, and peered through the chain mesh to check out the site. I didn't see any security cameras. I looked at the trailer. It was about thirty feet long, with a set of metal steps leading to a single door. The trailer was midway between where I stood and the back of the parcel. Among the vehicles parked outside the trailer were the pickup truck, an apple red Ford SUV, and a dark gray Cadillac Escalade.

Two men in work clothes and hard hats exited the trailer, heading toward the cement truck parked at the nearest side of the foundation. Then a van bearing the logo of an electrical company pulled up to the entrance. The driver stopped and bantered with the guard for a moment, then drove through, heading for the parking area outside the trailer.

The trailer door opened again. A man in a dark business suit exited, heading down the steps, his hand out as he punched a button on the remote. He got into the Cadillac and started it. As he drove out the gate, the driver, a man who appeared to be in his forties, glanced at me, then looked away. The Cadillac turned left onto the Embarcadero, heading toward downtown Oakland.

I turned back toward the work site. A man had just come out of the trailer. He was tall and broad-shouldered, dressed in gray slacks and a blue blazer over a green shirt, his wide shoulders straining the jacket. He wore a yellow hard hat and sunglasses. He crossed the work site, heading toward the gate where I waited. When he arrived, he stopped and took off his sunglasses, tucking them in the breast pocket of his shirt. He gave me a hard, assessing once-over with a pair of light blue eyes that resembled ice chips. I guessed his age as mid-forties. His skin looked as though he'd spent a lot of time outdoors.

"You wanted to see me?" he said in a rumbling voice.

"If you're Gary Manville."

"I am. What's this about?"

"Calvin Brady." I watched for his reaction. Manville didn't have one. But the security guard did. His eyes narrowed, looking at me as though he wanted to know more. Or perhaps he had something to tell me.

"Who are you and what do you want?" Manville demanded.

I handed him one of my business cards.

"Private investigator?" Manville growled. "Who hired you? Why?"

"My client's identity is confidential. As to why, I'm looking into Brady's death."

Manville glared at me. "As far as I know, it was an accident. Look, the guy is barely cold. They probably haven't even done an autopsy yet."

"They haven't, according to Detective Portillo."

"You talked to the cop."

"I spoke with Detective Portillo, yes."

"I don't have to talk to you." He pivoted and started to walk away.

"Suit yourself, Mr. Manville. I usually get answers to my questions, one way or another. Really, it might be better if you did talk with me, to clear up any concerns about Brady's death on your work site."

"I don't have time for this crap." Manville flipped his hand up in a dismissive gesture. He turned on his heel and walked back onto the site, heading for the trailer. He got into the red SUV and fired up the engine.

"I guess I touched a nerve," I said.

"I guess you did." The security guard flashed a smile. Then he smoothed it off his face and stepped back as the SUV approached the entrance. Manville didn't look at me as he drove past, turning left onto the Embarcadero.

I traded looks with the security guard. Then I took a business card from my bag and handed it to him. He tucked it into his pocket and turned his attention to the departing electrician's van.

As the van drove off the site, I walked back to my car. Before I unlocked the door I took one last look at the Cardoza property, my eye drawn to the two docks that stretched into the Estuary.

Is that where Cal went into the water? I wondered.

Chapter Six

≈≈≈≈≈≈≈≈≈≈

W HEN I RETURNED to my office, I began researching the various players in this drama. Manville Security
was a recent addition to the list of Bay Area security
companies, in business just over five years. In various state and
county filings, Gary Manville was listed as the sole proprietor and
the agent for service of process. The company's website told me
that Manville provided security for retail establishments and work
sites, and included links to testimonials from clients. I started a
background check on Manville.

Then I focused on the Cardoza Development Corporation
and the company's waterfront project. The company president was
Roland Cardoza, with Stephen Cardoza as chief executive officer.
Roland and Stephen were father and son. Cardoza Development
was headquartered here in Oakland, with an office in City Center.
It looked as though they were building a lot of market-rate housing
developments all over the East Bay, in both Alameda and Contra
Costa counties.

I did a search on Hasseltine Construction and discovered that
it was a subsidiary company of Cardoza Development. The company's website listed Brice Cardoza as the site manager for this latest
project on the Embarcadero. Further research on Roland Cardoza
told me that Stephen was the oldest of three children. There was a
daughter in the middle, married and living in Southern California.

Brice was the younger son. According to a recent article in a local business journal, Stephen had taken over more of the day-to-day running of Cardoza Development after his father had a stroke two years earlier.

The article was accompanied by a color photograph of Roland with his two sons. Roland was tall and had thinning gray hair. His sons were also tall. I recognized Stephen, the older, as the man I'd seen driving the Caddy off the construction site. He looked like a stereotypical businessman, with short brown hair and a well-tailored blue suit. The younger son, Brice, had a big, well-muscled frame and a sunburned, outdoorsy look, his shaggy hair a lighter shade of brown. Brice was the man I'd seen this afternoon, arriving on the construction site in the white pickup.

The Internet provided me with information on the Cardoza project, contained in articles written in various publications during Oakland's lengthy planning and approval process. Like the nearby Brooklyn Basin project, the Cardoza development had been proposed years ago, promising to repurpose unused industrial land by constructing buildings with retail space on the ground floor and market-rate condos on the upper floors. It was like several other projects they had built over the past ten years, in Oakland and other East Bay cities.

Roland Cardoza was wealthy and so was his son Stephen. They both lived in the Oakland hills, while Brice lived in a condo near Lake Merritt. Roland had grown up poor in San Leandro, the city to the southeast of Oakland. His family was of Portuguese descent, his grandparents having immigrated to the United States as a young married couple. Once out of college, Roland had worked for various businesses in the Bay Area. He married and started his own business in Oakland. He was in his early seventies now, and a widower. Stephen was divorced. Brice had never been married. I found several photographs of both brothers, taken at different functions. In each of the pictures, both Stephen and Brice were accompanied by different women.

Another article told me the site of the current Cardoza development had been part of a World War II shipyard. In the postwar era, the shipyard gave way to several warehouses. The Cardoza family had bought the land and the warehouses sixteen years earlier. They had purchased the adjacent property, location of the defunct marine supply business, about two years ago. Then they tore down all the buildings, leveling the site.

During the planning and approval process, the project had the support of several members of the Oakland City Council, citing the need for more housing in Oakland. On the other side of that argument were the project's opponents, including several waterfront environmental groups interested in preserving public access to the Estuary shoreline. Also opposed were two groups concerned with the cost of housing in Oakland, which had skyrocketed in recent years. They were all for housing, it appeared, but they wanted it to be affordable, not market-rate, like the Cardoza and Brooklyn Basin projects. A smaller group of people, concerned about being displaced from the shoreline, had also expressed opposition to the development. I found an article about a waterfront protest that had targeted both work sites.

Another set of articles in the local business journal told me who the architects were and provided illustrations of what the Cardoza development would look like when it was finished. A search netted a newspaper article about Chinese investors buying up all sorts of residential projects in the Bay Area. Stephen Cardoza was quoted, pointing out that unlike the Brooklyn Basin project, which did have Chinese investors, Cardoza Development was not only an American company but one that was based right here in Oakland, California.

I printed out various articles and photos. Then I picked up my phone. There was someone I wanted to talk with and we were long overdue for a good conversation.

My friend Davina answered her cell phone on the second ring, a lilt of laughter in her voice. "Jeri Howard. That's the funniest thing. I was just thinking of you, and here you are calling me. How are you?"

"Fine. And you? Let's get together and catch up. Lunch tomorrow? Your favorite restaurant."

"I'm always up for my favorite restaurant. I can do tomorrow. How about twelve-thirty?"

"See you then."

I noted the appointment on my calendar. The restaurant in question was in downtown Berkeley. Perhaps I could meet with Madison Brady afterwards, since I'd be near campus. My office phone rang. I picked it up and heard Madison's voice on the other end, her words urgent.

"Jeri, someone tried to break into Dad's apartment this afternoon."

"When? What happened?"

"His neighbor interrupted some guy and he ran."

"Did the neighbor report this to the police?"

"I don't think so. She called me and I came over right away. I'm at the apartment right now."

"I'm on my way. Give me your father's address." I shut down my computer and grabbed pencil and paper, quickly scrawling the address Madison provided. "Call Detective Portillo and let her know about this."

The man who'd tried to break in could be some opportunistic burglar, I thought as I locked my office and headed downstairs.

Or he could be a killer.

Chapter Seven

≈≈≈≈≈≈≈≈≈

CAL'S APARTMENT was on Wesley Avenue in a hilly neighborhood to the southeast of Lake Merritt, bordered by Lakeshore Avenue and Interstate 580. I angled my Toyota into a parking space half a block away and headed up the sidewalk. The three-story stucco building had seen better days, its green paint faded and peeling in places. Wooden window frames splintered, showing signs of rot. The mustard-colored awnings over the windows were torn in places. To the right of the front door was a row of mailboxes. I found the one that read BRADY and pushed the button below the nameplate. A few seconds later I heard Madison's voice, sounding tinny and distorted with static. "Who is it?"

"It's Jeri."

"Come on up. It's the third floor, at the front, the door on the left."

There was a loud buzz and a click indicating the door had been unlocked. I entered the building's foyer, where I saw a stairway to my left, covered with shabby beige industrial carpet that showed the dirt and the traffic pattern. I took the stairs up two flights and looked toward the front of the building, seeing two doors marked 3-A and 3-B. I knocked at the door for 3-B and Madison opened it.

"Thanks for coming over, Jeri."

"Did you talk with Detective Portillo?"

"I left a message for her. Dad's neighbor Agnes was leaving just as I got here. She said she'd be back in half an hour or so. I asked her to tap on the door when she gets home, so you can talk with her. The person she saw didn't get into the apartment, but he—she's sure it was a man—was trying to open the door with a set of keys. He must have Dad's key ring."

"That's a good guess. They didn't find any keys with the body?"

Madison shook her head. "Dad's car was at the work site, but no keys. When the police notified me about Dad's death, I told them I have keys to his car and apartment. They took me to the site to get the car. I was planning to come over here this afternoon anyway, to start packing up Dad's things and look for the title to the car. I don't know if I'm going to keep it or sell it. If I keep it I'll have to get the registration put in my name, and that means getting insurance. And finding a place to park it. Up until now I haven't had a car. I live in Berkeley, on the south side of campus, and you know what parking is like there."

I nodded. "Practically nonexistent."

She pulled the door open wider and beckoned me to enter. "No need for us to stand in the hall. Please, come in."

I stepped into Cal's apartment and looked around. It was a studio, about the size of the apartment above my garage, with plain furniture that looked as though it had been purchased at IKEA or Cost Plus. To my right was a daybed covered with comforter and pillows. Nearby doors opened onto a bathroom and a walk-in closet. A laundry basket in the back corner of the closet held faded jeans and a couple of wadded-up shirts. Two pairs of black socks hung from the rail above the bathtub. In front of me was a small round table and two chairs. The kitchen had a small refrigerator, microwave and four-burner stove. A thin residue of coffee darkened the bottom of the carafe in the drip coffee maker on the counter. Angled in front of the TV was a worn recliner. Books and CDs filled a nearby bookcase.

The table held a carton of crackers and a container of hummus from Trader Joe's, both open, and a stainless steel water bottle. A blue plastic file box, the kind that was readily obtainable at any office supply store, rested on the seat of one of the chairs. The lid, which had a handle affixed to the top, was open. A couple of folders had been pulled out of the box. I looked at the handwritten labels. One read CAR and the other read APARTMENT. The second chair held a large box of trash bags. Empty cardboard boxes crowded the remaining floor space.

"Want some crackers?" Madison asked.

"No, thanks."

"I never got around to lunch." She stuck her hand inside the box and pulled out a cracker, using it to scoop up hummus. She gestured at the boxes. "I've got to pack up Dad's stuff. I called the company that manages the building and told them Dad was dead. The woman I spoke with said I should get his stuff out of here as soon as possible. So I was planning to come over here anyway. Then Dad's neighbor called me about someone trying to get in."

"That seems hasty on the part of the management company," I said. "It's only a week till the end of October."

"I'm sure they want to jack up the rent while they've got the opportunity. I know from rent increases. I'm paying an exorbitant amount of money to share an apartment near campus with four other people while I work on my master's. Our rent is going up next month." She grimaced.

"Rents are going up all over Oakland and Berkeley."

I'd read a recent news article saying that Oakland rents had increased 88% in the past few years, as people who were priced out of apartments in San Francisco came across the bay to Oakland, which was supposed to be more affordable. It wasn't anymore. That percentage was a huge number. Now people were being priced out of Oakland.

Rental increases weren't limited to apartments, either. I thought of the letter I'd received about the increase in my office rent. As for living accommodations, I was glad that I'd bought my house several years earlier, when housing prices were less volatile. The rent from the garage apartment helped pay my mortgage.

Madison dusted cracker crumbs from her hands and took a sip from her water bottle. "Just a week to deal with all of this. Plus I have a research paper I'm working on for school. Never rains but it pours, right?" She shook herself out of her funk. "Enough of that.

I've got to pack Dad's stuff and figure out what to do with it. A friend of mine says I can stash some things in her garage for the time being. The clothes can go to the Salvation Army. I'll put an ad on Craigslist, see if I can sell the furniture. I'm going to keep the TV. It's newer than mine. A couple of guys I know told me they would help me haul the stuff away."

"We should take some of it to my office," I said. "The papers and files, anyway. That way I can examine them more thoroughly."

"Yes, I figured you'd like to take a look." She pointed at the closet near the front door. "That coat closet, that's where Dad kept his files. There are more file boxes in there. The first one I opened had what I was looking for, which was the information about Dad's car, and the rental agreement for the apartment."

Madison looked at the time on her iPhone. "We'd better get busy. I have to be back on campus for a meeting at six."

"Let's focus on the files and papers." I reached for a cardboard carton. "All the other furnishings can wait. I'd like to take your father's computer as well. We'll transfer everything to my car and I'll take it up to my office."

I set all four file boxes by the door and went to retrieve the laptop computer I'd seen on the table near the recliner. When I picked it up, I found an address book underneath. I tossed it into the carton.

"I'll take the answering machine, too." I unplugged it and added it to the box.

Madison and I began unloading the contents of the bookcase. "Dad used to hide things in the pages of books," she said.

"That's good to know. I'll take the books, too, and look through them."

A wicker basket held bills to be paid. Next to this was a stack of books, four hardbacks, from the Oakland Library, the Lakeshore branch that was a few blocks from here. The check-out receipt tucked into one of them said the books were due the following week. I riffled the pages of the library books, finding nothing except a card from a pizza delivery place that had been used as a bookmark. I set the books aside to be returned to the library.

We quickly packed up the books, both hardback and paperback. Cal's taste ran to thrillers and science fiction, as well as history of all sorts and some biographies. As for the CDs, Cal liked jazz, both instrumental and vocal. Those went into the box as well, though I didn't see anything stashed in between.

On the third shelf of the bookcase, I found a wooden box with a carved lid. I opened it, revealing an assortment of photographs. Most of them were pictures of Madison, from infancy through her childhood and teen years. The most recent photo was a snapshot of Madison and Cal. He looked much as he had at Errol's funeral, although dressed more casually. It looked as though the photo had been taken on the campus, with Wurster Hall in the background. It made sense. Madison was a master's student in City Planning, which was located in that building. I turned the photo over and saw a brief inscription in pencil, reading "Dad and Maddy, June."

"That was earlier this year," Madison said. "He came to campus to have lunch with me. One of my friends took the picture."

I delved further into the box, finding pictures from Cal's past. I recognized him as a teenager, standing between two people I took to be his parents. Madison confirmed this, glancing through the photos. "My grandmother and grandfather. I never met them. They died before I was born." She swept her hand around the room. "This is all that's left of my father. It's not much to show for a life, is it?"

"More than a lot of people have."

"When he got sober, after he'd lost so much, he said at least it was good for one thing. He'd gotten rid of a lot of stuff, literally and figuratively, he said. Stuff that was dragging him down, and he was starting fresh, without clutter. Not many possessions, just basic life."

She got to her feet. "He did have enough possessions to keep me occupied packing them up. I'll have to come back this weekend. But I think this is everything that could be considered files and papers."

I straightened and looked at the boxes to be transported to my car. "I hope there's an elevator in this building."

Madison nodded. "It's just past the stairs."

"I have a folding dolly in the trunk of my car. I'll go get it."

I had just reached the front door when someone knocked. I opened the door. Standing in the hall was an older woman, in her sixties, I guessed, with graying hair brushing the collar of her red quilted jacket. She had a large black bag looped over one shoulder and she held a leash. The small dog at the end of the leash was female, a mixture of brown and black, and looked as though she had some terrier in her bloodline. The dog wagged her tail and yipped.

The woman looked at me with a frown, clearly wondering who I was and what I was doing there. "Is Madison here?"

"Yes, she is."

Madison joined me in the doorway. "Hi, Agnes. Come on in. Jeri, this is Dad's neighbor, the one I was telling you about. And this is Zuzu." She held out her hand to the dog, who snuffled it eagerly and yipped again. "Agnes, this is Jeri Howard, a friend of mine, and Dad's. She's a private investigator. I'd really appreciate your telling her what you saw earlier this afternoon."

"Private investigator, huh?" Agnes entered the apartment and looked around. She sat down in the recliner and gathered Zuzu onto her lap. "I don't know what time it was, maybe two or thereabouts. I was heading out, going over to the library to pick up a book they have on hold for me. I heard someone out in the hall, sounded like it was next door. I thought it must be Cal. I hadn't seen him for several days, so I opened the door to say hello. It wasn't Cal. I didn't see whether he had keys or if he was using something else. I pulled my cell phone out of my pocket, went to the camera feature, and started taking a video."

"That was quick thinking," I said.

Agnes shrugged. "I don't know how useful it will be. I'm not a very good movie maker. Anyway, I opened my door wider and said, 'Hey, what are you doing?' This guy turned around. He saw that I was recording him with my phone and he grabbed for it. I slammed my door shut before he could get it though. I yelled that I was going to call the police. He took off down the stairs. I went to my front window and looked down in time to see him run down the sidewalk. He headed down Wesley. I didn't see him get into a car or anything. I called Cal's cell phone number and it went straight to voice mail. So I called Madison. She told me her father was dead. I was shocked. How terrible! He lived next door to me for over two years, and he was the nicest man."

"But you didn't call the police," I said.

"The Oakland cops?" Agnes's voice turned cynical. "They're not gonna do anything. They can't even keep up with the murders in this town, let alone a break-in that didn't happen. The guy didn't get into the apartment, and he could have walked right in the building. A lot of the tenants aren't too careful about security. Can't even be bothered to make sure the front door is closed and locked."

I let the comments about the Oakland police slide. There was a lot of truth to what Agnes said about the lack of incentive to investigate the incident.

"Can you describe the man you saw?"

"Medium height, medium build. Definitely a man. He was wearing sunglasses and a gray hoodie, pulled up over his face. And gloves. I really couldn't see his face."

"May I see the video?"

"I warn you, it's not very good." Agnes rummaged in her voluminous shoulder bag and pulled out an iPhone. She loaded the video. It was a few seconds long. I watched it three times. It was wobbly and didn't show me much. As Agnes said, the man had worn jeans and a gray hooded sweatshirt, with the hood pulled up and hanging over his forehead. The hood and the large sunglasses he wore obscured his face. I saw enough to tell me the intruder was probably a man, though it could have been a woman. The gloves he wore meant there wouldn't be any fingerprints on the door or handle.

"Could you email the video to me?" I asked.

"Sure thing. Give me your address."

I gave Agnes my business card and she promptly sent the video to my business email account. I would study it on a larger computer to see if I could glean any more details.

"Hey, Agnes," Madison said. "We found some books Dad had checked out of the library. Would it be possible for you to return them next time you're down there? They're due at the end of the week."

"Oh, sure. Hand 'em over. I'm back and forth to the library all the time."

Agnes tucked the library books into her bag. She unlocked her own apartment and she and her dog went inside.

Madison's cell phone rang. She answered the call as I headed downstairs to get the dolly from my trunk. When I returned, she told me Detective Portillo and her partner were on their way over. They arrived about twenty minutes later, after Madison and I finished loading the last of the files and boxes into my trunk. Grace introduced me to her partner, whose name was Mike Fisker. I hadn't met him before, but I'd heard from Sid that he was a new addition to the Oakland Police Department, having moved to the Bay Area from Los Angeles. He was in his early forties, I guessed, with a sharp manner. I had the feeling he didn't like private investigators getting involved with his case. It was an attitude I'd encountered before.

Grace and Fisker talked with Agnes and looked at the video. They thought the neighbor's description, and the video, were inconclusive. Could this be an opportunistic break-in? If so, why come all the way to the third floor? Was the intruder using a lock pick, or Cal's keys, which had not been found on the body?

Ordinarily, I would have advised Madison to have the lock changed on her father's apartment. In this case, there wasn't much point. She was giving up the apartment as soon as she got the furniture and the rest of her father's possessions moved out.

I left at the same time as Grace and her partner, watching them get into an unmarked car parked down the street. After they drove away, I knocked on a few doors in that block, asking if anyone had seen a man in a gray hoodie running from Cal's building. But it was a neighborhood full of apartment buildings, where most people were at work. Those who did respond to my knock shook their heads and shut their doors.

I drove back downtown and parked in the lot near my office building. Then I transported the boxes up to my office, piling them on the floor near my desk. By the time I was finished it was nearly six. I felt as though I'd gotten my exercise for the day.

Before I left the office, I called Zachary's Pizza on College Avenue, near my home, and ordered a thin-crust pizza loaded with sausage, pepperoni, salami, bacon and cheese. Damn the calories!

After I picked up my pizza I went home. I had purchased the wood-framed house on Chabot Road several years ago, flush with some fat checks from a number of successfully completed cases and satisfied clients. The money had provided a down payment. Each month I made extra payments to the principal with the goal of paying off the mortgage sooner. The house had been in disrepair when I first saw it, but it had good bones. It was built on a hillside that sloped down away from the street. The upper level, which had a working fireplace and hardwood floors, contained the living room, dining room, kitchen and half-bath, while the lower level had a large bedroom and full bath, an alcove for my home office, and a room for storage and a washer and dryer. From the bedroom, French doors led out to the patio, where I had a table and chairs and a propane gas grill.

The house was a probate sale, which meant the owner had died and it was for sale "as is." I'd been working on fixing the "as is" items, making improvements that went beyond new paint inside and out. That included rebuilding the rickety front porch and the equally unstable stairs that led from the main floor back deck down to the backyard. The front yard was small. I'd replaced the grass in front and back with drought-tolerant succulents and native grasses. In the back I'd built raised beds for flowers and vegetables. In addition to putting in drip irrigation, I'd spent the money for a gray-water recycling system. Even so, the drought had left many of my trees looking stressed. Now I was planning on putting in rooftop solar. The backyard got morning sun and I was debating about putting another set of solar panels out there.

As I pulled into the driveway next to Darcy's bright yellow VW, I was pleased, as always, with the sight of my house. I'd accomplished a lot since I'd signed the papers making it mine.

I got out of my car, pizza box in hand. Just then, Darcy opened the front door of the garage apartment and headed down the stairs to the driveway.

When I'd first met Darcy several years ago, she was a rebellious teenager. Her parents and later her grandmother had hired me to get her out of a couple of scrapes, one more serious than the other. She hadn't been on good terms with her mother then, but their relationship had improved. She was intelligent and adventurous, and I was pleased that she'd grown into a very interesting adult. She had been a good tenant and I was sorry to lose her, but glad she was moving to another phase of her life.

"Pizza from Zachary's, yum," she said when she joined me on the driveway.

"Come in and help me eat it."

"It's tempting. But I have a dinner date with some friends." She unlocked her VW and reached in, hauling out several cardboard cartons. "More boxes so I can pack up for the move to Boston. It's a studio apartment. You'd think I wouldn't have acquired so many things."

"As I always say, the stuff expands to fit the space available, plus two boxes."

"I'll be out by Thanksgiving," she said, piling the boxes on the driveway. She locked her car. "You can advertise now and see if you can rent it starting December first."

"I haven't decided what I'm going to do," I said, revisiting my earlier thoughts about the possibility of moving my office to the apartment. "I'm sure I won't have any trouble renting it. Now, if you'll excuse me, my pizza is getting cold."

I unlocked my front door and stepped into the small entry hall, to be greeted by my old tabby, Abigail, and my black cat, called Black Bart after the famous California outlaw. They importuned me with meows, claiming that they were perishing for lack of food. Their cries diminished not one whit when I pointed out that there was perfectly good cat food in their bowl. If I read their response correctly, their complaint was the food wasn't fresh.

I poured myself a glass of tea from the pitcher I kept in the refrigerator. Then I grabbed a handful of paper towels to use as napkins, sat down at the table, and opened the pizza box. I bit into a slice. Ah, bliss!

The cats were not supposed to get on the table and they knew it. I also knew that while I was out, they probably did the merengue on the table and the kitchen counter. Right now Black Bart hopped onto an empty chair and then onto the table. He stuck out a stealthy paw, trying to snitch a bit of pepperoni from the pizza.

I leaned toward him, my hand shooing him off the table. "No, you may not eat pepperoni. You would just barf it all over the floor and I'd have to clean it up."

He gave me a dagger stare and made a huffy sound as he hopped down. I had rescued him several years ago when the scrawny black kitten showed up on my patio. He was scrawny no more. Given the thud he made when he landed on the floor, it was clear that Black Bart had not missed any meals since he came to live with me.

I ate my fill of the pizza and closed the box, stashing the leftovers in the refrigerator. As I washed my hands at the sink, the phone rang. I looked at the readout and saw that the caller was my father. I answered and carried the phone to the living room, where I stretched out on the sofa, settling in for a chat.

"I made reservations for next week," Dad said. My birthday was coming up and Dad was taking me out to dinner, along with Dan Westbrook, the man I'd been seeing since June. I had selected a new restaurant in Oakland, a place I wanted to try, since I'd heard good things about the food.

Dad taught history for years, at California State University in Hayward, now known as Cal State East Bay. Since his retirement, he kept active with his newfound passion for birding. He was planning a fall trip to Klamath Falls, Oregon, and a spring trip to the Big Bend National Park in Texas. His usual buddy is the widow of a fellow Cal State professor, though sometimes I go with him.

The conversation turned to Brian, my younger brother. He and his wife were currently seeing a marriage counselor. Back in August, Brian, who was a schoolteacher in Petaluma, had gone missing. When my sister-in-law, Sheila, had alerted the family, I had returned from a hiking trip and set about finding my brother. My search made me aware of some serious problems in my brother's marriage. I'd always thought Brian and Sheila had a great relationship. They had been together a long time and had two young children. I was worried when I learned about the widening cracks in what I'd assumed was a strong marriage. My parents were equally dismayed. Mother and Dad were divorced and my own marriage had foundered. I didn't want Brian and Sheila to go down that path. The counseling should help. At least I hoped it would.

I looked at the clock. It was twenty minutes until the start of my t'ai chi class, which was at a nearby school. I grabbed my car keys and left the house.

Chapter Eight

≋≋≋≋≋≋≋

D AVINA ROKA once told me that her Hungarian sur-
name meant red fox. Indeed, her hair was that color. But
foxes don't have Davina's wild mane of curly red hair, tum-
bling down past her shoulders. Today her hair was set off by her
outfit, a forest green shirt decorated with coppery sequins, worn
over form-fitting black jeans.

I was meeting her for lunch, as promised, at her favorite restaurant in downtown Berkeley. I'd parked around the corner on
Kittredge Street, near the western perimeter of the University of
California campus, then I walked half a block to Shattuck Avenue.
On the corner I skirted panhandlers and students who were either
talking on their phones or sending text messages. Either way, they
weren't paying attention to where they were going.

Angeline's Louisiana Kitchen was located a few doors down
on Shattuck. I stepped inside. Davina was waiting for me near the
hostess station. We greeted each other with hugs, then the hostess
showed us to a table at the back of the restaurant.

"I'm havin' a beer," Davina drawled. Hungarian ancestors or
not, Davina had been born in New Orleans. She'd lived in the Bay
Area for many years, but she still had the accent.

"Wish I could, but I have an appointment with a prospective
client later this afternoon. It wouldn't do to show up with beer on
my breath."

Our server appeared at the table and I ordered unsweetened iced tea. Davina asked for an Abita Turbodog, a dark beer we both liked. "I'll let you have a sip," she added with a wicked smile. "I don't have to worry about my breath, since I'm just going to class."

I picked up the lunch menu and glanced at it, knowing I'd probably order what I usually did. Angeline's made a wonderful jambalaya, though from time to time I was seduced away from that particular entrée by the gumbo or the red beans and rice.

When the server returned with our drinks, we agreed to split an order of hush puppies. I went with jambalaya as usual. "It's my favorite. I'm so predictable." I handed the menu to the server.

"Sometimes you are, and sometimes you aren't," Davina said. "I'll have the crawfish étouffée. Not as good as my mama's, but pretty damn good. It's great to see you, girl. What's goin' on with you? You still dating that good-lookin' guy?"

The last time I'd seen Davina, a few months ago, had been here in Berkeley where the good-looking guy and I were having a quick dinner before attending a performance at Freight and Salvage, a music venue over on Addison Street. Davina walked into the restaurant and I introduced her to Dan.

"I am." I brought her up to date on my relationship with Dan as we ate our way through the hush puppies, slathering the little cornmeal balls with honey butter. Then the server brought our entrées and refreshed my iced tea.

When Errol had retired, I decided to continue as a private investigator, a sole practitioner. My coworker Davina took time off, visiting Europe. Then she'd gone to work for a nonprofit in Oakland, finally deciding she would go to law school. That's where she was now, in her final year at the School of Law in Boalt Hall.

She told me about her adventures, and I told her some of mine. Then I said, "You heard about Errol."

Her smile dimmed a bit. "I did. Minna called me. I guess she called all the people who used to work at the Seville Agency. I'm so sorry I couldn't make it to the funeral. I had classes that day and I just couldn't take the time to drive down to Monterey and back. Did you go to the service? I hope there were a lot of people there."

"Yes, I did go, and there were lots of people, some of whom I hadn't seen in ages." I savored a spoonful of jambalaya.

"That's why I was thinking of you last week. Because of Errol. You worked for him a lot longer than I did." Davina smiled again, her fork poised in midair. "I wasn't cut out to be a private investigator, but it was fun while I did it. And useful. I learned so much, about people and the law and procedure. I know it will help me working as a criminal defense attorney."

"I'm sure it will." I swallowed another mouthful of jambalaya. "Cal Brady was there."

"Cal?" Davina's face brightened as she took another bite of her étouffée. "How is he? I always liked him."

"I know you did." I sipped my iced tea. "I'm sorry to tell you that Cal is dead."

"What?" She set her fork on her plate, shock widening her eyes.

"His body was found in the Estuary Sunday morning."

"My God, what happened? How?"

"I don't know. But I intend to find out."

She reached for her beer and took a generous swallow, processing the news. "Cal dead. He was…" Her usually robust voice sounded subdued. "He was a man who had his ups and downs, that's for sure."

"It's been a long time since we all worked for Errol," I said. "I didn't know Cal very well. I didn't even know he had a daughter. Or a wife. But I think you knew him better than I did. You dated him for a while."

"I did go out with him," Davina said. "Despite that, I don't think that I knew him all that well. It took me a while to figure out he had a drinking problem. As is the case with a lot of alcoholics, he was good at hiding it. But it caught up with him eventually."

"What can you tell me about Cal?"

She took a sip of her beer. "He and his wife were divorced. That happened while he was still in the Navy, a long time before he came to work for Errol. I knew about that, and the daughter. I broke it off because I decided dating someone I worked with was a bad idea. But that wasn't the only reason, of course. Once I figured out he was an alcoholic, I decided I didn't need that in my life. His drinking got worse. It became harder for him to hide it." She fingered the beer bottle. "After what happened with that stakeout assignment that went south, I don't blame Errol for firing him. Eventually Cal went to AA and got his act together. Or so he told me."

"You saw him after he left the agency?"

She nodded. "Now and then, just around. You know the Bay Area. Live here long enough and you're gonna run into people you know. The first time was a few years back, I don't remember exactly when. He told me he had gone through detox and he was going to AA. He said it was really difficult, but he was determined. The last time I saw him was about six months ago, early May, I think, before spring semester ended. He was with his daughter, Madison, at Caffe Strada. That's where everyone on the southeast side of campus goes to get caffeinated. Madison is in grad school at the College of Environmental Design, in Wurster Hall, which is right next to Boalt Hall. We were all in line to get lattes and a nosh, so we sat and talked while we drank our coffee. Cal told me he was sober and I believed him."

"He was at Errol's funeral. He told me then he was sober, and had been for several years."

"Good for him. What a tragedy that he's dead, after getting himself straight. I was impressed by his daughter. She seems like an intelligent young woman. This must be hard on her." Davina toyed with the remains of her étouffée. "Errol's funeral was just last week, and you saw Cal then. How did you find out he was dead?"

"Madison came to see me yesterday at my office. She claims Cal was murdered."

Davina looked stunned. "That's crazy. Who would want to kill Cal Brady?"

"No idea. But I told her I would look into it."

We finished our entrées. The server cleared away our plates and asked if we wanted dessert. "Let's share an order of beignets," Davina said.

"Fine by me." The server departed with the plates and our order. "What else can you tell me about Cal?"

She thought for a moment. "He was from somewhere back in the Midwest. He went to the University of Wisconsin, so I'm guessing he was a native. He was in an ROTC program, which is how he wound up going into the Navy."

"What did he do in the Navy? And where?" At one time there had been a number of Navy bases in the Bay Area, such as the Naval Air Station on Alameda, and the Naval Station at Treasure Island, in San Francisco Bay. There was no longer much of a Navy presence here, except for recruiters and annual visits by the Blue Angels, the Navy precision flying team, during Fleet Week. Now most of the bases were located in Southern California.

"He mentioned San Diego. Other than that, I don't know. He can't have been in San Diego the whole time he was in the service. I know the military moves people around every couple of years. Cal got out and I don't know why he didn't make a career of it. Of course, the military is not for everyone."

"I wonder why he moved to the Bay Area when he got out of the Navy."

The server appeared at our table with two plates, two forks and a bowl of beignets, the light fluffy pillows covered with powdered sugar. We each helped ourselves to one. I cut mine in half and took a bite. Fried dough—delicious.

Davina raised her napkin and brushed powdered sugar from her lips. "Y'know, I think he came up here because his ex-wife was in the area. She remarried. Cal wanted to be where he could see his daughter on a regular basis. Madison got her undergraduate degree at one of the Cal State campuses. Then she worked before applying to grad school at Berkeley."

I took another bite of my beignet. "When you saw him last spring, did he say anything about his job?"

"He mentioned something about working on the waterfront. He was a security guard at some big development. Is that the Brooklyn Basin project I've heard about?"

"No, the development where Cal was working is called the

Cardoza project. Did he say anything specific about the job or the site?"

She shook her head. "No. We got to talking about development in general. Madison was interested because she's working on a master's degree in city planning and she'd done some research about infill housing."

"Housing built on former industrial sites," I said.

"That's right. I was interested because I worked at a housing nonprofit in the East Bay. That was before I decided to go to law school. The people I worked with were studying gentrification and how it's displacing people all over the Bay Area. Cal said this development wasn't like that because the place used to be a shipyard and some warehouses, with no housing in the area."

"That will change," I said. "Both Brooklyn Basin and the Cardoza development will provide market-rate housing, with retail and businesses on the ground floor and apartments above."

"The kind of housing that some people call 'stack-and-pack.' And all market-rate, none of it affordable, I'll bet."

I nodded. "You're probably right there. They'll charge what the market will bear, which is damned high now."

"You're telling me," Davina said. "All the people who can't afford to live in San Francisco are discovering Oakland. Rents are going through the roof."

"I've heard the 'stack-and-pack' term before. Usually it's derogatory. But one size doesn't necessarily fit all. I'm sure these developments will attract a lot of people because they are located on the waterfront. But neither site is close to transit."

"I suppose once the developments are built, AC Transit will have to change or add bus routes."

"Waterfront living isn't for me," I said. "I prefer my house with a yard, so I can at least plant a garden. These planned communities that builders are putting up now, the houses and landscaping are bland and boring. I grew up in Alameda. I like the older towns with distinctive houses and a mix of styles." My house in the Rockridge neighborhood of Oakland had some Craftsman touches.

Davina frowned. "Getting back to Cal, you said his body was

found in the Estuary and Madison says he was murdered. Do you think this has something to do with his job?"

"Possibly. Madison told me he was on the night shift. I've also learned that the site manager told the police that he'd reprimanded Cal for drinking on the job."

Davina scooped another beignet from the bowl. "It's possible he started drinking again. But I'm not buying that. Are you?"

"I don't know." I speared a beignet with my fork. "Alcoholics do have lapses. But I saw Cal last week and he was sober. He didn't look or act the way he did when he was drinking. Maybe something happened and he fell off the wagon. Or maybe someone is trying to make it look that way."

As we worked our way through the beignets, we talked about our days at the Seville Agency, and some of the other operatives who had worked with us. "Whatever happened to Elaine Ponsonby?" I asked.

Davina wiped powdered sugar from her mouth again. "She's in Sacramento, working as a legislative aide for a state senator."

I nodded. "That doesn't surprise me. She was always political. Duc Ngo joined the FBI. He's working out of their office in San Francisco. I saw him over in the city a year or so ago, at the Ferry Building farmers' market."

"Duc in the FBI." Davina laughed. "I guess I can see that. Say, remember Leo Walker?"

I made a face. "I do. And not fondly, I assure you."

Leo had never been my favorite coworker. He was a few years younger than me, cocky and arrogant, with the attitude that he was smarter than everyone else. He was going to be the greatest private investigator in the Bay Area, according to Leo. His hubris got him in trouble more than once. He made mistakes. He clashed with other operatives, including me. Leo had a habit of taking credit for other operatives' work, especially if it was good. If the outcomes were bad, he would blame others for his errors. I'd been on the receiving end of Leo's machinations and I didn't trust the guy. Errol noticed. He was a good judge of character and he quickly realized that hiring Leo had been a mistake. Leo moved on, less than a year after he had joined the agency. After he'd gone, Errol told me that he'd been on the verge of firing him.

Davina laughed at my expression. "He was a bit full of himself. I wasn't all that fond of him either. I saw him a few months ago."

"Where?"

"Downtown Berkeley. He greeted me as though I was his long-lost sister. Believe it or not, after he left Errol's employ, he worked for the same housing nonprofit as I had."

"I can't see Leo working for a nonprofit. Not enough money to suit him. He was a hustler then and probably still is."

"I don't doubt it," Davina said. "As for the nonprofit, he didn't last long, from what I hear. There was something—" She stopped as the server delivered our check. "I believe he left that job under a cloud. But I don't know what happened. If it comes to me, I'll let you know. When I saw him, he told me he was a consultant, but he didn't give me any specifics. He gave me a business card but I didn't keep it."

"Anyone can be a consultant these days," I said. "Just print up a card."

I had managed to get powdered sugar all over my front. I brushed it away. Davina and I split the check and left the restaurant. I offered to give her a lift back to her corner of the campus. "I'm meeting Cal's daughter. Since I was coming to Berkeley, it seemed like a good time."

"Despite the fact that I need to walk off that lunch, I'll accept," Davina said. "That gives me more time to prepare for my afternoon class."

We rounded the corner to Kittredge and I unlocked my car. I headed east, up Durant past Telegraph, the busy avenue south of campus, eyes scanning for a parking space. Parking was always a crap shoot near campus. As I approached the intersection of Durant and College Avenue, I spotted a car pulling away. As soon as the vehicle cleared the curb, I grabbed the space.

"Wow, do you have parking karma," Davina said as we got out of the car. I fed the meter and we walked along College to where it ended at Bancroft Avenue, on the UC Berkeley south perimeter. On our left was Caffe Strada, the coffee shop that Davina had mentioned earlier. As was usually the case, every table was full and there was a line out the door as people queued up to get coffee and pastries. I was always amazed at how many students and professors seemed to spend their days at Strada. As we passed the outdoor patio, conversations were in full voice, in several different languages, while at other tables, people worked on laptop computers.

We crossed Bancroft and stopped in front of the round pool with a fountain in the center, a few steps from the sidewalk. Davina gave me a hug and we parted. She walked briskly toward Boalt Hall.

Kroeber Hall was to my left. It was where the anthropology department was located, as well as a museum and gift shop. Ahead of me was Wurster Hall, home of the College of Environmental Design. Wurster, built in something called the Brutalist style back in the 1960s, was renowned as the ugliest building on campus, ironic since it housed architecture, as well as landscape architecture and city planning, where Madison was getting her master's degree. I thought Evans Hall, which housed mathematics, was also in the ugly building category. Dwinelle Hall, where I'd obtained my history degree years ago, was farther away, near Sproul Plaza. Dwinelle was home to several departments and it was a large and sprawling building known as a labyrinth. I'd often thought that once I entered those corridors, I'd have to leave a trail of crumbs, like Hansel and Gretel, to find my way out.

Madison and I had agreed to meet at two o'clock. While I waited for her, I sat on the wide perimeter of the fountain and watched people, always an interesting activity on the campus. A few minutes later I saw Madison approaching from Wurster Hall, her blue backpack slung over her shoulders. Her face was drawn, as though the pack contained the weight of the world. Not surprising. With her father's death, and the questions surrounding the way he died, that was to be expected.

I stood up and waved at her. When she saw me, her face brightened and she quickened her pace.

"Hi, Jeri. Thanks for meeting me."

"I don't have a lot to report. I haven't gone through the boxes yet. I have an appointment at three. I'll start on the boxes when I get back to the office."

"Let's get some coffee," Madison said. "I need some caffeine to get me through the afternoon."

"Sure." We walked across Bancroft Avenue and joined the line that stretched out the door at Caffe Strada. "You look tired."

She sighed and blinked away tears. "I had a rough night. Thinking about Dad. I loved my father. Now he's gone."

I squeezed her hand as we moved closer to the counter. "We'll get to the bottom of this."

"I know. Then there's that attempted break-in at his apartment. Packing up his things. I have to go over there again this afternoon. I've got a paper due and I'm finding it really hard to concentrate on schoolwork. And this place where I'm living—well, it's just one hassle after another."

We were at the counter now and I saw Madison eyeing the pastries. "My treat," I said. "What will you have?"

"A mocha and a brownie."

I nodded at the man behind the counter. "And a latte." I paid the tab and we stepped aside to wait for our drinks. When we had them in hand, we stepped out the side door to the patio. Every available seat was taken, so we went back across the street to the fountain and sat on the perimeter.

"What's up with your living arrangements?"

Madison unwrapped the brownie and took a bite, washing it down with a sip of coffee. "Too many people in too small a space. I told you I was sharing an apartment with four other people, none of whom I knew before I moved in. It's a two-bedroom, with two people in each bedroom. I'm the fifth wheel. My room is actually a walk-in closet off the living room. I use a folding screen for a door. I have a futon and a desk and I keep my clothes in a bunch of stackable plastic crates. The building is really old and a lot of things are falling apart. Right now we have a leaky faucet in the kitchen and the landlord is dragging his heels about fixing it. I took the place because my share of the rent was relatively cheap, for Berkeley. Now it's going to be more expensive. The rent's going up."

I shook my head, remembering my student days. I, too, had shared apartments near campus, some of them in similar states of disrepair. But the rents back then weren't as crazy as they were now. I'd always had my own bedroom, at least. The thought of paying a large sum of money to share a bedroom or live in a closet was hard to imagine. But that was the reality for students these days.

Once again I thought about the garage apartment. Darcy was moving out. But I still hadn't ruled out the possibility of giving up my Franklin Street office and using the apartment for business purposes.

"I'm going to look for a new place to live once the semester is over." Madison broke off another chunk of the brownie. "Mom says I could live at home, in Walnut Creek, but I need to be close to campus. Living at home and commuting is another set of problems."

I sipped my latte. "How were things between your father and mother? I know they divorced a long time ago, when you were young. Did they talk?"

"They did. I'd say their relationship was cordial. They talked on the phone now and then. That's pretty good for a divorced couple, I think."

"It is." I thought of my own parents, who had remained friendly after their divorce. "I'd like to talk with your mother. I want to see if your father may have said anything to her about things going on at work, or something that was on his mind."

"I can arrange that. She works, so it would need to be in the evening or sometime this weekend. Let me talk with her and I'll call you."

We finished our coffees. Madison slung her backpack over her shoulder and headed back to Wurster Hall. I retrieved my car and drove away from the campus.

I had a meeting with a prospective client who had an office in a business park near Sixth and Dwight Streets in West Berkeley. A couple of hours later, after moving the client from prospective to actual, I returned to my office with a contract and a retainer check. The mail included several other checks, always welcome, and a brochure about an upcoming conference sponsored by the National Association of Legal Investigators. I checked voice mail and email, returning calls and responding to messages. Then I went to the Internet and looked up the FBI's office on Golden Gate Avenue. I picked up the phone. It took me several transfers before I got to Duc Ngo's voice mail. I left a message asking my former coworker to call me.

I looked at the video again, the one the neighbor had shot Tuesday afternoon when someone tried to get into Cal's apartment. Blown up on my desktop computer monitor, it was still shaky and grainy. I paused the video and peered at the face that had been obscured by sunglasses and the hoodie pulled low over the forehead. The intruder was a man, I was betting on it. He was probably white. At the point when the intruder had turned toward the neighbor who was filming him, he raised his arm. I saw the glove on his hand and the cuff of his gray hoodie. Was that a mark on his left wrist? A tattoo? I enlarged the image, focusing on the hand, but the mark on the wrist remained tantalizingly unidentified.

I closed the video file and looked across my desk at the file boxes and cartons sitting on the floor in front of my filing cabinets. This was the stuff I'd brought from Cal's apartment. It was time to sort through the contents. Maybe I would find something that explained his death.

I remembered what Cal had said when I saw him after Errol's funeral, that he'd like to be a private investigator again. What if he had started an investigation of his own? That might be the reason he wanted to talk with me. If he had in fact been murdered, it could be he'd stepped on someone's toes.

Okay, what would Cal be investigating? Could it have something to do with his job at Manville Security? Something about the Cardoza development? Shenanigans going on at the work site? Or it could be completely unrelated to any of those. I didn't have a clue at this point what Cal was doing and whether it had gotten him killed.

I picked up the first file box and set it on my desk, opening the lid. Then I pulled out file folders, opening them one by one. Cal kept personal records, like most of us. I sifted through them, hoping for clues about the man.

He was, as Davina had guessed, a Wisconsin native. I found his birth certificate, listing a hospital in Eau Claire and a birth date in February. He had an undergraduate degree in Mechanical Engineering from the University of Wisconsin, the big flagship campus of the system located in Madison. I wondered if he'd named his daughter after the university town, or whether that had been his wife's idea. I knew the name was popular for girls. Cal had participated in the Naval Reserve Officers Training Corps at UW–Madison, and he had been commissioned as an ensign in the Navy after graduation. He'd served a total of eight years and four months in the Navy. I found his discharge papers in one of the folders.

One folder was full of documents pertaining to Cal's veteran's benefits. Next was a thick folder labeled "Medical." I opened it and saw that Cal had obtained his medical care from the VA clinic in downtown Oakland. But he'd gone through an alcohol treatment program at the VA hospital in Martinez, in Contra Costa County.

I found a folder containing his divorce papers, granted at the time he was living in San Diego. I glanced at these, seeing that his ex-wife's name was Linda. Behind this was Cal's passport, which had expired six years ago. And that was it for the contents of this file box. I put the folders back inside and set the box on the floor, picking up another box. I pulled out folders, finding tax and banking records, as well as bills paid and miscellaneous receipts.

The third file box contained something I was looking for—employment records. A cursory glance through the files showed me that a handful of papers pertained to Cal's tenure at the Seville Agency. Most, however, were records of Cal's most recent job, with Manville Security. I set the folder aside so I could examine it in more depth.

I went through the fourth file box, but I found nothing indicating whether Cal had been conducting an investigation of his own, nothing that provided me with any reason someone would kill him.

I opened a box containing books from Cal's bookcase and picked up the first volume, a trade paperback about the Lewis and Clark expedition. He'd been using a business card as a bookmark. I pulled the card from the book and looked at it. It was from a place called the Bayside Ballroom, located in Oakland. I tucked the card back into the book and glanced at the clock. It was a quarter to five and I wanted to go to my bank to deposit those checks before going home. I'd wait until the following day to go through the other boxes.

Chapter Nine

M Y CASE LOAD this month included pre-trial investigative work for a local attorney whose client was the plaintiff in a civil lawsuit in the Alameda County Superior Court. Since I had a meeting with the attorney scheduled the following week, I set aside time Thursday to write my report. I'd just finished when the phone rang.

I picked up the receiver. "Howard Investigations."

At the other end of the line I heard a man's voice, rich and deep. "This is Nathan Dupre calling for Ms. Howard."

"I'm Jeri Howard."

He chuckled. "Cool. I never talked to a private eye before."

"How can I help you, Mr. Dupre?"

"Maybe it's the other way round," he said. "I'm a security guard at the Cardoza work site. I saw you the other day when you showed up at the gate, asking to see Gary Manville. Before you left, you slipped me your card."

I leaned back in my chair. "You looked as though you had something to tell me."

"I do." Dupre laughed again. "When you started asking questions about Cal Brady, you damn sure got Manville riled up."

"Do you know why?"

"I got a theory or two. I figured we could talk about that. And Cal."

"Mr. Dupre, I would be happy to buy you a cup of coffee. Pick a time and place."

"That would be cool," he said. "It's my day off and I've got to do some grocery shopping. I'll meet you at eleven o'clock, at the Peet's on Lakeshore Avenue, near Trader Joe's."

"Sounds good. I'll be there."

At ten forty-five, I left my office. I drove a few blocks to Lake Merritt, downtown Oakland's jewel. The lake was at the other end of the channel that led to the Inner Harbor, and it was fed by several creeks, most of them subterranean since they'd been paved over years ago. Today was sunny, the sky blue and cloudless, with a bit of autumn chill in the air. The sidewalks were full of people who lived or worked in the area, walking around the lake, dodging the Canada geese who acted as though they owned the place. Since the area was a wildlife sanctuary, I figured the geese did. Ducks, mostly mallards, paddled the lake's smooth surface. Cormorants sunned themselves on a wooden float and seagulls wheeled above. A pelican landed, skimming along the water.

I drove to the neighborhood, parked and walked down Lakeshore Avenue to Peet's Coffee, where I claimed a table. At ten minutes after eleven, Dupre showed up, bearing shopping bags from Trader Joe's. He came through the door and greeted me with the same cheeky smile I'd seen the other day when he was working at the Cardoza site.

"Sorry I'm late," he said, setting the bags on the floor. "There was a line at the checkout."

"Coffee's on me. What will you have?"

He glanced at the menu board. "A pumpkin latte, large."

Much as I like pumpkin, eggnog, ginger and peppermint, the flavorings that proliferated at this time of year, I didn't care for them mixed with coffee. I ordered Dupre's pumpkin latte and a plain version for myself, along with a couple of Snickerdoodles, big sugar cookies with a dusting of cinnamon. I waited at the end of the counter, then picked up the coffees and carried them back to the table.

Dupre took a sip and grinned. "That hits the spot. How long have you been doing this private eye gig?"

"A long time." I sipped my coffee and quartered one of the cookies, taking a bite.

"You make a decent living at it? Well, you must, if you've been doing the job that long."

"Decent enough."

He reached for the other cookie and broke off a chunk, popping it into his mouth. "Cal was a private eye once. At least that's what he told me." He stopped and took another hit from his latte. "I'll bet you knew him back in the day. That's why you're interested. I'm betting it's his daughter that hired you."

My standard operating procedure when faced with such statements was to neither confirm nor deny. "How long have you worked for Manville Security?"

"Nearly four years for Manville, close to eleven years working as a security guard. Before I got the gig with Manville, I was at another security company in Oakland. I was looking to make a change and I liked the salary and benefits Manville was offering. I like Gary, too. He can be a hard-ass at times, though."

"Have you worked at the Cardoza site long?"

"May of this year. That's when they started grading and excavating. So that's five months. We've got round-the-clock security, three shifts a day."

"Why round-the-clock security?"

Dupre swallowed more coffee before answering. "Loss prevention, that's what they call it. There's a lot that can happen on a construction site if it's not guarded. One big problem is scavengers coming on the property, stealing metal. Especially copper. There's a big market for copper. They grab it and take it to recyclers to get the money. These days you've got to have guards all the time, and even then people get in. There's a fence around the property but that doesn't always keep people out."

"Have you had incidents?"

"With people trying to get on the site? Oh, yeah. There are lots of homeless people living on the waterfront, from Jack London

Square all up and down the Embarcadero. And the Lake Merritt Channel. Quite a camp there, and it's a mess. With all the development that's going on, the homeless guys get displaced. Someone's always telling them to move along. At our location, the folks at the nearby restaurants and marinas complain about them, and we've had problems at the site, too."

He sipped his coffee and continued. "They don't get in the front gate, because that's visible to the Embarcadero and the traffic there. The whole site is surrounded by a fence, but that doesn't stop anyone. A few weeks ago, we found out someone had taken a bolt cutter to the chain. Whoever did it helped themselves to some tools and all the copper they could find."

"Even with a security guard on duty?"

"The guards are supposed to walk the site during the shift," Dupre said. "But there are times when we're inside the trailer, using the john or having a snack. On this particular night, the guard was inside the trailer catching some Z's. Gary Manville fired his ass the next day. We figure it was homeless guys that got in. There are enough of them hanging around. You can buy a bolt cutter at any hardware store. That section of the fence was replaced, of course."

Homeless people stealing supplies from the work site didn't explain how Cal Brady wound up in the water.

"As a matter of fact, we got homeless people living on boats out on the Estuary." He laughed. "Well, I guess if they're living on boats they're not exactly homeless. But they aren't legal. If they were, they'd be living at one of the marinas. I know, because I hear the marina people complain about them. There's this one woman who anchors her boat off shore near the work site. She's got a dinghy. Sometimes at night she rows ashore and ties up at those docks that are at the back of the work site, left over from a boating supply store that used to be there. She dumps her trash, on our site and other places, like the Starbucks. I've run her off a time or two, and so have the other guards."

That was interesting. If the woman spent a lot of time in the Estuary near the Cardoza development, could she have seen something the night Cal died?

"The other situation we had to deal with was protesters," Dupre said. "The Cardoza brothers don't want people to come onto the property and sabotage the equipment or the site itself. Just for the hell of it, or to make a statement."

I took another bite of my cookie. "What sort of protesters? Why would they sabotage the Cardoza development?"

"Hey, this is the Bay Area." Dupre shrugged. "Around here, somebody's always protesting something. The way I heard it, the Cardozas got into a pissing contest with the environmentalists, back when the project was on the drawing board. They got all their approvals and permits from the city so work started in May. There were people with picket signs, out front at the Embarcadero gate. The Cardozas were upset about that, I can tell you. They acted like they were under assault. They wanted the cops to arrest the protesters. Seems they never heard about free speech and freedom of assembly." He laughed.

"What was it about? Pollution, wildlife?" With all the shipyards and boatyards along the Estuary, pollution due to spills was an issue.

"It's about being able to get to the shoreline," he said.

"Shoreline access," I said. "The Bay Trail."

The result of legislation passed back in 1987, the Bay Trail is a network of hiking and bicycling trails aimed at encircling both San Francisco Bay and its northern neighbor, San Pablo Bay. When completed, the trail will be approximately 500 miles long, connecting the shoreline of all nine Bay Area counties and forty-seven cities. About two-thirds of the trail has been completed since the legislation passed, over 300 miles. I knew Dan, who wrote hiking guidebooks, had walked a lot of those miles.

There are gaps in the trail, of course. The ability of ordinary citizens to get to the water, whether the ocean coastline or the bay shore, is a hot-button issue in California, with a coastline that stretches 840 miles. That was the reason for the creation of the California Coastal Commission, which frequently butts heads with landowners who want to close off their oceanfront property to the public. There is an ongoing case in the Bay Area concerning a landowner who owns coastal property and wants to block access to a local beach. The California Coastal Commission and the Surfrider Foundation took him to court.

Public access is no less important for the shoreline of San Francisco Bay. Those building the Bay Trail have spent nearly thirty years working with city and county governments as well as individual landowners, painstakingly filling those gaps. I knew the Brooklyn Basin project had touted its plans to include trails as part of its development. That project was the high-profile one, reported extensively in the news. The Cardoza project, on the other hand, had garnered less attention. In my Internet research, I had located a copy of the original plans, which didn't include a shoreline trail. Subsequent versions did show a narrow paved path, which would link with the public trail that ran along the waterfront behind the businesses like the hotel and the Starbucks, just north of the work site.

"The Bay Trail is supposed to ring the entire bay," I said. "There have been problems, I understand, with property owners who don't want to give an easement at the shoreline for the Bay Trail."

"Yeah, that sounds like the Cardozas. That was Stephen you saw leaving the site the other day, in the gray Caddy."

"I thought as much. What happened between the Cardozas and the protesters?"

"The way I heard it," Dupre said, "there was a lot of back-and-forth and arguing between the waterfront environmentalists and the Cardozas. Eventually the Cardozas agreed to give access to the shoreline part of their property. Kicking and screaming all the way, or that's the way I heard it on the grapevine."

"When I was at the site on Tuesday, I saw a lot of people going in and out of that trailer. What's it for?"

"That's where the security guards hang out between rounds," Dupre said with a grin. "Partly, anyway. Hanging out too much can be a problem. It sure was for the guy who was sleeping on the job and got fired. The trailer is an office and meeting place. Brice Cardoza, the site manager, the guy who is supposed to be in charge of construction, he hangs out there, too. He uses the trailer for talking with contractors, that sort of thing. The trailer has a living room and dining area at the front, a bedroom, a bathroom and a kitchen with a refrigerator and microwave, stuff like that."

I wanted to get a sense of the parameters of Cal's job. "You mention rounds. I'm guessing that means you walk the work site on a regular basis throughout your shift." Dupre affirmed this with a nod. "Tell me about your schedule."

"It's a typical schedule," Dupre said. "Three eight-hour shifts a day, with four guards rotating through the cycle. The day shift starts at seven in the morning, runs till three in the afternoon; swing shift is three to eleven; and the night shift eleven to seven the next morning. Five days on the same schedule, then off a couple of days, then back to work on a different shift."

"What's the routine, when you're on the site?"

"The guy that's reporting for duty checks in with the guy that's going off shift," Dupre said. "They talk about anything that came up during the shift, like maybe things missing, or problems with somebody trying to get on the site. Stuff like that. Like I said, we do the rounds, take breaks in the trailer. When I'm working nights or swing, I walk the site every hour or so. During the day I'm on the gate, like I was on Tuesday."

"Who was on duty before and after Cal's last shift on Saturday night?"

"A guy named Luton was the guard on swing shift. As for who would have relieved Cal Sunday morning, that would be me. I just came off five day shifts. Today and tomorrow I'm off. When I go back to work on Saturday, I'll be on the swing shift."

"What happened on Sunday?"

Dupre sighed. "I showed up about a quarter to seven. Cal usually met me at the Embarcadero gate when he was coming off duty. The gate was closed and locked, of course, it being a Sunday, not a work day. I unlocked the gate, drove in, locked up again. Cal's car was there so I figured he had to be around. I checked the trailer. He wasn't inside. So I walked around the site looking for him. Still no Cal. At that point I called Gary. He showed up right away. We looked around again. Nothing. Called Cal's cell phone. It went straight to voice mail. A couple of hours later we heard sirens, saw cop cars and an ambulance. But we still didn't put two and two together. Then the cops called Gary. That's how we found out about Cal's body." He grimaced.

"You say you looked all over the site for Cal. You didn't see Cal, but what else did you find?"

Dupre answered me with visible reluctance. "I found some booze bottles on the ground near the back fence."

I took a sip of my latte. "The story I'm hearing is that liquor bottles were found on the site after a night shift and that it happened several times."

"Three times," Dupre said. "Twice in September and once in early October. Each time it was after Cal worked a night shift. The rumor was going around that it was Cal, drinking on the job and leaving the bottles. But Cal said it wasn't him. I believed him."

"Why?"

Dupre drank more coffee, then set down his cup, his fingers drumming on the table. "I liked Cal. He never made a secret of being a recovering alcoholic. He was walking the AA walk. Said he had been down a hard road and he wasn't going back there again. We socialized some. He lived not far from here. We'd go out for a pizza or take in a movie at the Grand Lake. I never saw him take a drink, the whole time I knew him, and that's over three years. He drank coffee, iced tea, or water. That's all I ever saw Cal drink." He shook his head. "If he was drinking and hiding it, why leave the damn bottles where they could be found?"

I agreed. It didn't make sense. There had to be more to it than a bunch of empty liquor bottles.

"Besides," Dupre said. "Anyone could have left those bottles. For all I know the homeless guys tossed them over the fence. Although the fence is pretty high and I'm not sure those guys would bother, they'd just leave bottles wherever. They sure do that with their trash."

"I also heard that Cal was reprimanded for drinking on the job. Were you there when that happened?"

"Yeah, I was there. I relieved him that day. That whole thing smells funny, if you know what I mean."

"I don't. Please, enlighten me. Who reprimanded him?"

Dupre made a face, as though he'd tasted something sour. "Brice Cardoza, the site manager. His old man and his brother run the whole show. They own that construction company, so Brice is in charge. He's a real prick. Excuse my language."

"No offense taken. What happened?"

"Brice said Cal was acting drunk."

I took a sip of my latte. "Acting drunk? How?"

"Cal was a little off that morning, like he was really tired. He told me earlier in the week he'd been having trouble sleeping. That happens when you're on the night shift and sleeping days. The whole world is making noise when you're trying to get some shut-eye. The other reason was Cal thought he had a dose of food poisoning. He'd bought a tuna salad sandwich from a deli to eat during his shift. He said after he ate the sandwich he got sick."

"Makes sense," I said.

"It does to me. But Brice was making all kinds of snarky remarks, really riding Cal. He told him that obviously he'd spent the night boozing it up and that's why he was stumbling around like a drunk. Then he goes on to say he's going to complain to Gary Manville, that he won't tolerate anyone being drunk on the job, not his workers and certainly not the security guards. Then Gary Manville showed up for a meeting with Stephen and Brice, and Brice went through the whole song and dance again, for Gary's benefit."

He shook his head. "Man, it was like everyone got up on the wrong side of the bed that morning and they hadn't had enough coffee. Then the next week Cal switched around shifts, said it was so he could go to a funeral."

"Yes. I was at the same service. Someone we used to work with died."

"Well, that week there was a rumor going around that Cal hadn't gone to a funeral, that he was out drinking and had to stay home to sleep it off."

Interesting. I wondered if the rumor could be traced to Brice Cardoza, since he'd made such an issue of Cal's supposedly drinking. If Gary Manville, who actually was Cal's supervisor, hadn't formally reprimanded Cal, why was Brice getting into the act? Perhaps he and Cal had clashed. Was there bad blood between them?

"What can you tell me about Brice?" I asked.

Dupre made a disparaging sound, blowing air through his lips.

"You don't like the guy," I said.

Dupre laughed. "You figured that out, huh? No, I don't like him. He's an arrogant, entitled asshole. Excuse my French. You know the type. His daddy owns the company, so he's wonderful and the world owes him. The more I see of him, the more I'm glad I don't work for him directly. He's the kind of guy who yells at his workers in front of everyone. I hate that, when it happens to me and when it happens to other people. And he was on Cal's case a couple of times before the whole drinking-at-work thing came up."

I had always heard that, from a management standpoint, a supervisor should praise an employee in public and administer discipline in private. That was the way Errol had done it when I worked at the Seville Agency. Of course, not all employers were like that. I'd heard too many tales of bosses who bullied and hectored in front of other employees, making sure that one's coworkers knew exactly what was going on—and exactly what low esteem the boss held for the unlucky employee. I thought it was a bad way to manage people. Even if Cal had been drinking at work, the reprimand should have come from Manville, who was actually Cal's boss, and not Brice. That was jumping the chain of command, as the military types would call it.

"It sounds to me," I said, "like Brice is the only one belaboring the drinking issue."

Dupre's laugh was disparaging. "He's got no room to talk. Brice is the guy that goes over to the Biergarten every night after work. I've seen him there, drinking his way through a few beers. Sometimes he meets a foxy-looking blonde."

"Brice gives Cal a dressing-down in public," I said, "supposedly for being intoxicated, in front of Manville, the others, anyone who could listen. Why humiliate Cal in public? Was there bad blood between Cal and Brice?"

"Could be," Dupre said. "I thought it was because Brice is a monumental jackass. But it might be something else. Maybe he was getting back at Cal. Most of the time the security guards don't interact that much with the site manager. But it seemed like Cal and Brice rubbed each other the wrong way."

"When did it start? Did something happen to cause it?"

Dupre thought about it for a moment. "There was this guy that got hurt on the site. It was during the summer. He got buried in a trench and they had to dig him out. Cal was there when it happened, working days that week. He said the guy should have filed a worker's comp claim, but he didn't."

"That's a logical step after a workplace injury. I wonder why the man didn't."

"You ask me, I think some of Brice's workers are illegals. I've got no proof of that. Just got a feeling. A lot of these guys are Mexican and they don't speak English very well. And it's like a revolving door. I don't see the same guys at the work site for very long."

That would explain why the worker hadn't filed any sort of a claim. If he was in the country illegally, he could be picked up by the U.S. Immigration and Customs Enforcement, ICE, and deported. There were supposed to be legal sanctions against hiring undocumented workers, but in reality, a lot of employers dodged that bullet. They wanted workers on the cheap, people they could pay a marginal wage and people who weren't protected by health insurance or labor laws.

"Cal talked with this guy, I don't remember his name. But Cal told me it was a shame he was being treated like that. He was hurt pretty bad, Cal said."

I mulled this over. "Cal talked with the worker after the accident and encouraged him to seek compensation."

Dupre nodded. "I think so. Anyway, Brice would have figured that it wasn't any of Cal's business, that he was interfering. I'm not sure, but that could be what triggered it. Seems to me it was after that accident that Brice started riding Cal. That's when the booze bottles started showing up at the work site."

An attempt to discredit Cal? How would Brice find out that Cal was a recovering alcoholic? Then I recalled what Dupre said earlier in our conversation, that Cal had never made a secret of it. People talked. Maybe Brice had overheard something.

I wanted to speak to the worker who had been injured on the job, but Dupre reiterated that he couldn't recall the man's name. "I'll scout around, see if I can find out."

"Don't get in Brice's crosshairs," I told him. I would go back to my office and go through the papers that I'd transported from Cal's apartment. If Cal was conducting any sort of investigation, maybe it was into Brice's business practices.

"On the phone you said you had a theory about why Manville got riled up when I started asking questions about Cal."

"What happened to Cal was just one more damn thing that's gone wrong. It's the Cardozas. Gary's usually Mr. Cool, totally in control. But working for that bunch is getting to him. Those guys are real difficult. They keep nitpicking, grousing about this or that, threatening to fire Manville Security and hire another firm."

"I want to talk with Gary Manville," I said.

"He blew you off at the work site," Dupre said. "I'll talk with him, see if I can convince him to call you."

"Thanks. Who else would be on that work site during the night shift?"

"Brice," Dupre said. "Sometimes when I'm working the night shift, he shows up and spends some time in that trailer."

"Alone?"

"The times I've seen him he was by himself. He could have had company, someone in the car, that I didn't see because I was walking my rounds."

"How long had you known Cal?"

"Since he came to work for Manville. That's over three years ago. Cal had some gaps in his work history, because of the drinking. Cal told me Gary hired him because they knew each other in the Navy. They were stationed together, San Diego, I think it was. Manville did the whole twenty years in the service and retired with a pension. That's when he started the security company. When Cal came looking for a job, Manville took him on."

"What else can you tell me about Cal?" I asked. "I know he was divorced. Did he mention his private life? Family? Friends?"

"He talked about his daughter a lot. He was really proud of her.

Said she was smart, going to be a city planner or something like that. She's going to school over in Berkeley. I don't think he had many friends. Although…" Dupre smiled. "He was taking dance lessons."

"Really?" I tried to picture Cal Brady on the dance floor, and failed. Though now that business card from the Bayside Ballroom made sense.

"He told me he'd always wanted to learn how to swing dance," Dupre said. "He found a place that teaches all sorts of dancing, including swing. He signed up and told me he really enjoyed it. Said it was good exercise. I said to him, man, with all the walking we do at the work site, I don't know that you need any exercise. To tell the truth, I think he wanted to meet people. Well, women. And the dance class was a good way to do that. About a month ago he told me was interested in this woman he'd met in class. They went out for coffee after class, two or three times, I think. He said he was planning to ask her out again, for dinner and a movie."

"I'd like to talk with her," I said. "Did Cal give you the woman's name?"

Dupre thought for a moment, then shook his head. "I don't know that he ever told me her name. Just said she was about his age, mid-forties, and divorced, like he was. As for the place, I don't know the name."

But I did. It was on the business card Cal had been using as a bookmark.

Nathan Dupre looked at his watch. "I really should go before my frozen food thaws out. If I think of anything else, I'll let you know. And I'll talk to Gary, I promise."

He departed, carrying his bags from Trader Joe's.

Chapter Ten

B Y THAT TIME it was past noon. I bought a sandwich at a nearby shop and ate it at a table by the window, watching people as they went by on Lakeshore Avenue. Then I headed back to my office to prepare for my afternoon appointment with an insurance adjustor about a disputed claim.

The client's office was located on Broadway, about ten blocks from my own office. It was a fine afternoon, the air crisp and the sky blue, still warm though it was late October. I enjoyed these lingering fall days. I decided to walk. It took about fifteen minutes to reach my destination, just past Twenty-first Street, in the vicinity of the Paramount Theatre. The grand old movie palace had been built in the 1930s. After falling into disrepair in the 1970s, it closed. Then it had been restored to all its Art Deco glory. Now the Paramount was a venue for the Oakland Symphony and the ballet, and sometimes hosted a classic movie series on Friday nights. Dan and I had recently spent an evening there, enjoying a big-screen showing of Hitchcock's *North by Northwest*. I felt as though I was *in* the crop-dusting scene rather than watching it.

When I finished the meeting with the client, I went outside and stood for a moment on Broadway. I looked across the street, at a three-story building in the middle of the block. This was where I had earned my private investigator's license, working under Errol Seville's tutelage. During my six years as an operative, the firm had been located on the top floor. The building had not been in the best of condition then. Now the building was even more rundown than it had been back then. It looked abandoned, the windows on all three floors boarded up. But not for long, I gathered, from the scaffolding going up in front of the building. This part of Oakland was changing.

The area was called Uptown, with trendy bars and restaurants to match. Over on Telegraph Avenue, the block-long parking lot and garage that had served the old Emporium Capwell department store had been turned into condos and apartments. Like the Paramount, the Fox Theatre on Telegraph had been an opulent old movie palace that had fallen on hard times. Now restored, the Fox served as a musical venue. Capwell's had closed, replaced for a time by a rundown Sears store, while the old Sears building at Twenty-seventh and Telegraph had been turned into lofts. Another company was taking over the Capwell's building.

What would normally be Twentieth Street was called Thomas L. Berkley Way, named after a prominent African American lawyer and newspaper publisher who'd served on the Oakland Port Authority Board of Commissioners. At one time this stretch of Broadway had been Oakland's main downtown shopping district. Now Berkley Way was Oakland's small financial district, the wide street between Broadway and Lake Merritt lined with banks. The Kaiser Building and the nearby Ordway Building towered over the lake, while the new Catholic Cathedral of Christ the Light anchored the corner of Grand Avenue and Harrison Street.

These days a free shuttle, a small bus painted an eye-catching lime green, drove a daytime route between Grand Avenue and Jack London Square, and a nighttime route that extended even farther. Called the "Free B," the shuttle ran several times an hour, and busses were usually standing room only during the lunch hour. I walked down Broadway, past the Paramount, and paused at the shuttle stop, debating whether to walk back or catch the bus, which had not yet appeared. Then I glanced down the street. Here was the green bus, heading my way.

Back in my office, I updated the client's file. Then I called Dan, who was at home in Berkeley, working on the book he was writing about hiking in Sonoma County. We confirmed that I was cooking dinner for him tomorrow night. Then I asked, "Who would I talk to about the Bay Trail? Something's come up in a case I'm working on, regarding landowners who didn't want to grant access on some property on the Oakland waterfront."

Dan thought about it for a moment. "You might want to talk with a woman named Rachel Leverson. I spoke with her when I was writing an article about the Bay Trail. I have her card here somewhere. Just a minute."

He set down the phone. I heard him whistling in the background. A moment later he came back on the line. "Here it is. Rachel Leverson, and she's in Oakland." He rattled off a phone number and for good measure threw in the organization's address, which was on lower Broadway near Jack London Square, close to the waterfront.

"Thanks. I'll see you tomorrow night. Remember, you're bringing wine and dessert."

After ending the call, I looked up Leverson and the organization where she worked. It was an environmental group focused on San Francisco Bay. From what I found on the website, the group was leery of both the Brooklyn Basin and Cardoza projects.

I could just as easily interview Rachel Leverson over the phone, but whenever possible, I prefer to do so in person. That allows me to gauge reactions, facial expressions and body language. It also gets me out of the office.

I reached for the phone and called the organization, hoping to set up a face-to-face. When the receptionist answered, I asked to speak with Leverson. "Tell her I'm a friend of Dan Westbrook," I added. That got me through the gatekeeper. Leverson picked up the phone a moment later.

"I'm a private investigator," I said. "Dan is a friend. I am working on a case that involves the waterfront. Do you have time to meet with me this afternoon?"

"I've got a meeting later, but I have some time during the next hour. Are you in Oakland?"

"I'm just up the street from you, near Eleventh and Broadway."

"Come on down," she said.

I locked the office and went back over to Broadway, catching the green shuttle bus again. This time I rode the bus three stops down to Third Street. I found the address and went upstairs to a third-floor, bare-bones office. After I announced myself to the receptionist, I was shown to an interior office.

Rachel Leverson was a woman in her forties, stocky and comfortable in her body, dressed in what they call business casual, in a pair of navy slacks and a light blue blouse. She had a pleasant smile on her round face, short brown hair turning gray at the temples, and a pair of square-rimmed glass perched on her nose. She offered coffee, which I accepted, and asked how I knew Dan. We chatted for a few minutes, then I got to the reason I was here.

"As I told you on the phone, I'm working on a case involving the waterfront. I understand that your organization had some issues with the Cardoza development on the Embarcadero."

"The Cardozas." Leverson frowned and her expression radiated dislike. "We had such problems with that development."

"I understand that they were unwilling to grant access to the shoreline on their property."

She nodded over the rim of her coffee cup. "At first they agreed to do so. In the initial stages, when the development was going through the planning and permit process with the city, the Cardozas agreed to give an easement for a path along the shore, for walkers and bicyclists. It's supposed to be part of the Bay Trail."

"I know about the trail," I said, "from Dan, and reading about it, of course."

"It's been a long process getting the trail completed, and we have a ways to go," she said. "Early on, it was the father, Roland Cardoza, that we and the other environmental groups were dealing with. He was a nice older gentleman, willing to listen and compromise. Then he had a stroke and was out of the picture. The son, Stephen, became the point of contact." Again, Leverson made a face.

"I take it that Stephen Cardoza is less willing to listen and compromise."

"More like not cooperative at all. He's one of those 'my way or the highway' types. With him, it's all about the money. Initially that parcel they're redeveloping was smaller. But they bought up adjoining parcels and nearly doubled the size. The Cardoza project isn't as big as Brooklyn Basin, but the way housing costs are going up in this area, the company stands to make a lot of profit."

"How did it play out with Stephen Cardoza?" I asked. "I understand there were protestors at the gate when they broke ground."

"Yes. That was one of our strategies. Last spring when the Cardozas started actual construction work on the parcel, they started backpedaling, talking about how they weren't going to give access to the shoreline. They said people could walk along the Embarcadero if they wanted to hike along the Estuary. That is true in some sections of the Bay Trail. The trail's not always right there on the water, though we'd like it to be. The Brooklyn Basin planners were cooperating on the issue of trails and access. With the Cardozas, we went round and round for several months, trying to get them to live up to their side of the initial arrangement. We had a Memorandum of Understanding signed by Roland Cardoza and he's still the president of the company, even after the stroke. To tell the truth, I think they had someone in city government in their pocket."

"What makes you say that?"

"I don't know. Nothing I can put my finger on. Just a feeling." She shrugged. "Anyway, we finally told them, hey, you don't live up to what we agreed to in the MOU, we're taking you to court. That did the trick. So did the demonstration at the site. It gave us some visibility and made the Cardozas look bad. Which Stephen Cardoza most certainly did not like."

"I'm glad you and the other environmental groups are looking out for the health of the Estuary," I said. "The waterfront's changing, that's for sure."

Leverson agreed. "Much as I'd like to see open space replace the industrial leftovers, I know the city is going to succumb to the temptation to develop. Housing and retail will bring more people to the Estuary. Now I'm hearing talk about building a waterfront ballpark. I don't know where they would put it, but if they do it, that will really increase development. I just hope it's not at the expense of the Estuary."

I rode the shuttle back up Broadway, getting off at Eleventh Street. Instead of walking back to my office, I crossed Broadway and headed for the downtown area known as City Center. This redevelopment project began the planning stages in the late 1950s. It was once envisioned as a huge development that would include an indoor shopping mall, high-rise office buildings, a hotel and an above-ground parking structure. Seventy blocks were set to be razed for the development but the plans were scaled back to twelve blocks after pushback from downtown residents and property owners. As it was, residential hotels in the area were demolished after the people who lived in them were evicted. This area was once home to a large section of ornate apartment buildings, in the Victorian and Italianate styles, with ground-floor retail shops. But the city took the buildings through the eminent domain process and demolished them.

The only remnant of downtown the way it used to be could be found in the few blocks known as Old Oakland, the site of the Friday farmers' market that clustered along Ninth and Washington Streets. The historic delicatessen, Ratto's, which has been in business since 1897, was also slated to be torn down. Oakland residents vigorously protested and the deli was spared the wrecking ball. Other echoes of the past could be found in a block called Preservation Park, site of sixteen grand old buildings from the Victorian era. Five were original to the site, while others had been moved there to escape destruction.

Even after the City Center development went up in the 1970s and 1980s, the project struggled financially. The parking garage was underneath City Center. Inside there was a plaza with a fountain and a piece of outdoor art that reminded me of large, colorful pick-up sticks. Many eateries line the plaza, including the ubiquitous Starbucks and a cupcake shop with wares that looked tempting.

Cardoza Development was located in one of the business high-rises close to Fourteenth Street. As I approached the double glass doors that led inside the building, I saw a man in gray pin-stripes get off an elevator. I recognized him from one of the photos I'd found on the Internet. This was Stephen Cardoza.

He walked toward Fourteenth Street. I followed. He crossed the street to Oakland City Hall. Like several other buildings in the city, the hall was built in the Beaux-Arts style so prevalent in the late nineteenth and early twentieth centuries. It looked a lot like a tall wedding cake, sculpted out of white granite and terra-cotta. The triangular park in front of City Hall was called Frank Ogawa Plaza. It had been named after a civil rights advocate and the first Japanese American member of the city council. Ogawa was a California-born Nisei who, with his family, had been interned during World War II. A few years back, the plaza had been the site of the large Occupy Oakland encampment, when a sea of tents had covered the grassy area in the middle. Now, in midafternoon, there were a few people stretched out on the lawn and others sitting on the steps in front of the hall.

Cardoza walked to the steps and stopped. He looked at his watch and then at the front doors of City Hall, giving all the signs of waiting for someone. I hovered nearby, my cell phone out, as though sending a text message. A few minutes later a woman came out of the building. She looked to be in her thirties, with blond hair twisted into a roll at the back of her neck, above the collar of the floral print dress she wore. She came down the steps and greeted Cardoza, then she looked over her shoulder as another woman came out of the building.

This new arrival was older, with salt-and-pepper hair over a strong, square face. She wore a navy blue pantsuit with a bright red blouse and looked commanding as she strode toward Cardoza and the blond woman. She also looked familiar but her name escaped me. I snapped a few photos of the threesome. I wasn't close enough to hear what they were saying. Then they turned and headed across the plaza, led by the older woman. I followed, keeping a few paces back. They entered a café on the other side of the plaza and sat at one of the tables.

Interesting, I thought. The interior of the café didn't offer me much opportunity to eavesdrop. But it looked like a business meeting. It didn't surprise me that a developer like Cardoza knew someone at City Hall, or that he would meet with those people outside of the hall. I recalled what Rachel Leverson had told me during our talk. She had wondered if the Cardozas had someone in city government in their pocket. Maybe they did.

Chapter Eleven

~~~~~~~~~~~~~~~~~~

I TURNED and retraced my steps, heading back to City Center Plaza. I had to check out that cupcake shop. I looked at the offerings and saw a cupcake that contained coffee and chocolate, my favorite flavors. I bought two and carried them back to my office, where I started a pot of coffee. While water dripped through the grounds, I turned on my computer.

I did a search on the Oakland City Council, which has seven districts, plus an at-large member. Council members serve staggered four-year terms. Unlike the mayor's office, there are no term limits for the council. The web page I found listed the council members by district, with photos of each member. Here was a picture of the older woman I'd seen with Stephen Cardoza. Her name was Audrey DeSousa. She had been on the council for six years, which meant she had been reelected once. She represented a district in the Oakland hills, not mine.

I did another search, looking for articles about DeSousa. I saw a byline I recognized. Nyah Stubbins had once been a reporter for the *Oakland Tribune*. But she had left that position several years before when the newspaper went through another round of changes. It had once been independent, then it was purchased by a local newspaper group. Now it was folded into something called the *East Bay Times*. These days, with the advent of online editions and declining subscriptions, times are hard in the newspaper business.

Nyah was still writing, as a freelancer and a blogger, her focus on Oakland and its specific virtues and problems. I read her posts on a regular basis. She had her finger on the pulse of the city's politics and I was sure she could tell me about DeSousa.

I located Nyah's cell phone number in my contacts. She was usually busy, so I expected to get voice mail, but she answered.

"Can we get together? I have questions about the city council."

"I'm near the Tribune Tower right now," she said, naming the Oakland landmark at Thirteenth and Franklin, towering over what had once been the newspaper offices. Back in the 1920s, Harry Houdini had escaped from a straitjacket while dangling upside down from one of the upper floors. "Are you at your office? I'm just two blocks from your building. I'll drop by."

Nyah showed up ten minutes later. She was a tall, slender African American woman who wore her hair braided in cornrows that fell past her shoulders. Her earrings and necklace were African beads. She was from West Oakland. I'd met her years ago, when she was still a reporter and I was working for Errol.

"I heard Errol died," she said, after greeting me with a hug. I motioned her to the chair in front of my desk as I poured mugs of coffee for both of us.

"Yes, he did. I went to the memorial service last week. He was a good guy. I'll really miss him." I took a sip of coffee. "Say, I've got a couple of chocolate cupcakes here. Want one?"

She shook her head. "I just had coffee with a friend at Sweet Bar on Broadway and I must admit that cheesecake was involved. I'll pass on the cupcake. What did you want to ask me? You said it was about the city council."

"Specifically a city council member named Audrey DeSousa."

Nyah nodded, sipping her coffee. "She's been on the city council for about six years. Her tenure has been rather lackluster. She's been overshadowed by some of the more vocal and visible members of the council. DeSousa is very pro-development. Initially she was in favor of the coal project but I think she's backed away from it because of all the opposition from the mayor and other council members."

The coal project Nyah referred to was a controversial plan by a local developer to build a huge and expensive commercial development near the Outer Harbor, at the old Oakland Army Base that shut down in 1999. The development was set to include a recycling center, maritime support services and a rail line. The most contentious element was a proposed rail-to-ship coal-exporting facility. Millions of tons of coal would be shipped from Utah by rail to Oakland, where the coal would then be loaded onto ships for transport to China.

Opposition came not only from residents of West Oakland, the neighborhood that would be affected, but also from many environmental organizations, including the Sierra Club. Oakland city government, state legislators and the area's congressional representative were also against the coal shipping plan. In addition to the prospect of pollution from coal dust arising from coal being transported in open cars through the city, opponents cited climate impacts. When it comes to climate change and rising sea levels, Oakland, with miles of shoreline on the bay and the Estuary, will be on the front lines.

Nyah was very vocal in her opposition to the coal project. She was active in environmental justice, a social movement that focuses on fair distribution of environmental benefits and burdens. The part of town where she had grown up, West Oakland, had seen more than its share of the burdens. The neighborhood had long been an industrial center, with the port and the railroads. There were freeways on two sides, both busy, and a constant flow of truck traffic heading to and from the port. A sewage treatment plant was located near the base of the Bay Bridge anchorage. In the past there had been steel plants along the waterfront. Between the diesel trucks and diesel train engines, West Oakland had high rates of asthma. It also had a Superfund cleanup site, legacy of one of the chemical factories, now closed.

"There's a lot of opposition to that idea," I said. "We really don't need long trains full of coal coming into the port. It will be interesting to see how it all plays out. I know the developer has a long-standing relationship with the governor."

"The governor who is committed to action on climate change," Nyah pointed out. "We'll see...."

"What else can you tell me about DeSousa?"

"She's against the housing impact fee," Nyah said. "Not surprising since she's so pro-development."

"I've been reading about that. Is the fee supposed to generate money for affordable housing?"

"Also transportation and infrastructure," she said. "Other cities are doing it. Oakland needs to get onboard, with all the new construction that's planned or already in progress. The way it works, the city would impose a fee on new housing developments, whether single-family homes or multi-unit apartments. The fee will be graduated so that it takes more money from projects here downtown and less money from the low-income areas, such as East and West Oakland. DeSousa has already made several statements against the proposal. She has a lot of supporters who are developers."

"Including the Cardozas."

"Among others." She took another sip of coffee. "Why this interest in DeSousa and the Cardozas?"

"It relates to a case I'm working on," I said.

"I assumed it did. The Cardozas are building a multi-unit project on the Embarcadero, south of the Brooklyn Basin project. Market rate housing, of course. It's always market-rate, when people are desperate for affordable housing. Folks in West Oakland are getting gentrified out of their homes." She shook her head. "DeSousa is particularly close to the Cardozas. Roland Cardoza lives in her district, up in the Oakland hills. And he knew her father. A lot of Portuguese Americans live in San Leandro and that's where the DeSousas and the Cardozas are from. So the Cardozas provide DeSousa with lots of campaign contributions."

"Is she running for city council again? Her term's not up for a couple of years."

"Oh, no, not city council," Nyah said. "DeSousa is aiming at the state legislature in Sacramento. There's going to be a seat available in the California Assembly. It hasn't been announced yet, but the person who has that seat now is planning to run for Congress. DeSousa is going after the assembly seat."

It appeared the Cardozas had an ally in DeSousa. I thought again to the scene earlier, with Stephen Cardoza meeting DeSousa in front of City Hall. How did this relate to Cal Brady's death? Or did it have anything all to do with the murder?

After Nyah left, I replenished my coffee mug and ate one of the coffee-and-chocolate cupcakes. It was every bit as delicious as it looked. After I'd eaten the last morsel, I licked icing traces from my fingers.

I stood up and removed the lid from one of the boxes I'd brought from Cal's apartment. At the top was the book containing the Bayside Ballroom business card he'd been using as a bookmark. Nathan Dupre said Cal had been taking swing dance lessons. On the Internet browser I typed in the URL listed on the Bayside Ballroom card.

The ballroom was located on the Embarcadero, not far from the Cardoza work site. On weekdays the studio was open from noon until ten o'clock at night, and on weekends, ten o'clock to five. I clicked on the link that led me to the class schedule for the current month. The studio offered lessons in everything from bolero and rumba to salsa and tango, with foxtrot, ballroom dances and waltz in between. Most of the classes were taught in the late afternoon or evening, to accommodate working customers. Every other Sunday afternoon the place had a tea dance. On Thursdays there was a dance party in one of the facility's ballrooms. The other ballroom was where the Western swing dance class was taught on Thursdays, with a beginner's class at seven P.M. and an intermediate class following at eight P.M.

I was betting Cal had taken the beginner-level class. Today was Thursday. I'd go over to the studio later. According to Dupre, Cal had gone out for coffee, several times, with a woman in the class. If I got to the studio before the class started, perhaps I could talk with the woman.

I turned again to the boxes I'd brought from Cal's apartment. File boxes first, I thought, then the books. I lifted the first plastic file box to my desk and stood there, going through the contents. As I sifted through the contents of the box, I gleaned information about Cal's day-to-day life, but I didn't find anything that told me whether he was investigating something. I set the box on the floor and went through the other three boxes, netting the same result. Then I picked up the first box of books, mindful of what Madison had told me about her father's propensity for hiding things in the pages. If Cal had been investigating something, like the workplace accident Nathan Dupre told me about, perhaps he'd hidden his notes here.

I worked my way through a collection of science fiction and thrillers. Affixed to the cover of one of them was a yellow Post-it with the name "Lydia" printed in black ink. I set that aside and picked up a book about the building of the Panama Canal. This one had a folded slip of paper inside with the words "Vance Marine Supply." Was this the boating supply store that used to be on the Embarcadero? It was gone now, the land added to the Cardoza parcel. I did an Internet search on the business and discovered that it had been destroyed in a fire over two years ago. Arson had been suspected in the blaze, according to the brief news article. But there was no follow-up article to tell me whether arson had been proved. The store's demise explained how the Cardozas came to buy the parcel.

I picked up a thick hardcover book called *Blood and Thunder*, by Hampton Sides. It was a biography of Kit Carson and I'd read it when it first came out. It looked as though Cal had purchased the book used. The dust jacket was yellowed and torn in places. The price had been clipped from the front flap and another price had been written in pencil.

I opened the pages. My first find was a scrap of paper torn from an envelope. When I read the scrawled words it proved to be a grocery list. No help there. I riffled the pages. Here was something else, a piece of newsprint that had been folded in quarters. I pulled it out and unfolded it, looking at a newspaper clipping. One side contained an advertisement and the other was a photograph with a caption. At the top Cal had written "Oakland Tribune" and a date.

The photograph had been taken at an event held earlier this year at the Oakland Museum of California, which was on Oak Street near the courthouse. The museum rented out its spaces for events and this one had been a charity fund-raiser. I examined the photograph, which showed several people holding wineglasses and chatting. On the left side of the photo, wearing a tailored red-and-gray dress, was Audrey DeSousa. Standing next to DeSousa were all three Cardozas, Roland, the father, and his sons Stephen and Brice. On the right side of the photograph was the blond woman I'd seen earlier this afternoon with DeSousa and Stephen Cardoza. The caption identified her as Zoe Erland, a City Hall staffer. My guess was that Erland worked for DeSousa. I consulted DeSousa's city council web page and discovered that I was right. Erland was listed as the council member's aide.

Another link to the Cardozas, but why had Cal saved this photo? Was it because it pictured all three of the Cardozas? Or did it have something to do with Audrey DeSousa and her developer-friendly stance?

I set the photo aside and worked my way through the rest of the books in the box, finding nothing more of interest. The second box contained a lot of hardbacks, mostly about World War II. At the bottom was *The Rising Sun*, John Toland's book about the war from the Japanese viewpoint. The book was so massive that when it had been originally published in hardcover, it was in two volumes. Neither of the books in the box had dust jackets. A price written on the inside cover of the first book indicated that Cal had purchased the volumes at a second-hand book store. The binding was loose. I checked inside, between the binding and the spine of the book. Nothing there. I picked up the second volume, intending to check the same area. I didn't have to. Something slipped out, landing on the desk.

It was a slim notebook, about three by five inches, small enough to tuck into a pocket. I sat down in my chair and opened the notebook. I recognized Cal's handwriting. But reading what was written inside was difficult. Cal had been using some kind of shorthand of his own devising.

I kept at it, figuring out a few words, then others. It appeared that this was what Cal had been investigating, the accident at the Cardoza work site that had injured a worker. The worker's name was Manuel Álvarez and there was a phone number. Cal's notes indicated that Álvarez was indeed undocumented, as Nathan

Dupre had told me during our conversation this morning. After being injured on the job he'd been fired. No doubt that was what prompted Cal in his effort to help Álvarez.

I picked up the phone and called the number in the notebook but I got a message saying that the phone was no longer in service. It could have been a pay-as-you-go phone, sometimes called a burner, the kind of phone that wasn't tied to a wireless carrier. Instead one purchased the phone with a prepaid number of minutes. Once the minutes ran out, more could be added, or the phone could be discarded.

I read through the notebook one more time. It was time to have a talk with Brice Cardoza. He was the only person who had been saying, loudly and repeatedly, that Cal was drinking on the job.

I shut down my computer and left the office. It was late afternoon and it was possible most of the work force had left the Cardoza construction site. I took the Embarcadero, driving past Jack London Square. As I passed Fifth Avenue and the Brooklyn Basin development, I encountered a lot of traffic on the Embarcadero, but it wasn't as bad as the slowly moving traffic to my left, on Interstate 880, which was full of vehicles. It seemed that evening rush hour no longer took place in the evening, but started in midafternoon.

When I reached the Cardoza development, I pulled my car to the curb, looking at the work site. As I suspected, it appeared most of the construction workers had gone home. The gate that fronted on the Embarcadero was closed. A security guard emerged from a portable toilet at the back of the site and ambled toward the gate. Two vehicles were parked in front of the trailer. One of them presumably belonged to the security guard. The other was the white pickup truck with the HASSELTINE CONSTRUCTION logo. It looked like the same truck that Brice Cardoza had been driving when I'd seen him on Tuesday. About ten minutes after I arrived, a man came out of the trailer. From his build and his shaggy brown hair, it looked like Brice Cardoza. He unlocked the pickup and got in, starting the engine. The truck backed away from the trailer and headed for the gate, which the guard had opened. The driver waved at the guard and then turned left onto the Embarcadero.

The guard closed the gate. As the truck passed me, I confirmed that Brice was the driver.

After a quick look at oncoming traffic, I pulled away from the curb and made a U-turn. The truck headed past the Starbucks and the hotel building and paused at the stop sign, waiting for south-bound traffic to pass. Then it turned left, onto the short stretch of Tenth Avenue that ran from the Embarcadero toward the shore-line. The street was a dead end, terminating fifty yards or so west of the Embarcadero, in the looming shadow of the now-empty Ninth Avenue Terminal. The pickup turned left, into the parking lot of a restaurant called the Biergarten.

I had been to the restaurant before. As the name implied, the place had a wide selection of beers, many of them from Germany. The menu was loaded with wurst and schnitzel. On the right side of the building a walkway led down to several boat slips. To the left of the front door was a patio surrounded by a low wooden fence. The patio looked out over the water, with communal picnic tables of varnished wood, shaded by big white umbrellas. It was a good place to sit with a brew, a brat and a basket of fries, watching the boats and the sunset.

Cardoza wedged the white pickup into a parking space at the end of a row. He didn't get out of the truck right away. As I passed the vehicle, I saw him talking, one hand holding a cell phone, the other gesturing. I parked in the first available space, got out of my car and strolled toward the restaurant. Cardoza ended his call and got out of the pickup. As he approached me, I gave him a once-over. He looked to be about six feet tall, with broad shoulders and bulky torso straining his khaki slacks and light blue work shirt. His hair was light brown, curling at the ends as it had in the photo I'd found. He paid no attention to me as he stepped up to the front door and entered the restaurant.

It was a pleasant late-fall day. I hoped Cardoza would sit out-side, on the patio, which was visible from the parking lot and the path behind the hotel. I stood waiting outside, my phone in my hand, pretending to read a text message. I looked up as a car door slammed nearby. A dark-haired man with a thin face and a long nose walked past me, talking on his phone. I turned and saw Brice

Cardoza walking onto the restaurant's patio. Most of the tables were occupied, but there was an empty one at the far end. He sat down there, facing the door that led back to the restaurant. He leaned back and stretched one khaki-clad leg out on the bench.

The dark-haired man finished his call and entered the restaurant. I paced along the outer fence, my cell phone at my ear for camouflage as I watched Cardoza. He ran a hand through his hair, head tilted upward as he looked at the large board that listed the beer offerings. A server approached the table and he spoke to her, pointing at the board. The server departed and returned a few minutes later with a large stein of amber-colored beer. Cardoza took a long swallow and checked his watch. Was he meeting someone? He pulled out his cell phone, punched several buttons, and raised the phone to his ear. He turned toward me and I moved away from the fence, again pretending to talk on the phone. Cardoza ended his call and tucked his phone into his pocket. He drank some more beer, looking out at the boats on the water.

I walked toward the restaurant entrance as two men exited, getting into a sedan a few paces from me. The sedan backed out of the space, which was quickly claimed by a bright red BMW. The driver's-side door opened and a woman emerged. I recognized the floral print dress. It was Zoe Erland, Audrey DeSousa's City Hall aide, the woman who had been with Audrey DeSousa and Stephen Cardoza this afternoon. In the photograph she had been standing next to Brice at that museum event. Was she here to meet him now?

She passed me without glancing my way. When she went into the restaurant, I turned and walked back along the fence. She entered the patio and walked to the end where she joined Brice at the table, sitting down on the bench opposite him. She set the briefcase beside her. The server approached and the woman looked up and shook her head.

Girlfriend? Or something else?

As I watched the expressions on their faces and their body language, I didn't see any affection between the two of them. In fact, this had all the earmarks of a business meeting.

The server returned, setting a large basket of fries on the

table. Cardoza sprinkled salt over the fries and doused them with ketchup, then dug in, wiping his fingers on a paper napkin. He and Erland talked as he ate, but there was too much noise coming from the other restaurant patrons for me to hear them. I moved closer to the fence surrounding the patio but still I couldn't hear them.

Cardoza took another long drink from his beer. Then he reached into the pocket of his work shirt and took out an envelope that had been folded in half. He unfolded it. I was close enough to see that it was an ordinary business envelope, but there was nothing written on it. I raised my cell phone again, going to the camera. I quickly switched the setting from still photography to video and began recording Cardoza and Erland. He handed the envelope to Erland. She opened the briefcase at her side and slipped the envelope inside.

What had I just seen? A bribe? A payoff? Somehow I didn't think Cardoza was handing off a love letter to Erland.

Cardoza raised his beer to his lips as Erland got up from the table and walked away. I moved around to the front of the building. Before Erland left the restaurant I took a photo of the license plate on her red BMW and filmed her entering the car. Then I walked back toward the patio, where Cardoza was finishing his beer and fries. He wiped his hands again and pulled out his cell phone. When he finished the call he waved at the server, who brought him the check. As he stood he took his wallet from the back pocket of his khakis and tossed a few bills on the table. Then he walked toward the door leading into the restaurant.

I was waiting for him outside. "Brice Cardoza."

He stopped and looked at me, squinting a pair of pale blue eyes. "Yeah?"

"You're the site manager of the Cardoza development on the Embarcadero."

"Yeah. What about it?"

"I have a report of an accident at the work site, involving a man named Manuel Álvarez."

I'd been looking for a reaction and I got one. Cardoza frowned at me and growled, "Who are you? What do you want?"

"I'd like some information on what happened to Mr. Álvarez. I understand he was working in a trench and was injured when he was buried by dirt. I've been told Mr. Álvarez was fired. By you."

Cardoza's expression turned threatening as he moved closer. "That's bullshit. Who have you been talking to?" He took another step toward me. He was about six feet tall to my five foot eight and he outweighed me. He was trying to intimidate me but I held my ground.

"You've been talking to Álvarez," Cardoza said. Then the penny dropped. "Or Brady." Now his face was just a few inches from mine. I could smell the beer on his breath and see the fire in his pale blue eyes. "Whatever that drunk told you, it's a lie. Brady's a boozer and a loser. He got his ass fired from his last job because he was a drunk. Now he's dead."

"Yes, Brady's dead. What would you know about that?"

Cardoza stopped, anger turning to alarm. "What the fuck is that supposed to mean?"

"Just what I said. What do you know about Brady's death?"

"Nothing," he snapped. "Guy got drunk and went swimming in the Estuary. And if you're spreading a bunch of bull crap about that, you better watch your back, bitch." He brushed past me, deliberately knocking me off the sidewalk. I righted myself as Brice strode toward his truck. I stood and watched as he got into the driver's seat. He started the truck with a roar and backed out of the space, narrowly missing a car that was circling the parking lot, looking for a place to park. The driver of the car honked his horn and Cardoza responded with an upraised middle finger as he tore out of the parking lot.

I had certainly touched a nerve there.

Chapter Twelve

B RICE CARDOZA was a worm. It would give me great pleasure to take him down a peg. If he was responsible for Cal's death, I'd put him in jail for it. First, though, I had to figure out what had happened, and why. And prove it, in order to make charges stick.

Zoe Erland offered another avenue of investigation. I'd seen Brice pass that envelope to her. Why? What was in the envelope?

I drove to the Bayside Ballroom. It wasn't exactly on the bay, but the front of the building looked across the Embarcadero at the Estuary and the island that housed the Coast Guard base. I parked in the lot and headed for the front door, which was flanked by large plate glass windows that looked in on two large studios with wooden floors and floor-to-ceiling mirrors.

I entered the small lobby, where glass walls and doors on either side of a central counter led to the ballrooms. There were two people behind the counter. The man was dealing with customers, a young couple who were signing up for dance lessons. The woman behind the counter was talking on the phone. She indicated that she knew I was there, gesturing to tell me she'd be with me in a moment.

I stepped to one side and looked at the brochures and fliers arrayed at the end of the counter. In addition to classes, the venue was available to rent for events. It looked like the place had a full schedule, though. The larger room was to my right, called the Grand

Ballroom, where tonight at seven o'clock I could take a tango lesson if that suited me. At eight o'clock, tango would give way to a dance party, open to all for a six-dollar charge.

The smaller Terrace Ballroom, the location of the Western swing dance class, was on my left. I stepped past the soda machine and looked through the glass lobby window into the studio. The far wall of the room was a large mirror. The other three walls contained benches and chairs. I counted eleven people waiting for the lesson to begin. Most of them appeared to be middle-aged, though the young woman wearing a swirly red dress and low-heeled shoes was about thirty. Sitting on the bench to the left was an Asian man in black slacks and a yellow knit shirt. He leaned over and removed his street shoes. Then he took a pair of black dancing shoes from a cloth bag and put them on, tying the shoelaces. I noticed that several other men were wearing similar shoes, though the gray-haired man sitting by himself wore loafers with his gray slacks and checked shirt. Farther back I saw a door leading to a back room. To the left of this was a rack with a loudspeaker and some other electrical gear. Inside the back room I glimpsed a coffee urn and a sign that pointed out the location of the restrooms.

The woman behind the counter finished her phone call and smiled at me. "May I help you?"

"Who teaches the swing dance class?" I asked.

"That would be Suzette." The receptionist glanced at the big round clock on the lobby wall. It was nearly six-thirty. "The beginner's class starts at seven and the intermediate class at eight. They're both in the Terrace Ballroom. The cost is fifteen dollars for a walk-in. If you're interested, you can take all five classes in the session for sixty dollars. And," she added with a glance at the Grand Ballroom, "if you take the class you get free admission to the dance party."

"Not tonight, thanks. What I'd really like to do is speak with Suzette, please."

She looked curious, but got up from her chair and walked to the door leading to the Terrace Ballroom. She opened the glass door and beckoned to a slender woman who was standing near the equipment rack, wearing form-fitting gray slacks and a short-sleeved blue top with sequins decorating the sleeves. She appeared to be in her mid-thirties, with honey-colored hair braided in the back. Suzette walked up to the doorway.

"This lady would like to speak with you about the swing dance class," the other woman said.

Suzette gave me a friendly smile. "Certainly. What do you want to know? Let's step over here and I'll answer any questions you have."

We moved to the corner of the lobby, standing to one side of the soda machine.

"My name's Jeri Howard. I believe a man named Cal Brady was taking swing classes here. At least that's what someone told me."

She looked perplexed. "Yes, we do have a student named Cal. A tall man, in his forties. I don't really know much about people in the class, other than their names, and first names at that. The students come and go. Why are you asking?"

I pulled a business card from my bag and handed it to her. "I'm sorry to tell you that Cal Brady's dead."

She stared at the card, then at me. "How awful. What happened?"

"His body was found in the Estuary Sunday morning."

"I heard something on the news about a body." She looked stricken.

"Cal was a friend. I'm looking into the situation at the request of his daughter. I spoke with one of Cal's coworkers earlier today. He told me that Cal was taking swing dance lessons at a place near where he worked. This is close to his job site. Was he taking lessons here?"

She nodded. "For the past few months. He was a regular. Except when he had to work. He told me he was a security guard, and sometimes he had to work nights." She looked at my card again. "You're a private investigator? Is there something odd about Cal's death?"

I nodded. "I believe there is. So does his daughter. The person who told me Cal was taking dance lessons also told me he was interested in a woman he met here in class. Evidently they had gone out for coffee several times. I would really like to talk with that woman."

"Her name's Hilda," Suzette said. "I don't know her last name. But she's a regular. She's been coming to classes here for about six months. I could tell that she and Cal hit it off. I knew about the coffee dates, because I overheard them talking one night. She usually shows up about now. When she gets here, I'll point her out to you." She shook her head. "I am so sorry to hear this. Cal seemed like such a nice guy."

I knew that Bayside Ballroom would not be likely to give me Hilda's contact information. My best bet was to wait. I took a seat on the bench near the front door, watching as people entered the building and the clock on the wall ticked toward seven o'clock.

Ten minutes before the swing dance class was due to start, the outer door opened and a woman walked into the lobby toward the door leading to the Terrace Ballroom. Suzette met her there. "Hi, Hilda. Do you have a minute?"

The woman appeared to be in her mid-forties, the same age as Cal, with an oval face and a long nose. She was medium height, with dark brown hair pulled back into a short ponytail at the nape of her neck. Tiny gold studs decorated her pierced ears. She wore blue slacks with a buttoned shirt decorated with blue and yellow flowers.

Suzette steered Hilda toward me. I held out a business card. "My name's Jeri Howard."

"Hilda Camacho," she said, her voice low and pleasant. She looked at the card, perplexed. "A private investigator? What is this about?"

"I'm Cal Brady's friend," I said. "I'm sorry to tell you that Cal is dead."

"Oh, no." Sadness swept over her face and she blinked her large brown eyes. "That's terrible. He was such a nice man. What happened?"

"His body was found in the Estuary Sunday morning."

She gasped. "Did he drown? But how? He was working nights. That's what he said the last time I talked with him. Did something happen at the job site? Was it an accident?"

"Do you have a few minutes to talk with me?" I asked.

"Of course."

We moved away from the ballroom door, back to the bench where I'd been sitting. Once we sat down, I said, "I understand that you had gone out with Cal a few times, for coffee. Did he ever talk about his job, or anything that might have been bothering him?"

Hilda frowned. "It wasn't an accident, was it?"

"Why do you say that?"

"You're an investigator." She waved the card I had given her. "Cal was, too, at one time. At least that's what he told me."

"Yes, he was. Cal and I used to work together, a few years back. Then he left the firm."

"He told me he got fired, because of his drinking."

It appeared that Cal had been upfront with Hilda. "Yes, he was fired. I saw him recently at a memorial service. He told me he was sober, that he'd been going to AA."

She nodded. "He said he hadn't had a drink in nearly four years. He also told me about his daughter. She's in grad school over at UC Berkeley. He was so proud of her." I saw the glistening of tears in her eyes. "I really liked him. I'm sorry he's dead. Do you know when his funeral will be?"

"His daughter hasn't scheduled the service yet." As far as I knew, the autopsy was still pending. "If you'll give me your phone number, I'll call you as soon as I know something."

She recited the number and I jotted it in my notebook. Inside the ballroom, the students were on their feet in the middle of the shiny wood floor, the men facing the women, as Suzette demonstrated a move. Hilda looked into the ballroom and I wondered if she was going to get up and join the class. But she didn't. Instead she spoke. "It wasn't an accident, then."

"No. I think he was murdered."

"Who would do such a thing?" she asked, more to herself than to me.

"Did he talk about anything that was bothering him?" I asked again.

"We talked, after class, and we went out for coffee three times. He had asked me out for dinner and a movie, next week. They have this classic movie series at the Alameda Theatre. That's where I live, in Alameda. Anyway, the movie was *Lawrence of Arabia*. We both wanted to see it on the big screen. I didn't know him very long, but we really hit it off, you know. Like we'd known each other for a long time." She sighed.

"The last time I saw him was here at class, last week. He had just gone to that funeral and had had a couple of days off. He was starting his night shift days that Thursday, at eleven at night, but he came to class from seven to eight. We went over to Alameda and had coffee at the Peet's there on Park Street. We walked over to the movie theater, since it's nearby, and we looked at the classic movie schedule. That's when we made the date. Then he went to work."

"Did he ever talk about work?" I asked, moving the conversation back to my original question.

Hilda nodded. "He told me there was a man who got hurt on the job. Cal thought this man got a raw deal, because he was undocumented. The man who was in charge of the construction, Brice, I think his name is—Cal didn't like this guy Brice at all. Said he cut corners and treated the workers bad. As for the man who was hurt, Cal said he was going to figure out a way to help him. He didn't say how, but I knew he was looking into things there on the job, thinking that maybe he'd talk to Cal/OSHA. I don't know if he ever did."

That made two of us who didn't like Brice Cardoza. I waited, hoping that Hilda would remember something else that Cal had told her.

"Cal said…" Her voice trailed off. "Cal figured out something about that company that's building the development."

"Hasseltine Construction?" I asked.

She shook her head. "The Cardozas."

"Did he say what it was?"

"No. But he was really excited about it. Energized, you know what I mean? He said it could be dynamite."

I sat back on the bench, wondering what Cal had uncovered. It could be dynamite, all right. That information could be the catalyst for his murder.

Chapter Thirteen

WHEN MY FATHER retired, he discovered a passion for birding. I enjoy spending time with Dad and I've accompanied him on trips around the Bay Area. I already had the binoculars, a useful tool for a private investigator. I've acquired a few other things, including a copy of Roger Tory Peterson's *Field Guide to Birds of Western North America* and my own little notebook to write down the names of the birds I've seen.

It's a slippery slope. Next I'll be signing up for a birding class.

When I left my house early Friday morning, I wore the protective coloration of a birder, including binoculars and bird book tucked into my daypack with a bottle of water. I drove through Oakland to the Embarcadero. My destination was a strip of businesses located between the Brooklyn Basin development and the Cardoza site. I drove past the hotel near the corner of Tenth Avenue and the Embarcadero and pulled into the lot. I parked in front of the Starbucks at the end of the row and went inside, where I ordered a latte to warm me. It was chilly outside.

Coffee in hand, I left the Starbucks. There was a parking lot at the side of the building that ran all the way back to the water. Vance Marine Supply, the store that had burned several years earlier in the arson fire, was to the south. After the Cardozas had acquired the land, what remained of the building had been razed and the ground graded. Now a hedge and the high chain-link fence separated the parking lot from the Cardoza project. The only remnant of the boating supply store was the two unoccupied docks jutting into the Estuary, their emptiness contrasting with the boats tied up at the marina docks near me.

I walked through the side parking lot, heading back to the water. At the shore were marina docks, with gates barring the way to the boats themselves. The area behind the businesses and hotel, however, was part of the Bay Trail now. Instead of turning right, onto the trail, I angled to the left. Here the hedge was ragged and overgrown, hiding the parking lot from view. A dirt path led about fifteen feet along the shoreline until it came to a halt at the fence that surrounded the Cardoza construction site.

It was seven-fifteen in the morning. The guard on the night shift had been relieved by his day-shift counterpart. I stopped and set my latte on the ground. At the spot where the pavement ended, two ring-billed gulls fought over some morsel scavenged from a nearby trash can. I turned toward the Estuary and raised my binoculars, focusing on several birds in the water between me and the empty docks. They were Western grebes, diving for food. Three double-crested cormorants perched on the nearest dock, and a pair of mallards, male and female, paddled in the water below them.

After taking a sip of coffee, I focused the binoculars on the Cardoza work site and the trailer, seeing several vehicles parked in front, even at this early hour. One of them was the white pickup with the HASSELTINE CONSTRUCTION logo, the truck that Brice Cardoza had been driving last night. Next to it was the gray Cadillac belonging to his brother, Stephen. Nathan Dupre had told me about the early-morning meetings the brothers liked to schedule. As I watched, the daytime security guard exited one of the portable toilets, adjusting his trousers. He walked briskly toward the gate that fronted on the Embarcadero, just in time to meet a pickup truck.

I panned the binoculars back to the trailer. Then I looked at the empty docks behind the site. Out in the Estuary I saw a boat with a red stripe, probably the one Dupre had said was occupied by a woman who sometimes rowed ashore and dumped her trash on the work site. It was an old cabin cruiser, maybe thirty feet long. I didn't see any sign of her, but guessed she was aboard, since there was a blue dinghy tied up beside the boat.

"You birdwatching?"

I turned. A man stood at the spot where the dirt path joined the pavement. He was medium height, thin, with curly blond hair sticking out from under a gray watch cap. He was homeless, by the look of him. He and his layers of shabby clothing had seen better days. The small shopping cart a few paces back was a dead giveaway. It contained what looked like a small tent, a sleeping bag, and several canvas totes. The man appeared to be around sixty, but he could have been forty or even younger. Living on the streets is hard and adds years to the appearance.

I nodded. "Yes. Lots of water birds here."

The man nodded. "Oh, yeah. We get all kinds. Bufflehead, scaup, Northern shoveler. All kinds of grebes. I saw a merganser the other day."

"Sounds like you know your birds."

A smile lightened his worn face. "Yeah, well, I grew up on the coast."

"Do you stay in the area?" I gestured at the shopping cart.

He shrugged and the smile went away. "Here and there. What's it to you?"

I sipped my latte. "A body was found in the Estuary Sunday morning."

He nodded, his face wary. "Yeah, I heard about that. Up by Clinton Basin. A man's body, washed up against a fence."

"I think the body went into the water down here." I pointed. "Maybe even off those docks."

He looked over at the docks, his voice noncommittal. "Could have gone into the water anywhere."

I took out a business card and held it up. "Jeri Howard. I'm a private investigator. Did you see anything unusual, late Saturday night or early Sunday morning?"

He plucked the card from my hand, glanced at it, then looked up at me with a pair of hazel eyes in his lined face. "Why do you want to know?"

"The man whose body was found at Clinton Basin was murdered. He worked as a security guard at that construction site."

He didn't respond right away, as though he was mulling it over. I had a feeling he had seen something. I hoped my hunch would pay off.

"You got any spare change?" he asked.

"How about we go over to Starbucks so you can get some breakfast? My treat."

"Works for me. Coffee and some of those breakfast sandwiches would taste real good this morning."

"What do I call you?"

"Tony." He stuck the business card in his pocket.

I led the way to the front of the building. Tony didn't want to leave his shopping cart unattended. He sat down at one of the outside tables.

"I'll order," I said. "You can have anything you want."

He must have had the menu memorized. He rattled off his choices. I entered the coffee shop and queued up at the counter. When it was my turn, I placed the order, adding an almond croissant for myself. Tony wanted four breakfast sandwiches and four scones, along with a large coffee. I paid the tab and waited until my name was called. I stuck his coffee and mine in a tray and carried it outside, a large paper bag of food in the other hand. I sat down next to Tony and took my croissant out of the bag, breaking off a piece. He unwrapped his first breakfast sandwich, egg with bacon and cheese, and tore into it. I suspected he hadn't eaten in a while.

I waited until he was on his second sandwich. "Do you know anything about the boating supply store that was on the lot by those unoccupied docks?"

"Just that there used to be one," he said, around a mouthful of egg and cheese. "I've only been hanging out here for a year or so. That was before my time. But I heard that store burned down. I also heard somebody torched it. The rumor mill, so to speak."

"Did the rumor mill have any theories about who torched the store?"

Tony wiped his hands on a napkin and knocked back some coffee. "The usual, saying the store owner must have lit it up himself, to collect on the insurance money."

I shifted to the more current topic. "What did you see last Sunday?"

He reached into the bag and took out one of the scones. "I was sleeping back there where you were looking at birds. The Starbucks closes at eight. I wait until the people that work there leave, then I go back there. That hedge provides some good cover. Nobody can see me, except from the water. I got a one-person tent I can set up real quick, and a down sleeping bag. That night, I was tucked in, nice and warm, asleep. Then I woke up. I guess it was because I heard voices."

"Could you make out what they were saying?"

He shook his head and took another bite of the scone. "No. Just voices, shouting. Then I heard a splash. That made me curious. I crawled out of my tent and got up. I saw a couple of people down on one of those docks that sticks out from the construction site. There's lights at the end of the docks so nobody runs into them after dark. Anyway, that night, I could see those people, but I couldn't tell what they were doing. I figure they must have tossed something in the water. Whatever it was, it made a big splash."

I fought down the picture of Cal's body being thrown off the dock into the water. "You say people. Were they men?"

"Yeah, I think they were men," Tony said. "One of them was good-sized, tall and bulky, it looked like. I figured it was a man. Besides, the only people I've seen on that construction site are men." He stopped and smiled. "Well, maybe not all."

"What do you mean?"

"Lydia, the tattooed lady." Tony grinned. He sang a few bars of the song from the Marx Brothers movie, *At the Circus*. "She doesn't have any tattoos, not that I can see. I haven't gotten that close. I talk with her now and then. She's a character." He gestured with one hand, pointing out toward the water. "She lives on that cabin cruiser out in the Estuary, the one with the red stripe on the hull."

Lydia. That was the name written on the Post-it I'd found on one of Cal's paperback novels when I was going through those boxes. Could it be a coincidence? A different Lydia? Or had Cal known Lydia, the woman who lived on the boat? I wouldn't know for sure unless I could talk with her.

"Tell me more about Lydia," I said.

"I've seen her at the construction site. At night she rows her dinghy ashore to get rid of her trash. And her pee bucket."

I could have done without the image of the pee bucket. But people have to relieve themselves and they don't always have access to flush toilets.

"She figures she can get away with it because at night there's usually nobody at that construction site except the security guard," Tony said. "She's had run-ins with the guards a time or two, though."

"Did you see her that night?" I asked.

"Oh, yeah, she was up. When I heard that splash, I thought it was Lydia coming ashore in her dinghy." Tony reached into the sack and pulled out a scone. He took a bite and chewed. "I saw her on the boat. She had a lantern and she was moving around on deck. It was about the time I got out of my tent and saw those guys on the dock."

"What else did you see?"

"That's about it. Those two people, they walked up the dock onto land, heading for that trailer that's on the construction site. They must have gone inside, because I didn't see them after that. Me, I got back in my tent and burrowed back down in my sleeping bag. Here on the water, it's cold that time of night. Sunday morning, the people from the building here rousted me out. I took down my tent and moved farther down the Embarcadero, other side of the construction site. Later in the day I heard about that body, on the grapevine. I didn't think much about it. Monday I came back up here, by the Starbucks. I saw the cops at the construction site." He shook his head. "I thought those guys on the dock had maybe dumped something in the water. But a body? No, that didn't ever occur to me. Damn."

"How can I get in touch with Lydia?"

Tony put the rest of the scone in his mouth and crumbs dribbled as he spoke. "Not sure. Give me another one of your cards. If

I see her next time she comes ashore, I'll give it to her and tell her to call you. She's got one of those burner phones. So do I."

He gave me his phone number and I handed over another business card, for Lydia. I sweetened the deal with a few bills from my wallet, and hoped he'd follow through.

I returned to downtown Oakland and the lot where I park my car. Instead of going up to my office, I took a large canvas shopping bag from my trunk and set out toward Broadway.

One of my favorite Friday activities is the Old Oakland Farmers' Market. A two-block stretch of Ninth Street from Broadway to Clay Street is closed to traffic. Vendors set up on either side of the street, selling produce, prepared food, and crafts. I didn't have any appointments this morning, but I did have plans to cook dinner for Dan tonight.

I strolled along the booths, examining the produce and buying vegetables and fruit, including broccoli and salad fixings. Now that it was late October, we were into what I call apple-and-orange season, but there were still strawberries. We hadn't yet had a drenching rain to signal the end of the growing season. I bought a three-pack of big red berries and a few persimmons to go with the apples I already had at home.

I headed back to my office and left my purchases on the credenza behind my desk, then checked my messages. Madison Brady had phoned. I returned the call.

"Jeri, have you found out anything new?" she asked. "Have they done the autopsy yet? I haven't heard anything from the police since Tuesday, when someone tried to get into the apartment."

"I haven't heard anything either," I said. "I'll call Detective Portillo. I've been looking through your father's boxes. I found a notebook. It appears he was looking into an accident at the work site. A man was injured in a trench. Your father thought the man got a raw deal because he was undocumented."

"That sounds like something Dad would do," Madison said. "Looking out for the underdog. But I can't see it as a reason for anyone to kill him."

"I agree. I'm guessing that he uncovered something else while he was checking out the accident. I'll keep looking." I added, "Did you know your father was taking swing dance lessons?"

She laughed. "Yeah, he told me about that. He said it was fun and good exercise. And he tried to talk me into coming with him to class. I wish I had. I'm sorry, I didn't think to mention the dance class. How did you find out?"

"I talked with one of the guards that he worked with. He told me." I paused. "He also told me that your dad had gone out a few times with a woman he met in class."

"Really? Now that he didn't tell me."

"Her name is Hilda. I talked with her yesterday. She was really upset about his death. It seems they had a date next week."

Madison sounded subdued now. "I'm sorry to hear that. If you'll give me her name and number I'll get in touch with her."

Hilda Camacho had given me her contact information. I told Madison I would contact Hilda to see if it was all right to give Madison her phone number.

"Listen," Madison said. "You wanted to talk with my mother. I spoke with her and she's available tomorrow at one in the afternoon. Would that fit with your schedule?"

I didn't have anything on my calendar for Saturday, except a visit with my friend Cassie, and that would be a case of my dropping by whenever I got around to it. "Sure, tomorrow works. Give me the address." I grabbed a pen and wrote down the address, which was in Walnut Creek, in Contra Costa County.

After I'd ended the call with Madison, I turned to the computer and checked my email. I was writing a response to a client when my office phone rang.

"Nathan Dupre tells me I should talk with you," Gary Manville said in his brisk, no-nonsense voice. "I can see you at two at my office."

Chapter Fourteen

≈≈≈≈≈≈≈≈≈

ANVILLE HUNG UP without so much as a good-bye. This should be an interesting interview. I hoped he would thaw out enough to give me some information about Cal and his tenure at Manville Security.

I worked steadily for a couple of hours, eating a quick lunch at my desk from provisions I kept in a small refrigerator in my office, topped off with the cupcake left over from yesterday. Then I left, heading over to Broadway where I caught the free downtown shuttle. I got off at Grand Avenue and walked over to Telegraph Avenue. As I walked along the street, I had a prickly feeling between my shoulder blades. Was someone watching me? I turned and scanned the people on the sidewalk. Nothing. I resumed walking until I reached the address I was looking for. I went inside. According to the board listing of tenants next to the elevator, the security firm was on the fifth floor.

Manville Security's front office was small and utilitarian, furnished in shades of gray, right down to the chairs and the herringbone pattern on the low-pile industrial carpet. The only note of color was provided by the young woman at the reception desk, who had a streak of fuchsia in her black hair. Her long nails were the same shade, with sparkles at the end. How could anyone type with nails that length?

She looked up. "May I help you?"

"Jeri Howard to see Gary Manville. I have a two o'clock appointment."

"I'll let him know you're here." Her impressive fingernails danced over her phone console and she cocked her head to one side, listening to the voice emanating from the headset at her ear. Then she disconnected the call and smiled at me. "Please have a seat, Ms. Howard. Mr. Manville will be with you shortly."

I sat down on one of the gray-upholstered chairs and examined a stack of magazines and newspapers on the end table. The available reading material consisted of that morning's *San Francisco Chronicle*, which I'd already read, the *Wall Street Journal*, which I had no desire to read, and several security industry publications. I picked up one of the security magazines and leafed through the pages, looking at ads and headlines.

A few minutes later, the receptionist told me I could enter the inner sanctum. She hit a switch that unlocked that door. I went through it to an interior hallway, where Manville stood in a doorway. He was dressed much as he had been on Tuesday, in gray slacks, this time worn with a pale green knit shirt. He didn't say anything, but motioned me into his office.

The surface of his desk was relatively bare, with a large coffee mug sitting next to his telephone. A miniature San Francisco Forty-Niners helmet served as a paperweight for a slim stack of file folders. On the wall behind the desk I saw several plaques with pictures of ships and engraved brass plates, relics of Manville's service in the Navy. The window on my right looked out at Telegraph Avenue, the view, such as it was, obscured by a set of Venetian blinds.

There were two client chairs. I sat down in one of them. Manville sat down in his own padded office chair and steepled his hands together. He stared at me, eyes cold in his square face.

He didn't say anything so I opened. "Thanks for agreeing to talk with me."

His face stayed chilly, as though he was already regretting that decision. "I'm only doing this because Nathan Dupre talked me into it."

"I appreciate that."

"Look, Ms. Howard, what is your agenda?"

"My agenda? Finding out what happened to Cal. Madison Brady asked me to look into her father's death. She doesn't believe it was an accident. Neither do I. Cal was murdered."

Manville frowned. "Have they done the autopsy?"

"No results yet, at least nothing I've heard. But I don't think he was drinking. My best guess is, someone incapacitated him in some way, perhaps a blow to the head, and dumped him into the water to drown."

"Son of a bitch," he said, his voice almost a whisper.

"That surprises you?"

"I was..." He hesitated. "I was entertaining the suspicion that Cal had started drinking again."

"That's because whoever killed him wants everyone to think that." My voice took on a conciliatory tone. "Let's back up and start over, Mr. Manville. We both want to find out what happened to Cal. Give me some background on your relationship with him. When did you meet Cal? How well did you know him?"

Manville considered this. Then he picked up his mug and pointed at it with his other hand. "You want some coffee?"

I smiled. Finally the guy was thawing out. "No, thanks. I'm coffee'd out right now."

He got up from his desk and moved across the room, where a tray on top of a small refrigerator held a drip coffeemaker and several mugs. He poured himself a warm-up and returned to his desk.

"We were in the Navy together," Manville said, settling back into his chair. "I met him in San Diego. We were both freshly minted ensigns at the Naval base down there, assigned to the same destroyer. We both came to the Navy from ROTC, so we had that in common. I was single. He was married at the time, met his wife while he was in college. Madison was just a kid then."

He took a sip from his mug. "At some point his wife got tired of being a Navy wife. She left Cal, got a divorce, got custody of Madison. She remarried. It happens. I've been married and divorced, too." He paused. "I guess Cal had a drinking problem all along. I didn't notice until later. It got worse, but the change was gradual. He was good at hiding it."

"Alcoholics frequently are," I said.

"I don't think Cal ever wanted to make a career of the Navy," he said. "When he decided to leave he came up here. His ex was living in the East Bay with Madison and her new husband. Cal wanted to be close, so he'd be able to see his daughter. That must have been about ten years ago. We stayed in touch, phone calls and the occasional email. He talked about going to graduate school and I guess he did take some classes. He told me he was working as a private investigator. Then I didn't hear from him. The last phone number I had for him was disconnected and my emails bounced back."

Manville set the coffee mug on his desk. "A couple of years later, I retired from the Navy. I'm from the Bay Area, grew up in El Cerrito, so I came back. About a year or so after I started my security firm, Cal showed up, here at the office. Said he'd seen an article in the local business journal about me starting up. He wanted a job. I asked him about the drinking, because I knew it had gotten worse those last couple of years in the Navy. Cal told me he'd gone through a treatment program courtesy of the VA and that he had been going to AA ever since. He swore he was clean and sober. I believed him. I decided to take a chance on him. He worked for me over three years, and we never had a problem. Until…" His voice trailed off.

"All right, my turn," I said. "I knew Cal because we both worked for a private investigator named Errol Seville."

Manville nodded. "I recognize the name. That's the man who died a couple of weeks ago. Cal asked for time off so he could go to the funeral."

"That's right. I saw Cal at the memorial service. He told me he was sober. I believed him. I worked for Errol a long time. When he retired, I set up my own shop. Cal worked for Errol a couple of years. Then Errol fired him for being intoxicated on the job."

"I knew about that," Manville said. "Cal told me, at the same time he told me about going to treatment. He felt bad about that and wanted to be upfront with me."

"Did you tell anyone else?"

He frowned again. "Of course not. That was confidential, between me and Cal."

"Then how did Brice Cardoza find out about it?"

"I don't know that Brice did."

"Then why was he accusing Cal of drinking on the job?"

Manville stared a hole in his desk. "Something happened at the job site. Two, maybe three weeks ago. I was there because the Cardozas wanted a meeting. They do that a lot, schedule meetings at the site, first thing in the morning. Cal had the night shift. When the day shift guard relieved him at seven o'clock that morning, he said Cal was stumbling around, slurring his words. Then Stephen and Brice showed up, early. Brice hit the roof. When I got there a few minutes later, Brice jumped all over me and Cal, saying Cal was a lousy drunk. He wanted me to fire Cal. It was a major clusterfuck. Excuse my language."

I nodded, ignoring the profanity. "What was Cal doing all this time? What did he say?"

"He told me it must have been something he ate or drank. He apologized to me, several times. Brice wasn't having any of it. He's a pain in the ass, by the way."

"I've met the man, and I agree."

"In addition to Brice having a meltdown, Stephen was giving me the eye. He's a cold fish. The Cardozas are not the easiest people to work for. They're demanding. They keep making noises about firing me and hiring a larger security company. So in retrospect, I didn't defend Cal the way I should have. And I'm sorry for that."

"What was your impression of Cal's behavior that day?"

He didn't answer right away, taking refuge in his coffee mug. "I have to say, it reminded me of times in the past when I'd seen Cal drunk. I was really taken aback when I showed up for that meeting and Brice started complaining about Cal boozing it up on the job. I put him off, but Brice wouldn't let it go. He kept hassling me. He wanted me to fire Cal, kept asking when I was going to get rid of that drunk, as he called him. When Cal took time off to go to that funeral, Brice made some snarky remark about how Cal must have gone on a bender and was home sleeping it off. Even now, with Cal dead, he's making with the snide remarks. He said Cal must have gotten drunk and fallen into the water. Now you tell me Cal was murdered. Who the hell would want to kill Cal Brady? Why?"

"I don't know," I said. "But I intend to find out."

Chapter Fifteen

≈≈≈≈≈≈≈≈≈≈≈

I LEFT MANVILLE Security and took the elevator down to street level. I stepped out to the sidewalk and walked in the direction of my office, savoring the sunny afternoon. When I reached the corner of Telegraph and Grand Avenue, I headed down Grand. I was waiting for a walk signal at Broadway when I heard a voice behind me say, "Jeri Howard, is that you?"

When I turned and saw who had spoken to me, I knew who it was immediately. I had never cared for my former coworker. I wasn't particularly glad to see him.

"Leo Walker."

Leo flashed a wide, friendly smile, a twinkle in his hazel eyes. "The very same."

He was in his thirties now, a year or so younger than me, medium height and build, casually dressed in gray slacks and a red knit shirt worn under a lighter gray sports jacket. His wavy blond hair curled around his ears and spilled onto his forehead. In his left ear I saw a tiny gold stud. He had a tattoo as well, on his left wrist, a spider with a black body and purple legs, the design visible under his jacket cuff as he raised his left hand and pushed a strand of hair away from his face. He carried a nylon briefcase with a shoulder strap, slung over his right shoulder.

Interesting that my former coworker should turn up on an Oakland street corner just two days after Davina and I had talked about him. Coincidence? I'm wary of coincidence.

"How are you?" he asked. "I haven't seen you in a long time."

"It's been several years." The light turned green. We walked across Broadway.

Leo gestured to his right. "You know, every time I see this neighborhood, I think about that year I worked for Errol. They're gonna tear that building down and build something else."

"There's a lot of that going on, all over Oakland," I said. "Errol died a couple of weeks ago."

"Did he really? I'm sorry to hear that," Leo said. "Did he have another heart attack?"

"Yes. His memorial service was last week."

"I'm sure it was well attended."

"It was. There were a lot of people there. I saw Cal Brady." Introducing Cal's name into the conversation was deliberate. I wanted to see what reaction I got from Leo.

During the time I had worked at the Seville Agency, workplace friendships developed. So had workplace rivalries, some of them edged with dislike. Davina and I had been friends back then and we'd stayed friends. Cal and Leo, however, had been rivals. There was friction between them from the start. Cal was already working at the agency when Leo came on board. Cal, his alcoholism at that point hidden, was the older, supposedly steadier operative. Leo was the young hustler, brash and sometimes rash.

Cal and Leo had butted heads while working on a job. Errol had to step in and give both of them a talking-to. When Cal lost his job, Leo took great pleasure in his rival's comeuppance.

What was it he'd said?

The boozer is a loser. Drunk on the job. About time he got his ass fired.

Which was, now that I thought about it, almost the same thing Brice Cardoza had spewed at me last night.

Leo smiled but his words had a nasty edge. "Cal the loser, huh. Is he still boozing it up?"

"Went to AA," I said, "and sobered up."

"Well, I guess that happens." Leo didn't look convinced at the veracity of my words, however. "What about you? I know you're still a private investigator. I see your name in the papers every now and then."

"I am. It keeps me busy. What are you doing these days?"

Davina had told me that Leo was working as a consultant, after leaving the nonprofit where she'd worked—under a cloud, she'd added. What kind of a cloud? I wanted to hear Leo tell me what he was doing. These days, it seemed as though anyone doing anything could wear the label consultant.

"A little bit of this, a little bit of that." Leo flashed the easy smile again, as we continued walking along Grand. "After I left that job with Errol I took some classes in project management through the UC Berkeley Extension. Then I got a job with a nonprofit here in Oakland, working on housing issues."

"Are you still with them?"

"No, I've moved on. Worked with a couple of local businesses, here in Oakland and over in San Francisco. I've just been doing a variety of things." He grinned. "Trying to decide what I want to be when I grow up."

"Who says we have to grow up?"

"Hey, I hear that. Davina's in law school over at Berkeley," he added. "I saw her a few months back. I'm sure she'll make a terrific attorney. So what are you working on?"

"Nothing particularly glamorous. I do a lot of insurance work for local attorneys, things like that. It pays the bills." I looked at my watch. "I need to get back to my office. Do you have a card, Leo?"

"Sure. And I'd like yours."

We exchanged business cards. I saw the bright green downtown shuttle bus rounding the corner from Broadway. "I've got to catch that bus. Good to talk with you."

I quickened my pace, reaching the shuttle stop at the next corner a few seconds before the bus did. When the shuttle opened its doors, I stepped aboard. As I claimed a seat, I turned and glanced back. Leo still stood where I'd left him, watching me from the middle of the block. There was something odd about the look on his face.

Odd indeed. Call me suspicious, but I thought the whole encounter was peculiar.

The shuttle bus turned onto Webster Street and Leo disappeared from view. I rode the shuttle as it circled back to Broadway and headed downtown. I got off at Twelfth, walked a block over to Franklin Street and went upstairs to my office. My answering machine light was blinking, indicating that I had messages. I played them back, making notes, and returned several calls. Then I called Davina Roka. I got her voice mail, so I left a message asking her to call me as soon as possible.

I switched on my computer, checked my email, and made notes on my conversation with Gary Manville. An hour later, my phone rang. It was Davina. "What's up?"

"I ran into Leo Walker this afternoon," I told her. "Or he ran into me. I had the strangest feeling that it was deliberate."

I gave her an overview of my encounter with Leo. "Is it just me? I think it's curious that he turns up after we were talking about him on Wednesday. He mentioned that he'd worked for that nonprofit in Oakland. You told me you thought he'd left under some sort of cloud. Was he fired?"

"I don't know. And I don't remember what I was told, other than there was something off about the way he left. The nonprofit is called New Start East Bay. It's located down at Jack London Square." She gave me the address. "Best thing to do is go down there and talk with someone."

"Can you give me a name?"

"Pilar García. She's an admin assistant, been there for years. Drop my name if you think it will help."

"I will, thanks." When we ended the call, I looked up the nonprofit on the Internet and reached for the phone. I was out of luck, though. Pilar García was away from the office and would return on Monday.

I leaned back in my chair. When I'd mentioned Cal's name, Leo didn't act as though he knew Cal was dead. That wasn't really surprising. There had been very little media coverage. I didn't watch television news so I didn't know whether the local stations had covered the story. A few column inches in the local newspapers had mentioned that the body of an unidentified man had been found in the Estuary. A few days after that, a brief follow-up mentioned that the body had been identified as that of Calvin Brady, and that the Oakland police were investigating. That was it.

I recalled the prickly feeling I'd felt while walking along that block of Telegraph Avenue leading to the office building where Manville Security was located. Had I been followed? By Leo?

I took out the business card Leo had given me. It contained no physical or mailing address, just an email address, and a phone number that was probably a cell phone. He said he was a consultant. As a consultant he could be working from home. There were also a number of co-working sites in Oakland, places where self-employed people could show up and work at communal tables. In fact, there was just such a site on Broadway near Grand, where I'd encountered Leo.

I logged onto my Internet browser and began searching for Leo Walker. I didn't find much. If he was a consultant he had a sketchy online presence.

Why did I have the feeling that my encounter with Leo had been no accident? What was the reason for my suspicion?

I couldn't put my finger on just what was bothering me. But over the years, I had learned to trust my gut, and my gut was telling me to beware.

Chapter Sixteen

~~~~~~~~~~~~~~~~~~~~~~~~

D
AN WAS COMING over for dinner tonight, and I
had a few hours to get ready. There were a couple of stops
I wanted to make first, though.
I left my office and headed down Broadway, detouring through a
neighborhood called the Valdez Triangle. An organization called
the East Bay Intergroup was located on Twenty-seventh Street,
and they hosted Alcoholics Anonymous meetings, seven days a
week, at all hours. I wanted to talk with Cal Brady's AA sponsor,
and this was the best place to start. Anonymity was one of the
important pillars of the program, so my request was met with a
great deal of skepticism and resistance. I handed out business cards
and kept repeating my spiel. Cal was dead and I was looking into
what had happened. I hoped that his fellow AA members could
give me a lead.

That done, I headed for my Rockridge neighborhood, where I
was fortunate enough to snag a parking space on College Avenue
near Claremont Avenue, on the Oakland–Berkeley border. Parking
in this area could be difficult and sometimes near impossible. I'd
already stocked up on fruits and vegetables at the farmers' market.
I went into the Ver Brugge butcher shop, where I bought a small
roasting hen. I was tempted to go into La Farine, the nearby bakery.
I resisted. Dan had promised to bring wine, bread and dessert.

Shopping done, I drove home to Chabot Road and parked in

the driveway. I carried my shopping bags inside. I was greeted at the door with the hungry-kitty song-and-dance. Abigail and Black Bart were undeterred when I pointed out that there was food in their bowls. Of course it was dried and crusty. Definitely not fresh. Chastened by their meows, I opened a can of cat food and dished up some of the fishy stuff. Then I unloaded my produce onto the kitchen counter, piling fruit in an oversized ceramic bowl.

Unlike my mother, who is a gourmet chef and restaurant owner, when I'm cooking I keep it simple. What could be simpler than roast chicken and steamed broccoli? I unwrapped the hen and set it in my roasting pan, seasoning it with salt and pepper. Then I took a lemon from the fruit bowl, pierced it in several places with a paring knife, and stuck the lemon into the bird's cavity, along with several garlic cloves. The chicken went into the oven and I washed my hands, reaching for a head of broccoli. I rinsed it, cut it into smaller pieces, scooped the florets into my vegetable steamer, then tossed the leaves and stem ends into the green recycling bin.

Dan was due at six-thirty, so I'd steam the broccoli when he arrived. I got out my dishes and flatware and set the table. I paused to look at my handiwork. I was so used to eating alone or on the fly that it was good to take some time to make things look nice. On that note, I needed to pick up some of the clutter in my living room. I grabbed a couple of books I'd been reading and stacked them on the top step that led down to my bedroom. Then I ran the vacuum cleaner. The noise sent Abigail and Black Bart scurrying down the stairs to hide. When I'd finished vacuuming, I, too, went downstairs. I stashed the books on a bookcase and changed my clothes.

Dan arrived on schedule, a bottle of Chardonnay in one hand and a shopping bag in the other. "What's in the bag?" I asked as I kissed him.

Dan was tall and rangy, and he looked good in his faded jeans, worn with a blue-and-gold plaid shirt. His hair was dark, with a few strands of gray at the temples, and it curled around his ears. His blue eyes sparkled with good humor and laugh lines wrinkled his face. He grinned as he shook the bag with a flourish. "As promised, wine, bread and dessert. I stopped at La Farine."

"Good. I was tempted to go in there when I was shopping on the avenue this afternoon."

He carried the bag to the kitchen and removed a loaf of bread. "That kalamata olive bread we both like. And…" He did a mock drum roll on the table. Then he took out a bakery box and opened the lid, revealing an assortment of the bakery's delectable tartlettes, with flaky crusts and fillings of both fruit and cream. There was one with apple and another with a poached pear.

I pointed. "That one with the hazelnuts and chocolate, that's mine."

"I had a feeling you'd say that. Good thing I got two of those. And one each of the pecan butter rum and cranberry hollandaise."

"You're making my mouth water."

"So is the smell coming from the oven."

"Roast chicken." I turned on the stove burner to steam the broccoli. "Everything will be ready in a few minutes."

"Great. I'll open the wine."

He knew where to find the corkscrew and the wineglasses. While he removed the cork I got out a cutting board and sliced some of the bread. He handed me a glass of Chardonnay. I sipped the wine. It had a smooth, buttery taste that I liked. "Very good."

"One of my favorite wineries," he said. "It's in western Sonoma County, near the Russian River. I picked up a couple of bottles while I was up there researching my book."

Dan brought me up to date on his writing project. He was nearly finished with the Sonoma County hiking book. He told me his publisher had approached him about doing another hiking book, this one about the Eastern Sierra. He was definitely interested, since his parents lived on the other side of the mountains.

I took the roasting pan from the oven and set it on a trivet. The chicken smelled wonderful. The broccoli was done. I transferred it to a serving bowl. I sliced a lemon to squeeze over the vegetable, then set both bowls on the dining room table, along with the butter dish and a salad.

I returned to the kitchen and moved the chicken from the roasting pan to a platter. "Dinner is ready."

Dan carried the platter to the dining room table and we sat down. He carved the chicken and served pieces onto each plate. I passed him the broccoli and salad.

Dan cut into his chicken and took a bite. "Delicious."

"Thanks. It's the lemon and garlic in the cavity. That's the one trick my mother taught me that stuck." I drizzled my broccoli with lemon juice and poked one of the florets with my fork.

As we ate, we talked about our families. I'd met Dan last June while working on a case with ties back to the 1940s, when my grandmother Jerusha had been a bit player in Hollywood. Dan's grandmother, Pearl Westbrook, had also been a bit player, and she'd been one of my grandmother's housemates. Grandma Jerusha had died several years ago, but Dan's grandmother was very much alive, living in Lee Vining in the Eastern Sierra, near Mono Lake. Dan's father, Carl, was with the Forest Service. His mother, Loretta, had been born and raised in Lee Vining. In fact, she was Native American, one of the Kutzadika'a people, also known as the Mono Lake Indian Community, whose ancestors had lived around the lake for centuries.

Dan was the oldest of the Westbrooks' three children. Like me, he was in his late thirties, and like me, he was divorced. His marriage, which had been over for several years, had resulted in two children, a boy and a girl. They lived with his ex-wife and her second husband in Fresno. Dan and I had been seeing each other regularly since June. That was nearly five months ago and the relationship had deepened from friendship to romance. Sometimes I felt as though things were moving faster than I'd like.

"How's your brother?" He sopped up some of the juices from the chicken with a bit of bread, then served himself more broccoli.

I frowned. "He has recuperated from being kidnapped and held prisoner. Physically, anyway. He and Sheila are seeing a counselor. I sure hope they can repair whatever is going on with their marriage."

The conversation moved to my upcoming birthday. Dad was taking Dan and me out to dinner, at a new restaurant that had opened in Oakland. I told Dan about Dad's traveling plans, his birding excursions to Klamath Falls this fall and to Texas in the spring.

"My dad is planning to retire at the end of the year," Dan said.

"Good. I know your mother will enjoy having him around full time."

"Or maybe not." Dan grinned. "I'm sure she has a long to-do list for him."

When we were done with dinner, we cleared the table and cleaned up the kitchen. I made a pot of coffee to go with the tartlettes and we sat on the sofa, talking and munching the pastries. They were all good but I pronounced the hazelnut–chocolate concoction the clear winner. Because, after all, there's chocolate and then there's everything else.

Our conversation wound down as the cats appeared from their hiding places, each claiming a lap. I snuggled into Dan's shoulder and sipped coffee.

"Have you ever thought about getting married again?" Dan asked.

I straightened and set my coffee mug on the end table, running my fingers through Abigail's tabby fur. She purred contentedly. I looked at Dan. Where had that question come from?

"I haven't given it much thought," I said finally. "Have you?"

He ruffled Black Bart's ears. "Sometimes."

My marriage to Sid Vernon, a homicide cop, had been impulsive and short-lived, with no children other than Sid's daughter, Vicki, who was living with her mother in San Diego when Sid and I were married. Looking back, I'm not sure why I decided marrying Sid would be a good idea. I suppose we were in lust. It hadn't taken me long to decide it wasn't working. I moved out and filed for divorce. I was doing the right thing for myself in ending the marriage, but Sid had taken the breakup badly. It took a while to get past the resentment that had lingered on both sides. Fortunately we had both moved on, resulting in our current, cordial relationship.

As for Dan, his marriage had lasted longer and he had the children. I knew Dan was close to his kids and kept in touch with them via email and Skype. He also visited them frequently, something he was able to do because, like me, he was self-employed.

Marriage. I felt awkward about the turn this conversation was taking. I straightened and reached for my coffee mug. "Want a refill?"

"Sure." I collected Dan's mug and walked to the kitchen to get the coffee. When I got back, he suggested watching a movie. We sorted through my DVD collection and agreed on a couple of Humphrey Bogart movies, *Dead Reckoning* and *Dark Passage*. We settled back on the sofa to watch.

Dan spent the night. Over scrambled eggs and English muffins the next morning, we talked about the Bay Trail, since he had hiked a good portion of it. I didn't tell him about the case, other than saying I was looking into the death of a former coworker whose body had been found in the Estuary. Now that he was dating a private investigator, Dan knew not to ask too many questions.

I finished my coffee and got up to get the pot. After I poured coffee into my mug and his, I said, "I really would like to take a look at the waterfront from the water."

Dan grinned and reached for the blackberry preserves, spooning a generous portion on his buttered English muffin. "I know a guy with a boat."

Chapter Seventeen

~~~~~~~~~~~~~~~~~~

LINDA FULMER, Madison Brady's mother, lived with her second husband and their two sons in Walnut Creek, out in Contra Costa County. On Saturday, I gave myself plenty of time to get there. I knew from experience that traffic on Bay Area freeways never seemed to let up. I reached the interchange of Interstates 580 and 680 and took the exit, driving through a commercial district, then into a pleasant residential neighborhood south of the downtown area.

It was a sprawling one-story house with a double garage, with a square Honda SUV in the driveway. I parked at the curb and walked up to the front door. The woman who answered the bell was in her early forties, dressed in beige slacks and a green blouse. She had hazel eyes, her blond hair cut short enough to show off small gold earrings. I saw a hint of Madison in her mother's features, the shape of the face and the long nose.

"Mrs. Fulmer, I'm Jeri Howard. I appreciate your agreeing to talk with me."

She favored me with a tight smile as she motioned me to enter the house. I stepped into a hall with white walls and bamboo flooring. Photographs hung at intervals on the walls. The one closest to me looked fairly recent, showing Mrs. Fulmer with her husband, Madison, and two boys of middle-school age.

"I'm doing this because Madison asked me to," Mrs. Fulmer

said. "She's having a hard time dealing with her father's death. Which is no surprise. He was her father and they were fairly close, despite the divorce. I don't know that I can help much. Cal and I were married for eight years. We got divorced when Madison was seven. I haven't seen him very often since then. But we did talk on the phone. From what Madison said, you want to know if he said anything to me about his work situation."

"Yes, I would like to know if he did. But also, I'm trying to get a sense of Cal, of who he was. I want to know him better."

"You worked with him," she said. "At least that's what Madison told me."

"True. But it was a short time. And how well do you know your coworkers?"

"Point taken. Would you like some iced tea? I have a pitcher in the refrigerator."

"That would be great. Thanks."

"Here's the living room. Make yourself comfortable. I'll be with you in a minute."

She headed down the hall toward the kitchen I glimpsed at the back of the house. I went through a doorway on my left to the spacious living room furnished in a mix of styles. Here an Oriental rug in shades of green and gold covered the wood floor. A gray-and-white cat curled up in the middle of a white towel on one of the armchairs, in an attempt to keep the cat hair off the upholstery. I approached the cat and held out my hand. It deigned to sniff the proffered fingers, looking at me with knowing green eyes.

"That's Nemo," she said, returning to the living room with two frosty glasses on a small tray. "He thinks he owns the place."

"I know. I have two cats of my own. Thanks, Mrs. Fulmer."

"Call me Linda. I'll call you Jeri. It's easier that way."

"Certainly." I took the glass she offered and sat in the armchair that wasn't occupied by the cat. She sat down on the sofa. After taking a drink, I set my glass on a coaster and took a small notebook from my bag. "When did you first meet Cal?"

She sipped from her glass. "Our junior year in college. We were at the University of Wisconsin in Madison. And no, Madison is not named after the town. I just like the name."

I smiled. "You must get that question a lot."

"I do." She seemed to relax a bit. "Cal was in ROTC. I'm from Wisconsin Dells and he was from Eau Claire. We both liked to hike and we met on a day hike. We started living together. We got married after he was commissioned in the Navy. We went to San Diego. I got pregnant there and Madison was born in the Naval hospital."

"Did you like being a Navy wife?" I remembered what Gary Manville had told me the day before, about Cal's marriage.

She grimaced. "I hated it. I should have known what I was in for, marrying a guy in the ROTC program. When Cal was commissioned, he was assigned to a destroyer that was based at Thirty-second Street. That's what they called the Naval station down there. He was gone a lot. I might as well have been a single mother."

"How long were you in San Diego?"

"About three years. The Navy moves people all the time, all over the place. After we left San Diego, we went to Mayport, Florida, and then to Great Lakes, which is near Chicago. I was fine with Great Lakes. At least Illinois is next to Wisconsin and I could go see my family." She sighed. "Then Cal got orders to Guam. I told him, I am not going. I don't care if it is a United States territory. I am not dragging myself and my kid to some little island halfway around the world. That was the last straw."

"Is that the only reason the marriage broke up?"

She didn't answer right away. Then she shook her head. "No. The marriage had deteriorated over those last few years. It was on the rocks a long time before he got orders to Guam." Her face took on a brooding look.

"What did you do after the divorce?"

"I went back to Wisconsin for a while, living with my folks. Then I got a job at the university. There are twenty-six campuses in the system, and I was in Milwaukee. That's where I met my husband. He works in health care. He was working for a company there, and then he got a job in the East Bay. We've been in California for fifteen years. Madison is twenty-three. My husband and I have two other children. Darren is twelve and Craig is fourteen."

"A mutual friend told me Cal moved out here after he got out of the Navy so he would be close to Madison."

"Yes, he did. I wanted him to see her whenever he could. Madison's his daughter, too. So he moved here to the East Bay. I think he was living in Oakland all that time."

"I knew him when we were both working as investigators for the Seville Agency in downtown Oakland. He started working there about seven years ago."

She nodded. "Yes, that's about the time he got out of the Navy and showed up here. I don't know why he didn't stay in the Navy the whole twenty years, to get his pension. I thought he liked it. Anyway, that's the job he was fired from, for drinking."

"Yes. We worked together about two years. He was let go five years ago. I didn't see him again until we both showed up at Errol Seville's funeral a week and a half ago. He told me he'd stopped drinking."

"That's true, he did." Linda sighed. "Let me backtrack a bit. I know Cal drank quite a bit. All those guys in the Navy do. I didn't think much about it. I guess the alcoholism came on gradually. Or maybe he was just good at hiding it. After he was fired from that job where you knew him, he hid it sufficiently to get another job, in Sacramento. Then he moved to San Jose, still another job. I don't know what sort of jobs. I didn't ask. That was when Madison was in her first year of college at San Jose State."

She paused for another sip of tea. "The spring after Madison started college, Cal disappeared, just dropped out of sight. No phone calls, nothing. Madison was upset, frantic. Cal's phone had been disconnected and when she wrote to his address, the letters came back. She wanted to go to the police and report him missing. We didn't do that. My husband and I thought we might be able to locate him through the Veterans Administration. Which we did. It took us a while, though. We finally figured out he had checked himself into a substance abuse program at the VA medical center in Martinez. At first he didn't want to see Madison, or anyone else. But when he got out of this program, he went back to Oakland. Someone had offered him a job, Madison said. Someone he knew in the Navy."

"That's right. Gary Manville. Did you ever meet him?"

She shook her head. "I can't say that the name is familiar. We met a lot of people during those years when Cal and I were married. Every duty station, it was like a revolving door. Then he was in the Navy another four years or so before he got out."

"Manville owns a security company in Oakland. Cal worked for him for nearly three years, as a security guard."

"Madison mentioned the name of the company but the name doesn't mean anything to me." Linda took another sip of her iced tea. "Cal and I parted amicably, and we've kept in touch, because of Madison. When his parents died, he put the money he inherited in an account in Madison's name, for her college expenses. She was a minor, then, and I was on the account as her guardian. Now that she's an adult that's changed. Cal did the right thing by his daughter, instead of drinking it all away, even if he had to live in his car or couch-surf."

"In your recent phone conversations with Cal, did he say anything about his job or his work situation?"

She thought for a moment. "There was someone he didn't get along with. This person didn't work for the security company. It was a man at the job site. I know it was bothering Cal but he wouldn't give me any details. He said it wasn't my problem, it was his."

Brice again, I thought. I probed further, but she didn't have much more to tell me. Cal had kept the details of what was going on at the Cardoza work site to himself.

Chapter Eighteen

CASSIE TAYLOR and I have been friends for a long time. We met when we were both working as legal secretaries for a law firm in San Francisco. Then we went in different directions. I got my private investigator's license. Cassie went to UC's Hastings College of Law in San Francisco. Once she got her J.D., she hung out her shingle with two other lawyers, Bill Alwin and Mike Chao, forming the law firm of Alwin, Taylor and Chao, with offices in the Franklin Street building.

When I decided to go out on my own as a private investigator, I took an office on the same floor as the law firm. I'd been there ever since, with Cassie just down the hall. Except for the last few months, when she'd been on maternity leave, first awaiting the baby's birth and then bonding with her new son.

On Saturday afternoon, I parked at the curb in front of Cassie's house, a one-story Victorian cottage on Alameda Avenue. It had been a fixer-upper when Cassie and her husband, Eric, bought the house and they had made numerous improvements. The house was painted pale blue. The yellow trim around the windows and on the porch railings was complemented by big pots of yellow and bronze chrysanthemums.

I rang the bell. A moment later, Cassie answered the door.

"How are you, and my godson?" I asked.

"He's sleeping right now. But you can take a peek. Eric's out riding his bike, so we'll have some girl time."

She ushered me inside. The small living room was a bit messy, with baby stuff strewn here and there. Photos of the new baby decorated the tables and bookcases. It looked as though Cassie had been taking advantage of her son's nap to catch up on some work, judging from the open laptop computer sitting on one end of the sofa.

Cassie led the way down the hallway to the small bedroom that had been turned into a nursery. We stood over the baby's bed and looked down at little Matthew Taylor Lindholm, who had been born in August. Cassie is African American and her husband is from Minnesota, with Scandinavian and German antecedents on both sides of his family tree. My godson, their first child, was a beautiful mixture of both gene pools, his eyes blue and his soft skin a creamy café au lait. At the moment, his eyes were closed. He was scrunched up on his stomach, a yellow blanket covering his pale blue shirt, his head, covered with soft dark curls, tilted to one side.

"It's amazing how much he's grown in three months," I said.

She smiled. "Isn't it? He changes every day. Want some tea? I just put the kettle on."

We headed back toward the living room, just as a whistle sounded. I followed her to the kitchen, where she gave me a choice of teas. I picked Darjeeling. I normally drink tea black, but today milk and sugar appealed to me, so I doctored my mug and took a sip.

Cassie reached across the counter for a round red-and-gold tin. She pried it open and displayed what was inside. "My mother made shortbread."

"Mmmm, looks good." I took a square of buttery cookie and bit into it. We carried our repast to the living room. Cassie set the computer on the end table and took a seat on one side of the sofa, putting her feet on the nearby ottoman. I took the other end of the sofa and sipped my tea, a wonderful accompaniment to the shortbread. "What's happening with you?"

"Besides motherhood and keeping up with work? Not much." Cassie took a piece of shortbread out of the tin. She had only taken one bite when we heard the baby waking up from his nap. Cassie got up and went down the hall, returning with little Matthew. She unbuttoned her blouse and unfastened her nursing bra, putting the baby on her breast. Once he was settled, contentedly suckling, Cassie picked up her discarded shortbread. "Is there something on your mind?"

I chuckled as I reached for another cookie. "There is. You read me like a book."

"We've been friends a long time. I pick up on the signals. What is it? You and Dan?"

"Maybe. Kinda, sorta. Oh, hell, I don't know. I'm probably reading more into it than there really is."

"I'm not going to know if you don't tell me," she said, her mug poised at her lips.

"I cooked dinner for Dan Friday night, and he asked me if I'd ever thought of getting married again."

"Ah," Cassie said. "Seems like a simple question. And it sent you into a tizzy."

"I'm not in a tizzy."

"You've definitely had a reaction."

I thought about it for a moment, hiding behind my mug of tea. "I have. Out of proportion, I might add. I'm getting way ahead of myself. My reaction is ridiculous. It's not like Dan proposed. It was a conversation, a brief one at that. But…"

"But…If he did propose? What would you say?"

I shrugged. "I'm not sure. My first and only marriage turned out so bad. I just don't know if I want to go there again."

"It wouldn't be going there again," Cassie said. "It would be something new and different. I don't blame you for being a bit, shall we say, gun-shy? You and Sid weren't suited."

"Why did I marry him? Was it just lust? I've asked myself that question over and over. To get married, and then have to go through the whole damn breakup."

"I have a theory, for what it's worth." Cassie took another cookie and bit into it. "We're all of an age. When we got into our thirties, no matter how liberated we think we are, there's that little voice at the back of the brain wondering about marriage and family, warning us that the biological clock is ticking. I heard it. I'm sure you did, too."

"I'll admit to that. But you didn't go out and marry a much-older cop with a lot of baggage. And then leave him less than two years into the marriage."

"Better you left him than stayed with him to be miserable." She washed down her cookie with a swallow of tea. "It's not like I waited for Eric to show up on a white horse. I almost married that guy I met in law school." She shuddered. "Thank God I came to my senses and escaped that relationship. What a jerk he turned out to be."

"I remember him. Never could figure out what you saw in him."

"Maybe it was lust, like you said. He was certainly attractive." A smile teased the corners of her mouth. "Just ask him."

We looked at each other and dissolved into the comfortable laughter of old friends who'd shared a lot through the years. Then Cassie looked thoughtful as she asked a question pertinent to women our age, whose biological clocks ticked for another decade or so and then wound down to silence.

"Do you regret not having children?"

I thought about it before I answered. "There was a time, in my twenties and early thirties, that I wanted to have a baby. Like a lot of women, I had the expectation that I'd get married and have children. It didn't happen." I shook my head. "I got over that desire to have a baby. By the time I hit my mid-thirties, I figured it just wasn't in the cards. I decided not to worry about it. So I guess the answer is no, at this stage of my life, I don't regret not having children. I don't think I would have been able to do what I do if I had a husband and family. I will say, I enjoy having Vicki as my stepdaughter," I added, referring to Sid's daughter from his first marriage.

"That's a good comment about doing what you're doing without a husband and family," Cassie said. "Now that I'm married and I have this little one…" She smiled down at the baby. "I have to look at that work-life balance thing. I enjoy my career as an attorney. It's what I want to do. I'm fortunate that Eric is such a supportive husband. But it's going to be interesting when I go back to the office." She gestured at the computer on the end table. "As you can see, I'm working from home. I'm going to ease my way in, working in the office part-time. Finding child care, of course, is a given."

"I'm sure you'll make it work."

Cassie looked at me and smiled. "*Have* you ever thought of getting married again?"

I laughed. "If I got married again, I'd have to clean out a closet."

"I know what you mean," Cassie said. "It's an adjustment to share my living space with Eric after having lived alone for so many years. Now I've got this little one. Just wait till he starts walking."

I looked at the baby in her arms. "He's not even at the crawling stage, so I don't think you need to baby-proof the house just yet."

"Getting back to the 'married conversation,' you haven't thought about it and you're not sure you want to."

"Just like a lawyer," I said. "Get the witness back on point. No, I can't say that I have thought about remarrying. I've been too busy figuring out who Jeri Howard is. I got married and divorced and I've had a lot of relationships since then. None of them have stuck. Maybe it's because I didn't want them to." I paused. "Dan feels different, though."

"Different how?"

I considered my words, drawing them out. "Feels like the relationship could be longer-lasting."

"Maybe even permanent?" Cassie asked.

"Permanent is such a...long-lasting word. At this stage of my life, I'm not sure I want that."

"Think about it. It sounds like he is." She smiled and shifted young Matthew to the other breast. "I could use a warm-up on my tea. Will you put the kettle on?"

"Sure." I got up, went to the kitchen, and turned on the stove burner. When the kettle whistled I made fresh tea for both of us.

I settled back in my chair and contemplated taking another cookie. Why not? Cassie's mother made such good shortbread.

"Don't eat all of that," Cassie said. "I'll give you some to take home."

"Thanks, I'll take it. Did you get the letter from the building manager about the rent going up? A twenty percent increase. That's a big jump in my overhead. It's going to hurt. I'm wondering if I can afford it." I took a bite of shortbread. "My lease is up in January. I'm debating the idea of working from home. Darcy, my tenant, is moving out of the garage apartment. I've got to investigate the zoning in my neighborhood before I make that decision, though. It would be convenient, but I like having my business downtown. It's easier for clients to find me, easier for me to go to the courthouse or the police department."

"Interesting that you should bring that up now." Cassie smiled as she cuddled the baby. "My partners and I have been talking about the rent increase. We knew it was in the works, even before the letters went out."

"How so?" I asked. "I didn't have a clue the rent was going up. Of course, I've been busy with cases."

"We knew because we've decided to expand. Our law firm is outgrowing its space. We've added two new associates in the past year, along with support staff like paralegals and admin assistants. We first thought we'd lease more space in the building. When Bill and Mike approached the landlord, they found out the rent increase was in the works. The landlord is planning some extensive remodeling to the building and he's using the rent increase to fund it."

"Lord knows the building needs an update," I said. "The landlord hasn't been all that good about keeping up the place. Remember that leak in the bathroom? That went on for weeks. And the cracked window in my office. I had to keep after him to replace that. If I stay, it sounds like in addition to paying more for the same office, I'll have to put up with the mess of remodeling."

"That's right. And we don't want the same space. We're bursting at the seams and we need room to grow."

"What are you going to do?"

Cassie grinned. "We're buying a building. The deal should close soon."

"Wow." I leaned back in my chair. "Where?"

"It's on Valdez Street, near Twenty-seventh and that building that used to be Biff's Coffee Shop."

I nodded. "I know exactly where that is."

"It's a one-story building, about nine thousand square feet, with parking in the back. It's got the right zoning. At one time it was a paint supply store that went out of business. The owner died and the heirs are motivated to sell. They want to settle the estate and get their money. So we put in an offer and they accepted. Lucky for us, because that neighborhood is going to change, big time."

"So I've heard."

The area Cassie was talking about was yet another Oakland neighborhood on the cusp of change. I'd lived and worked in the city for years and the changes that were happening were significant, and in some cases breathtakingly fast.

"The deal is supposed to close soon. Once that happens, the plan is to remodel. We've already got that in the works and are ready to jump in. I'm hoping we'll be ready to occupy the new place by January. Two-thirds of the building will be the law firm, and the plan is to turn the other third into offices for lease." Cassie stopped talking and smiled, looking pleased. I thought she was congratulating herself and her partners on making a good business move. Then her next words surprised me. "I'm getting ahead of myself, but that's okay. I might as well tell you now. Bill, Mike and I have already discussed this, Jeri. We are happy to offer you the opportunity to become our first tenant."

I was stunned for a moment. Then I jumped on it. "That's great! I accept. Details to come?"

"Yes, those pesky details," Cassie said. "I don't know how much the lease will be, or how long it will take us to remodel the building. I will say the wiring and the plumbing are better than what we have in our current location."

"Parking in the back is a real plus." I was paying by the month to park at the lot near my current location. I was guessing the rent at the new place would be higher, but not having to pay to park would help offset that. Parking for clients would be the icing on the cake.

The baby was asleep again. Cassie adjusted her nursing bra and top, then got up and put little Matthew back in his crib. When she returned to the living room, we talked a while longer, catching each other up on family. Then Eric came back from his bike ride and we chatted some more. When I left Cassie's house I didn't take my usual route home, over the Park Street Bridge and onto the freeway. Instead I drove through the Tube, the underwater tunnel that led from Alameda to Oakland. I headed up Broadway, past the Uptown block where the Seville Agency had once been located.

Uptown segues into the Broadway Valdez neighborhood, which roughly stretches from either side of Broadway from Grand Avenue to Interstate 580 and the Kaiser medical complex, which is a cluster of buildings around MacArthur Boulevard and Broadway. What used to be Oakland's Auto Row is considered part of Valdez. Car dealerships remain but many of them have been replaced by other businesses. If Uptown was now trendy, the buzz in Oakland was that Valdez would be next. Cassie and her law firm partners were making a good move, I thought, to get into the area before that happened.

Biff's, the landmark Cassie had referred to, was an old coffee shop, long closed, at Twenty-seventh and Broadway. The round building looked like a spaceship that had gotten lost and landed in Oakland. The building dated to the early 1960s, and its architectural style was called Googie, which I'd never heard of till I read a newspaper article on the old building. Biff's had operated for thirty years, dispensing burgers, fries and shakes to customers who sat in green Naugahyde booths. Then it had closed in the 1990s, the building boarded up and the lot fenced, while the city decided what to do with the land. Despite the fact that the building had its fans who wanted to see Biff's spruced up and reopened, it was likely the city would tear it down for a proposed housing development.

Valdez was a short street that ran only a few blocks, and dead-ended at Twenty-eighth. There were a couple of senior housing complexes located at that corner.

I pulled over and took a look at the building Cassie and her partners were buying. It was a bit down-at-heels right now, but from the outside, the one-story structure looked promising. A coat of paint and clean-up and the coming inside remodel would make it a first-class work space, a good location for the law firm, and for me.

This was a great birthday present, I thought, as I drove on toward home. Earlier in the week I'd been upset about the rent increase. Now I was feeling better about the situation. Change was constant these days, but this change promised to make things better, at least in my professional life.

Chapter Nineteen

S UNDAY MORNING I sat on an ottoman in my living room, putting on my tennis shoes. I managed to get the left shoe tied, but I hadn't yet tied the right. Abigail loves playing with shoestrings. Twice I made loops. Twice her paw snaked out and pulled the strings from my fingers. She looked pleased with herself. Relief came when Dan rang the doorbell. Abigail retreated, crouching under an end table. As I crossed the living room to the front door, my foot slipped out of the untied shoe.

Dan pointed at my shoeless right foot. "Nice look. Might not work on a boat."

"Abigail again." I opened the door wider. He entered and gave me a quick kiss on the cheek. "Let me finish while she's at bay."

I returned to the ottoman and put on the shoe, tying it without feline interference. Dan picked up a mouse-shaped toy and dangled the yarn tail in front of Abigail's nose. She batted at it with a quick, sure paw, knocking it from his hand. Black Bart was curled up on a fleece throw at one end of the sofa. As I got up from the ottoman, he opened one eye, then closed it, snuggling down for a strenuous day of sleeping. No doubt Abigail would join him soon.

Dan and I, on the other hand, were bound for the waterfront, where Dan's friend Mack had agreed to take us out on the Estuary this morning. Dan had a soft-sided cooler full of beverages. I had packed a large tote bag with a variety of edibles, as well as my wallet, phone, camera, binoculars and several layers of clothing. I knew from experience that the temperature on the water was likely to be cooler than on land.

Dan and I set off in his Subaru, driving through downtown Oakland and the waterfront. We took the Jackson Street exit off the freeway. The area we drove through had once been home to meat packing plants, warehouses, and parking lots. Now these buildings had been turned into apartments and condos, with new buildings constructed on the parking lots. Lakeside Metal was still there, at the corner of Fourth and Madison, a funky-looking building where all sorts of metal was recycled. Across the street was a one-story building that housed the administrative offices of Cost Plus Imports.

Dan turned right onto Oak Street and slowed. Ahead of us, bells rang out and the crossing arm went down barring the way. A whistle blew and a few seconds later the snub nose of an Amtrak locomotive came into view, heading south out of the Jack London Square station. I could tell from the time of day and the configuration of the cars that the train was the southbound *Coast Starlight*, heading from Seattle down to Los Angeles. After the train went by, the crossing arms lifted and Dan drove over the rails, turning left on the Embarcadero.

We crossed the Lake Merritt Channel and turned right on Fifth Avenue. This block-long stretch led to the Estuary. In addition to the marina at the very end of the street, there was a longstanding community of artists and musicians located here, giving the low-rise buildings a raffish bohemian atmosphere. A shop featuring salvaged items looked interesting. I'd have to come back and explore it.

There were two buses parked on the side of the street, looking as though people were living in them. Dan parked farther down, where the street ended, angling the car into a spot close to the gate that led into the marina. We got out of the car and took our gear from the trunk. Dan pulled out his cell phone and punched numbers.

"It's Dan. We're here."

A few minutes later a tall man appeared, walking up the dock. He was in his fifties, I guessed, with curly gray hair caught back in a ponytail and a luxuriant moustache. At his heels was a small female poodle with large dark eyes and a cream-colored coat.

The man opened the gate and stuck out a welcoming hand. "Mack Kelsey. Nice to meet you. This is Roxie."

"Jeri Howard." I took Mack's hand, which was big and calloused. Then I knelt and held out my hand so Roxie could inspect it. The dog trotted toward me and gave my fingers a thorough sniff, wagging her tail, slowly at first, then more quickly. I scratched the place between her ears. She groaned with pleasure. I stood up. "Thanks for taking us out on your boat."

"No problem. Any excuse to go out on the water. It's a gorgeous day."

It certainly was. In late October, we were past the warmest weather in the Bay Area. The daytime temperatures had dropped somewhat, but today was still projected to be in the high sixties. The sky was blue with just a few clouds here and there. Out in the Estuary, the sun glinted off the water.

"How did you two meet?" I asked as Mack led us back toward the docks. There were three, sticking out into the Estuary like fingers from a hand. I estimated that there were fifty to sixty slips, with boats of all sizes and varieties.

"Hiking the John Muir Trail," Mack said, referring to the mountainous Sierra Nevada trail that wound 211 miles from Mount Whitney to the Yosemite Valley.

"We were camped at Devils Postpile near Mammoth Lakes," Dan added. "Got to talking and hit it off. That was about four years ago. We hike, go out on the boat, and play poker now and then."

I frowned at Dan. "You never invited me to play poker? I love to play poker."

"We haven't had a game in a while." Dan laughed. "I'll bet you're a cardsharp."

"Seven-card stud is my game. I've been known to win a hand or two."

"I'll keep that in mind," Mack said. "We really should schedule a game. I'm always up for fresh green in my wallet. Here we are."

He waved toward his boat, the stern backed into a slip midway down the southernmost dock. The sailboat was a thirty-six-footer called the *Layla*, white hull gleaming in the sun. An orange dinghy was tied upside down on the bow. A set of plastic steps led up to the boat. Roxie trotted ahead and jumped up on the steps, then onto the boat. Dan and I followed with our bags. Mack directed us down the hatch to his cabin. Roxie led the way, nimbly climbing down the angled ladder. Mack's living quarters were a marvel of efficiency, with a small kitchen, an eating area and a built-in sofa that could double as a bed. At the head of this was a built-in stand-up desk with his radio and other equipment. Mack gave us the grand tour, showing us his aft sleeping compartment next to the head. Tucked under the bow was another small sleeping berth.

"Everything in its place," I said.

Mack laughed. "Yeah. Living aboard is different. You can't have a lot of stuff, and most people have stuff. When I decided to live on the boat, I pared down to the essentials."

Mack stowed the drinks Dan had brought in his refrigerator. I set down the bag I carried and pulled out clothing, putting on a warm vest and a zipper-front sweatshirt lined with fleece. If I got too warm, I could take off a layer, but I'd rather be warm than cold, I reasoned. I put on a blue knit cap over my short auburn hair. Then I got out my camera and binoculars, hanging both items around my neck.

I have been known to get seasick and any time on the open ocean or even the bay would have me upchucking over the side. But Dan assured me that this was different. We weren't going out into San Francisco Bay, just motoring along the Estuary so I could look at the waterfront from the water.

Mack grabbed an oversized book of navigational charts from the table near his radio. He slipped his iPhone into a holder with Velcro straps, which he then fastened onto his upper left arm.

We headed up to the deck. Roxie followed, jumping onto a plastic stepstool. From there she climbed up the ladder. Her tail wagged in anticipation as Mack buckled her into a bright red life jacket. Then he showed us where the people life jackets were located. "Not that I think we'll need them," he added. "This is just a trip up and down the Estuary, right? That's what Dan said when he called me yesterday."

I nodded. "I'm investigating the death of a man I used to work with. I want to look at the place the body was found, at Clinton Basin. And the place where he worked, a construction site on the Embarcadero."

"Got it," Mack said. "I know the construction site you're talking about. I saw the Oakland Police Department boat at Clinton Basin last Sunday morning. A guy who keeps his boat here at the marina found the body. He was out walking his dog."

I was sitting at a small table that pulled down, forward of the helm. Mack had put the navigational chart book on the table, open to the page that showed the chart for the area. I pulled it toward me and examined the page.

"It's lucky they even found the body," Mack said. "I'm surprised the tide didn't carry it out into the bay."

"Where would the current take him?" I asked.

"I need to know what time he went into the water before I can tell you that."

"I don't know for sure, but I can guess. He was a security guard at that construction site. He was working a night shift, eleven o'clock to seven in the morning. The last time anyone heard from him was a text message he sent to his daughter at one-thirty A.M. He went into the water sometime after that. So let's say two in the morning."

Mack took his iPhone from the case on his arm. He pulled up a website with information on tides and currents. "Okay, early Sunday morning. The first low tide was at eleven minutes after twelve. The current moves south about a mile and a half." He leaned over the navigational chart on the table and traced a line with his index finger. "At one-forty-five in the morning there's a slack tide."

"Slack tide means no water movement?"

"That's right. It means there's no movement either way in the tidal stream. Slack tide happens before the tide direction changes. I figure the body would have moved about two nautical miles south then it would move north." Mack's finger moved along the chart. "High tide that day, at the Golden Gate, was seven-thirty-five in the morning. With the tide movement and the current here in the Brooklyn Basin channel, the body could have moved all the way up through the Inner Harbor and out into San Francisco Bay. Remember, a fresh body usually sinks. A person with body fat comes up quicker."

"Cal was tall and lean."

"It's just a crapshoot that the guy's body got found at all. If it had gone into the bay, probably never would have been seen."

"The body was tangled with line," I said. "I'm guessing the line got caught on something that slowed the movement." I wondered if the killer had tied the line, and something heavy, around Cal's body. That way the body would definitely sink. It made sense, from the killer's standpoint, not to leave anything to chance.

"That's a likely guess."

While Dan and Mack cast off, I studied the navigational chart, noting the depth of the water in various places. In several locations the chart indicated obstructions such as submerged pilings and wrecks. I hadn't realized there were wrecks in the Estuary, but their presence made sense, given the amount of traffic on this body of water.

The *Layla* motored slowly from the slip, heading out into the Estuary. Roxie sat next to me, an old salt in her doggie life jacket.

"My boat draws about six feet," Mack said. "Most of the Estuary is thirty feet deep or more. As we get closer to the shore, it's maybe fifteen feet or less. So I'm not gonna be able to get real close to where that body was found. I don't want to risk running aground."

"I understand," I said. "Do whatever you can. I really appreciate this."

Mack headed around the end of Fifth Avenue Point toward Clinton Basin. I saw a woman in jeans and a jacket walking along the shoreline, accompanied by a black-and-white dog that looked like a pit bull. The dog ran ahead but its progress was stopped by a chain-link fence that ran out of land and went several feet into the water. I raised my binoculars to my eyes and adjusted the focus. This was where Cal's body had been found, washed up against this fence, line around his body. I lowered the binoculars and pulled out my digital camera, zooming the lens closer. I snapped a few photos.

Mack pointed. "There are a couple of submerged pilings near the mouth of the basin, and a wreck below the surface over there. So I don't want to get much closer than this." He moved the boat in a wide curve, heading back out to the main channel.

Now that I was out on the water, I realized that what I saw from my drives along the Embarcadero was the manicured side of the Estuary. From the water, there was another view, one of old rotting piers, trash washed up on the shoreline, caught in the fence where Cal's body had been found. A plastic water bottle floated in the current twenty feet or so off to port, while a splintered board bobbed in the boat's wake. I wondered what discards and detritus covered the bottom of the Estuary, under the dark water.

The boat motored along, the backside of the big Brooklyn Basin development off the port side, where huge pilings supported a large pier. A California seagull perched atop an oversized cleat. Three more gulls wheeled overhead. At the bottom of the pilings I saw a pair of Western grebes with black-and-white feathers and long yellow bills. They skimmed along the water's surface, then dived, searching for food.

At the helm, Mack turned the boat to port, moving out of what the navigational chart called the South Brooklyn Basin Channel into a smaller channel at the back of the buildings along the Embarcadero. The Ninth Avenue Terminal loomed above us, a huge structure built in the Beaux-Arts style, which dated from the 1920s and was expanded in the 1950s, constructed to handle non-container cargo. My reading about the Brooklyn Basin project told me that the terminal, some 180,000 square feet, would be demolished down to 20,000 square feet, with the portion that remained to be restored as an open pavilion for concerts and other events. At one time a historic preservation group had sued over the plans to demolish the terminal, but I wasn't sure how that had turned out.

We motored past the Biergarten, the restaurant where I'd had my parking lot confrontation with Brice Cardoza on Thursday. The establishment had several guest berths, so that people on the Estuary could tie up and go up the ramp for lunch or a beer. Marina docks, a dozen of them, stretched from the beer garden to the back of the Cardoza construction site. Boats were tied up at most of the slips, except for the last two docks, which were in back of the defunct marine supply store, the one that had burned in the suspected arson fire, the land subsequently purchased by the Cardozas to increase the size of their development. The docks interested me. It was possible that Cal had gone into the water here.

Mack waved in the direction of the empty docks. "I used to buy supplies at that store. It was a good one, had everything from hardware to electronics to engine parts to clothes. Hated to see it go. The Vances, that was their name, a husband-and-wife team. Older couple, really nice people. I know the company that's building that project wanted to buy the land."

"I suppose the company offered the Vances a lot of money for the property."

"They did. But the Vances didn't really want to sell. They had built that business up over a lot of years. I remember talking with Mr. Vance and he told me the developers were really persistent. They kept upping the money. Then there was a fire. The whole building went up. Total loss."

"I read about that, and the article said the fire was suspicious."

"Yeah, it was," Mack said. "I saw Mr. Vance a few days after it happened. Poor guy, he and his wife were up to their butts in investigators, from the fire department and the insurance company. He said there were signs that the fire had been deliberately set."

"An accelerant," Dan said. "But a place like that would have plenty of flammables on the premises."

"True enough. But Mr. Vance said something that stuck with

me. He told me the guy that was representing the developers was really putting on the pressure. Like it was intimidation. You know, sell me the property, or else."

"I'd like to talk with Mr. Vance," I said.

"He lives down in San Leandro. I got his number somewhere. When we get back to the slip I'll dig it out for you."

I raised my binoculars and scanned the Cardoza development site, which had nearly doubled in size once the Cardozas added the store land to their parcel. On this Sunday morning, there was one vehicle, a beige Honda, parked to the side of the trailer. I focused the binoculars on the trailer's windows and saw movement inside. Perhaps the security guard was taking a break.

Mack took the boat farther along the shoreline of the construction site. "Gets shallow along here. I'm gonna turn around."

The boat began to move in a wide circle. Now I could see the front gate of the site, the one that opened onto the Embarcadero. A security guard walked along the front fence. So who was inside the trailer?

The boat continued circling. From this angle, I saw another car parked in front of the trailer, a late-model silver sedan. Two men left the trailer. I lowered my binoculars and replaced them with my camera, zooming in and snapping pictures. I was sure the taller man was Brice Cardoza. The other man was shorter, slender, dressed in a gray hooded sweatshirt, his face obscured by sunglasses. I leaned forward, snapping more photos. Was this the man who had attempted to get into Cal's apartment last Tuesday?

The two men got into the silver car. The guy in the hoodie was driving. He backed the vehicle away from the trailer and headed toward the Embarcadero gate. I was too far away to get a look at the license plate, but once I downloaded the photos onto my computer, I could increase the size. Perhaps that would be enough to read the license number.

The security guard opened the gate and the car turned left, heading up the Embarcadero toward Jack London Square. As the boat turned, I noticed another vessel, offshore, about thirty yards from the shoreline. This boat, with the distinctive red stripe on the side, was the one I'd seen on Friday when I was on the Embar-cadero, looking at the site and talking with Tony, the homeless man. That day it had been just off the docks in back of the Cardoza site. Now it was at the other end of the site. On deck was a woman with a lean frame, wearing faded jeans and a green sweatshirt. A blue dinghy was tied to the side of the boat, bobbing gently in our wake as Mack steered his sailboat back in the direction we had come. Now I could see the name painted on the hull. In black letters above the red stripe, it read *Maysie*.

"That boat with the red stripe," I said, pointing. "The one with the woman on deck. I saw that boat in this area on Friday. A man I spoke with told me her name is Lydia and she lives aboard. Is that what they call an anchor-out?"

"I've heard them called a variety of things, anchor-out being the most common." Mack's face creased as he frowned. "Yeah, she's one of them. I've seen her around over the past year or so."

"Why the frown?" Dan asked.

"Some people think the anchor-outs are a big problem," Mack said. "Me, I don't know where I fall in that debate. All I know is the biggest problem me and other people have with the anchor-outs is that they dump their waste overboard. As in raw sewage going right into the Estuary. I've got a septic tank on this boat and I hook it up to the marina's waste unit. I use the marina toilets and showers. But the anchor-outs? Some of them use a bucket and dump their waste at a pumping station on shore. A lot of them just dump it over the side."

I looked at the water around me. "Not good."

"You got that right. You don't want to go swimming in that. Then there are thefts. Some people will steal anything that ain't nailed down and the anchor-outs get blamed. We got a lot of homeless people around here, but they aren't going to steal things like outboard motors, dinghies and oars. I've been lucky, I haven't lost anything, but a guy at my marina had his kayak stolen a couple of months ago. The manager of my marina had a generator and some lanterns taken. When people have gone to bed, the thieves start prowling around."

Late night, or early in the morning, I thought. Which was around the time Cal had been murdered.

"How do the anchor-outs get their boats?" Dan asked.

"A lot of the boats are abandoned," Mack said. "Squatters just move aboard and take the boats off shore. Having a boat is an expensive proposition. Say some guy buys a boat. Then he can't make the payments or pay the monthly rental for the slip. Guy just walks away, leaves the boat at the marina. I've heard of some people scuttling the boats, so they'll sink. It happened a lot during the recession. So the marina gets stuck getting rid of the boat. If the boat has sunk, they got to rent a hoist to lift it out of the water. Then they got to haul it someplace and store it, then break it up and get rid of anything hazardous. It's a mess. Of course, sometimes the harbormasters sell the abandoned boat."

"I imagine some of those boats end up anchored out here," I said.

"Yeah." Mack shrugged. "It's like the homeless people. They pitch tents and move in. You see them down by Union Point. There's a big bunch of them along the Lake Merritt Channel. It really looks bad over there. It's tough. I know people need places to live and it's damned expensive in this area. Rents are out of sight. But you've got trash everywhere on land and sewage being dumped into the water. Where do you draw the line?"

"Tough questions," I said. I looked back at the boat with the red stripe. "Does that boat stay in this general area?"

Mack nodded. "Yeah, pretty much. I see her in this section a lot. I've also seen her dinghy tied up at that dock by the construction site. I wonder if she might be responsible for some of the recent thefts from that marina next to the site."

Or dumping trash, I thought, remembering what Tony had told me on Friday.

Dan looked at me. "Jeri's wondering if she might have seen something the night of the murder?"

"You're right, I am. If Cal was killed around two o'clock and she was in the area, she could very well be a witness."

"I'll see if I can find out more about her," Mack said. "Got a

Coast Guard inflatable coming this way." He moved the boat farther out into the Estuary, steering clear of the fast-moving orange inflatable that had come from Coast Guard Island, home to two cutters. It looked as though the inflatable, with several crewmen aboard, was heading toward a large ship with a distinctive blue hull, with *Pacific Responder* in white letters high on the bow.

"That's an oil spill response vessel," Mack explained as his sailboat rocked in the inflatable's wake.

Marinas were spread up and down the Alameda shoreline on the other side of the Estuary, a forest of sailboat masts rising skyward. At the foot of Grand Street I saw a large boat belonging to the Alameda County sheriff's office. Now Mack motored along the backside of the Brooklyn Basin project.

"This development is going to be huge," Dan said, looking up at the piers that towered over us. "I've seen the plans. It will be on both sides of Clinton Basin."

I glanced up at Mack, standing at the helm. "What do you and your fellow marina dwellers think of all the development that's going on here at the waterfront, particularly this Brooklyn Basin development?"

"All these changes," Mack said. "It's got me worried. Me and a lot of other people."

"Why is that?"

"I'm hearing rumors that the next piece of land that gets bulldozed and developed might be Fifth Avenue. Which has a lot of small businesses and artists' studios and the marina, of course. There's a good-sized piece of land between Fifth and the Lake Merritt Channel. Big building there is a concrete supply place and then open land."

I nodded. "I know the property you're talking about."

"I don't even know what used to be there, but it's empty now. It's right on the water and it's ripe for development. Story I hear is that someone is buying the land and pushing for it to be a waterfront ballpark."

"Ballpark?" Dan said. "Since they built one over in San Francisco for the Giants, Oakland now wants a waterfront ballpark for the A's." At the look on my face, he laughed. "I know you're not a sports fan."

"Far from it. I think Oakland's public money would be better spent on the public schools and fixing the damn potholes, which are legion. One of them necessitated some expensive repairs on my Toyota a few years back. I get tired of cities throwing money and perks at sports team owners who are already rich enough to build their own damn stadiums. As a citizen of Oakland and Alameda County I'm already paying taxes for the last financial debacle that occurred when Oakland just had to lure the Raiders back from Southern California. Now the team wants to leave again. Let them."

"Not a football fan, huh?" Mack smiled. "Yeah, that waterfront ballpark comes up frequently these days. They were talking about building it up at the Howard Terminal. But I don't think that will work."

"Why not? Dan asked.

"I'll show you." Mack motored the boat past Clinton Basin and the Fifth Avenue Marina. Now we were at the place he was talking about, the open land between Fifth Avenue and the Lake Merritt Channel.

"I could see that as a location for a ballpark," I conceded. "But is it big enough?"

"They could build part of it on piers out in the Estuary," Dan said.

"Could do." Mack continued past Estuary Park and the backside of the area known as Jack London Square. I could remember when much of this land was open. Now it was crowded with apartments. The old Boatel was now the Waterfront Plaza. Here was the Oakland ferry terminal and the offices of the Port of Oakland. The *Potomac*, the presidential yacht used by Franklin Delano Roosevelt, was tied up here, open for tours and cruises during the summer months. Two smaller boats, both gray, were operated by the Oakland Police Department. A larger red-and-white boat belonged to the Oakland Fire Department.

A larger boat next to these had the name *Relief* on its hull.

"That's an old Coast Guard lightship," Mack said. "They were used as navigation aids years ago, anchored off shore where there was no rock to build a lighthouse. This one's open for tours, like the *Potomac*."

As we moved past those boats we were in Port of Oakland territory, with huge towering cranes looming overhead, used to move containers onto ships, like the huge vessel nearby, the length of several city blocks.

"The Howard Terminal is over there," Mack said, pointing at the shoreline. "It's at the end of Market Street. The land belongs to the port, which is why the city thinks it might work for a ballpark. The port would sign over the land to developers, the way they did with Brooklyn Basin. But I'm telling you, it won't work. It's close enough to Jack London Square, but quite a ways from downtown and BART. They'd need parking lots and shuttles. And the rail-road tracks run right in front of it. They'd have to build pedestrian bridges."

I waved in a northwesterly direction. "The Union Pacific rail yard is just a few blocks over there. These tracks are busy all the time."

Mack laughed. "Don't I know it. The marina's just a couple of blocks from the tracks. I hear train whistles all night long."

"They'd definitely need a pedestrian bridge over the tracks," Dan said, "like the ones at Jack London Square. Otherwise, I can just see some drunk baseball fans trying to play chicken with a train. That would be a recipe for disaster."

Mack nodded. "You got that right. A diesel locomotive does not stop on a dime."

"The site near Fifth Avenue would be a better location for a ballpark," I said. "At that point, the railroad tracks are on the other side of the Embarcadero."

"I hope it doesn't happen," Mack said. "The Fifth Avenue community is a good place. I'd hate to lose that."

Mack again took the boat in a circle. To my right I saw the ferry terminal on the Alameda side. Farther north the Inner Harbor would give way to the Middle Harbor, where I'd gone birding with my father. On the Alameda side of the Estuary was the former Naval Air Station, now called Alameda Point.

Mack waved a hand in the direction of the old Navy base. "I used to be stationed there. I was an aviation machinist's mate. Funny thing, I grew up in Nebraska. The Missouri River was the biggest body of water I'd ever seen, until I was about ten years old. My folks took us kids on a trip to Disneyland and then we went down to San Diego. That's the first time I ever saw the ocean. So here I am, come from the prairie and now I'm living on a boat near San Francisco Bay. That air station was bustling back in the day. Never thought they'd close it down."

"Development plans there, too. I know a lot of Alameda locals are wary of more housing being built on the old air station. If you're driving, there's only one way off the west end of Alameda, and that's going through the Tube," I added, referring to the twin tunnels that ran beneath the Estuary, leading from Alameda to Oakland. Both were two lanes wide and both were at capacity during morning and evening rush hour. Adding more cars to that mix would make traffic even worse, but plans for development continued.

"Nobody talks about the flooding," Mack said. "I was stationed at Alameda during one of those El Niño years, when it rained like a son of a bitch. That whole section there by the air station main gate was underwater."

"That part of Alameda was marshland in the early years," I said. "Alameda's only thirty-three feet above sea level. When you factor in climate change and rising sea levels, West Alameda looks like a flood zone."

"It is a flood zone," Dan added. "I've seen the inundation maps for the San Francisco Bay area. Most of Alameda would be underwater, and so would the Oakland waterfront."

There was still a lot of maritime industry along the Alameda shore. We were opposite Bay Ship, which had a huge covered dry dock, used for ship and boat repair. Two tugboats, squat workhorses of the waterfront, went by on our starboard side, heading toward Middle Harbor.

The wind had picked up and I was glad that I had on my layers of clothing. As we headed back, passing the Lake Merritt Channel once again, I looked off the port side to the land Mack had been talking about, the area that was rumored to be a potential site for a ballpark. I made a mental note to look into property transfers at the Alameda County Courthouse. Maybe I could find out who was buying the land, and why.

At the Fifth Avenue Marina, Mack backed the *Layla* into his slip. Dan held a boat hook and snagged the line, helping to position the boat. Once both men had tied the line on either side of the boat to the cleats on the dock, Mack unbuckled Roxie from her life jacket. We spent the rest of the morning sitting on deck, talking about other things as we drank beer and spread Brie on crackers.

Chapter Twenty

O N MONDAY MORNING, I downloaded the photos from my camera onto my office computer. I opened the files and examined the pictures I had taken the day before, concentrating on the shots of the two men I'd seen leaving the trailer at the Cardoza work site. The photographs had been taken from a distance with my zoom lens, while the boat was moving. Several of the pictures were blurry, but I saw enough to determine that the taller man was indeed Brice Cardoza.

As for Cardoza's companion, I couldn't tell much about him, though I was sure this was the same man who'd tried to get into Cal Brady's apartment on Tuesday afternoon. Like the blurry figure in the cell phone video shot by Cal's neighbor, the man wore sunglasses and had a hoodie pulled up over his head, obscuring his face.

I printed out the photos and examined them with a magnifier. The two men had driven away from the work site in a silver car. As I enlarged the photo I'd taken, I saw a stylized *L* in a circle emblem on the trunk. The car was a Lexus. I was able to make out most of the numbers on the rear license plate.

The DMV was not supposed to hand out information on car registrations to people like me, but I had contacts. It would take some time to get results, however.

Brice Cardoza had probably sent this man to get into Cal's apartment, using keys taken from Cal's body. He was after something, probably the information Cal had collected while he was investigating whatever was going on at the work site. But there had to be more to this than the workplace accident that had injured the undocumented worker. Cal had stumbled onto something that was much more volatile.

I stared at the photo printouts I'd spread out on my desk. Perhaps Nathan Dupre, the security guard I'd talked with on Thursday, could identify the man. If not, he could at least tell me which guard had been working at the construction site during the day on Sunday.

I looked back through my notes concerning my meeting with Dupre. He'd mentioned that starting Saturday, he would be on the swing shift for five days, working from three in the afternoon until eleven o'clock at night. I phoned him now.

The call went straight to voice mail. "This is Jeri Howard. Thanks for putting in a good word for me with Gary Manville. I talked with him on Friday. I have a couple of questions for you."

I ended the call and made another. The man who had owned the marine supply store next to the Cardoza property was Charles Vance. On Sunday, before Dan and I left the Fifth Avenue Marina, Mack Kelsey had given me Vance's contact information. I called and got voice mail. I left my name and number, mentioning that Mack had given me Vance's number and I wanted to talk about what had happened to the store.

I turned back to my computer and once again looked up the phone number for New Start East Bay, the housing nonprofit where Pilar García worked. She had been out of the office on Friday, but she was back today. However, she was in meetings most of the morning, I was told.

I drank my way through a pot of coffee while I went through my email and wrote reports on two cases, one an insurance investigation and the other a civil lawsuit. I fielded several phone calls and set up an appointment for a prospective client. Then I shut down my computer and left the office.

New Start was located in a two-story building at the corner of Clay and Third streets in the Jack London Square neighborhood.

I entered the building and glanced at the signboard on the wall, to find out which offices were located where. The nonprofit was a few doors down, on the right side of the central corridor, through a glass door with a logo painted on it. The office was bright and cheerful, painted pale yellow, with a large ficus in a colorful red-and-orange pot next to the window that looked out at the street. To my left I saw a desk and near the window, several low chairs grouped around a table. The desk was staffed by a receptionist, a young man in his twenties. Behind him an inner door led back to other offices.

"May I help you?" he asked.

"I'd like to speak with Pilar García."

He glanced at the round clock on the wall near the window. It showed a quarter to twelve. "I don't think she's gone to lunch yet. Let me see if she's in her office. Your name, please?"

"Jeri Howard. Tell her I'm a friend of Davina Roka."

The young man reached for his console, then stopped, hand in midair. "It looks like she's on the phone. If you'll take a seat for a few minutes, I'll buzz her as soon as she's off her line."

I thanked him, stepped over to the chairs, and sat down. I knew from my research that the nonprofit was, like others in the Bay Area, involved in building affordable housing. Its staff located and purchased likely parcels of land, developed them and managed the apartment buildings. Much of the housing was infill, built on former industrial sites throughout the East Bay. I leafed through the brochures and magazines on the table. Most of them had to do with housing—community housing, nonprofit housing, infill housing. One publication talked about housing equity. Another tackled the subject of gentrification, which was a big problem in West Oakland, where the Victorian-era workers' cottages were being bought up, remodeled and sold for lots of money, more than the long-term neighborhood residents could afford.

I glanced through a photocopied article about the Wood Street Station, a remnant of Oakland's railroad past. It had once been a major station for the Southern Pacific Railroad and later, Amtrak. Another Beaux-Arts building dating to 1913, it had been badly damaged in the 1989 Loma Prieta earthquake. Amtrak now operated out of newer stations in Emeryville and at Jack London Square station. The Wood Street Station was still empty and covered with graffiti, despite repeated efforts at preservation and rehabilitation. Now, I learned, the station was owned by Bridge, one of the local nonprofits that built affordable housing.

I heard the receptionist talking on the phone. I looked up as the inner door opened and a woman stepped out. She was short and slender, in her forties, I guessed, dressed in navy blue slacks and a blouse in a muted floral pattern. She had a few streaks of gray in her dark hair. She walked toward me, a pleasant smile on her face.

"I'm Pilar García," she said. "I understand you're a friend of Davina's. How can I help you?"

"I'm interested in a former employee of yours, Leo Walker."

Ms. García's smile disappeared and her mouth pursed, as though the mention of Leo's name tasted bad. The expression in her eyes turned wary. "He worked here at one time. I can't give you any more information than that. State employment rules prohibit us from doing anything other than confirming his employment."

From the look on Pilar García's face, I had a feeling she would like to say more than the rules and regulations would allow. She was a source worth pursuing. The clock on the wall was edging toward noon.

"I understand," I said. "Thanks for your time. By the way, I would appreciate it if you would call Davina, before you go to lunch."

She looked at me thoughtfully. Then she nodded. "I will."

I left the New Start office and headed for my car. I had parked on Clay, facing Third Street. Sitting in the driver's seat, I had a clear view of the building I'd just left. I sat and watched, telling myself I would give it half an hour or so.

At a quarter after twelve, the building's outer door opened and Pilar García walked out. She had pulled on a blue cardigan sweater and she carried a purse and a canvas tote bag. She waited for a car to pass, then she crossed Third Street and continued walking down Clay Street, past my car. It looked as though she was headed for the Embarcadero and the Estuary. I let her get ahead of me. Then I got out of the car and followed, leaving half a block between us.

Before she reached the Embarcadero I heard the long-and-short warning whistle of an approaching train. She stopped at the corner and I stopped farther back. The eastbound Amtrak *Capitol Corridor* moved into view, the sleek silver-and-blue cars gleaming in the autumn sunshine as the train headed toward its next destination. When the train had passed, she crossed the Embarcadero and kept going, heading toward the water.

She turned right, heading for the ferry terminal, where a pier jutted over the water. She strolled along the pier, to the end, where she stood for a moment, looking out at the water. On this sunny October afternoon several people sat on nearby benches, eating their lunches, some brought from home, others take-out from nearby restaurants. After a moment, she turned and retraced her steps, sitting down at an unoccupied bench. She reached into the tote bag and removed a book, a water bottle and wrapped sandwich. I let her get in a few bites before I approached her.

She looked up. "Okay, I called Davina. It's hard to get her on the phone. I had to wait for her to call me back. She vouches for you. She says you're a private investigator and you used to work with her, before she worked here. What's this all about? Something to do with Leo?"

I took out a business card and handed it to her. "I think it might very well have something to do with Leo. His name has come up in one of my investigations."

She examined my card, holding it carefully between her thumb and forefinger. She made a disparaging sound. Whether it was directed at me or Leo, I wasn't sure. Her next words left little doubt. "He ought to be investigated, after what he did."

"What was that?"

She put my business card on the bench next to her. "I shouldn't be talking to you."

"Oh, but you want to." I sat down beside her. "I could tell from your face. When I mentioned his name there in the office, you looked like you'd bitten into a sour pickle. Something happened. What was it?"

She thought about it for a moment while she took a bite of her sandwich and chewed. After taking a swallow from her water bottle, she said, "Leo was us for a few months, less than a year. He was an admin assistant. Usually we're really savvy when we hire staff. We look for people who are passionate about what we do. Somehow Leo got past the radar. He talked the talk, said he grew up poor in Oakland. He claimed his mission in life was to help build affordable housing. But his mission was something else."

"What did he do?

She paused for a sip of water. "One day another admin assistant was working late. She found Leo in an office where he wasn't supposed to be, going through a filing cabinet, looking at files. He gave her a story and left. The following day, she reported it to her supervisor."

"What was in the filing cabinet that Leo was searching?"

"A proposal, plus all the background and correspondence relating to it. We submitted a bid to build forty units of affordable housing on a parcel in West Oakland. The proposal went to the Oakland City Council's Community and Economic Development Committee. We had word that we were going to get the award. Then the committee turned around and gave it to another developer, a for-profit company. We found out later that some internal communications about that proposal had been copied and given to the other developer. The documents were used to put New Start in a bad light. We think that's what Leo was doing in those files, looking for information and copying it."

"Was there any proof that Leo passed information to the developer?"

She shook her head. "Not really. Other than the timing. Leo was where he shouldn't have been. That evening was the last time anyone saw him. He didn't show up for work the next day. He didn't answer his phone. His employment was terminated, of course, after we jumped through all the necessary human resources hoops. The next week, we found out we didn't get the award."

I nodded, agreeing that the timing, and Leo's actions, were suspicious. "What was the name of the company that got the award?"

"Cherrytown. They're buying up a lot of potential infill property all over the East Bay, putting up developments with retail on the first floor and market-rate housing on the upper floors. Someone heard later that Leo was working for Cherrytown and some other for-profit developers. We also heard Cherrytown was making contributions to several of the city council members on the development committee."

Money talks, I thought as I wrote the name of the company in my notebook. I left Pilar García to finish her lunch in peace and walked back to where I'd parked my car. Back in my office I turned on my computer and began searching for information on the company.

When I heard the name Cherrytown, I thought of San Leandro. The town had once been known as "The Cherry City" because of all the fruit grown there. But Cherrytown had an address in Stockton, in San Joaquin County, where they did grow lots of cherries. I needed to do more research on the company, to see if they were, as Pilar had said, buying up property in the East Bay. If they were greasing palms as well, that would require more digging.

It would have to wait, though. I had a meeting with a client in downtown Oakland in less than an hour. I reviewed the client file and headed out the door.

Chapter Twenty-one

WHEN I RETURNED from the meeting later that afternoon, my phone was ringing as I unlocked the office door. I hurried to my desk and grabbed the receiver. "Howard Investigations."

"Is this the infamous Jeri Howard?"

I laughed. "Of course. And this is the equally infamous Duc Ngo. It's about time you called me back. I guess the FBI is keeping you busy."

"It is," he said. "I was thinking of you, even before you called. I heard about Errol's death. I knew you'd be going to the funeral. Unfortunately I couldn't. I was out of town."

"It was a good memorial service, as those things go," I said. "A lot of people there."

"Listen, I'm about to go into a meeting. How about lunch? Can you come over to the city tomorrow?"

I looked at my calendar for Tuesday. It was relatively clear. "Sure. What time and where?"

"The Slanted Door in the Ferry Building, at twelve-thirty."

"See you then. It'll be good to catch up."

I settled into my office chair and listened to voice mail messages. Some were hang-ups, others were business-related. Madison Brady had called, wanting to know if I had heard anything about Cal's autopsy. I hadn't, so I phoned the Oakland Police Department. Grace Portillo wasn't in the office. I left a message.

The last voice mail was from Nathan Dupre, returning my call from earlier in the day. I glanced at the clock. He was on swing shift today, due to report at three. It was nearly two now. I called him back and he answered on the first ring.

"Got your message," he said. "The guard's name is Ed Falworth. He's on days through Tuesday. I'm just about to relieve him. He didn't know Cal all that well. Why do you want to talk with him?"

"I was on a boat in the Estuary on Sunday. As we went past the construction site I saw two men leaving the trailer. One of them was Brice. He certainly spends a lot of time on the site when it's not actually working hours."

"Yeah, he does. As to whether he's working, the jury's out on that. I've seen him there weekends and nights," Dupre said. "And when he's not there, he's at the Biergarten working his way through a few beers. Now, about the guy he was with. You don't know who he is?"

"I don't, and I'd like to find out. He was driving a silver Lexus."

"Silver Lexus?" Dupre sounded thoughtful. "You know, I've seen that car before."

"I have photos. Can we meet before you report to work?"

"Yeah, I can. Ordinarily I'd say let's meet at that Starbucks on the Embarcadero. But that's too close to the construction site. How about Peerless Coffee on Oak Street? I can be there in fifteen minutes."

I put the photos I'd taken on Sunday into a file folder and left the office, my stomach growling because I hadn't eaten lunch. I retrieved my car from the parking lot and drove toward Jack London Square.

Peerless Coffee had been an Oakland fixture since 1924, the business founded by an immigrant from what was then Yugoslavia. It was still owned by the same family. Originally Peerless had been located in Old Oakland, the same site as the Friday farmers' market. In the mid-seventies the company had moved to its current location, where the retail outlet fronted the large coffee roasting facility. The store sold coffee, tea, spices, and peanuts in the shell, as well as an assortment of equipment and paraphernalia for brewing beverages. Antique coffeemakers decorated shelves high on the walls. Peerless was one of the few things on the Oakland waterfront that hadn't changed.

I parked in the lot, but I didn't see Dupre. I was early, though. My stomach growled again as I got out of the car, sniffing the perfume of roasting coffee. I went inside and purchased a latte and a chocolate chip cookie. Back outside, I took a seat at one of the tables provided for customers. I was munching on my cookie when a gray Honda hatchback pulled into the lot and parked.

Dupre got out, wearing his Manville Security uniform. He walked toward me, gesturing toward the door to the Peerless retail outlet. "Can I get a coffee first?"

I saluted him with my own cup. "Far be it from me to get between a man and his caffeine."

Dupre laughed and went inside, coming out a moment later with the largest available cup. He took a sip and sighed. "Oh, yeah, I needed that."

I wiped my hands on a napkin and opened the file folder containing the printouts of the photos I'd taken on Sunday.

"That's Brice, all right," Dupre said, leaning over to examine them. "The other guy, I've seen him and his Lexus before, at the work site. He comes to see Brice, but not during the day. It's usually at night or on weekends."

"Do you know who he is?" I asked.

Dupre shook his head. "You got the license number on the Lexus. Can't you run that and figure out who the car belongs to?"

I smiled. "This is real life, not the movies. The Department of Motor Vehicles frowns on that sort of thing. In fact, they have all sorts of ways to prevent my getting that information."

"The privacy thing. I get it." He drank coffee and looked at his watch. "I've got to go to work. You want me to take that picture and show it to Ed Falworth, the guard I'm relieving?"

"I'd rather not. I don't want Brice to know I took photos of him." I also didn't want to run the risk that the photo printout might fall into the wrong hands. "Just ask Falworth if he knows the identity of the man who was with Brice at the site on Sunday."

"Will do." Dupre gave me a jaunty salute with his coffee cup and headed for his car. As he drove off, I finished my latte and cookie, once again examining the pictures I'd taken. Then I tossed my trash in a nearby can and went back into Peerless, where I bought a pound of French roast coffee beans.

I went back to my office. I had more work to do, updating the client file from my earlier meeting. By the time I finished it was nearly four-thirty. Might as well call it a day, I thought. The phone rang. I answered with my usual greeting. "Howard Investigations."

"Jeri Howard?" It was a man's voice and it didn't sound familiar.

I confirmed my identity, sensing the man's hesitation radiating over the phone line.

"My name's Raymond," he said. "I got your number from someone at East Bay Intergroup."

That was the place that housed Alcoholics Anonymous meetings. I had handed out my business cards at the facility on Friday. Perhaps that exercise had paid off.

"I'm looking for Cal Brady's sponsor," I said. "Would that be you?"

He answered my question with one of his own. "Is it true Cal's dead?"

"His body was found in the Estuary a week ago Sunday."

The man sighed. "Damn, that's awful. Yeah, I'm Cal's sponsor. I see him at meetings at least once a week. We get together for coffee every couple of weeks. And check in by phone every few days. I hadn't heard from him. That got me worried. I've been calling his cell phone and it goes straight to voice mail. Now I get a message saying the mail box is full. Then you show up at the Intergroup building, handing out cards and telling people Cal's dead. That's where I got your card. So it's true? Damn. What happened?"

"Cal's body was found in Clinton Basin, near the Fifth Avenue Marina. I think he was murdered, Raymond. His daughter has asked me to look into it." He didn't say anything. "Look, I know you and Cal were in AA. Believe me, with the work I do as a private investigator, I understand the importance of confidentiality. But I need to know if Cal talked with you about anything that was going on at work. I think he was investigating something on his own. That may have led to his death."

Raymond hesitated. Then he said, "Okay, I'll talk with you. I get off work at five. I can meet you then. How about Farley's on Grand? It's not far from my office."

"Not far from mine, either. I have short hair and today I'm wearing a blue shirt."

"I wear glasses and my hair's going gray," he said.

I worked at my desk a while longer, then I locked my office at ten till five and headed downstairs to the lot where I parked my Toyota. I was planning to go home after I talked with Raymond. At this time of the day street parking wasn't difficult. I found parking near the corner of Broadway and Grand and fed the meter. Farley's was in the middle of the block. There were two men at the tables outside, talking and drinking coffee. Inside the coffee shop a woman with a laptop sat at one of the tables. In a nearby chair a man was reading a newspaper, sipping from a cup at his elbow.

I stepped up to the counter and ordered. This was my second coffee shop meeting of the day. Some days it seemed that I subsisted on caffeine, much of it purchased in places like this. Coffee shops were convenient for meetings, though, neutral ground outside of my workplace and that of the person I was meeting.

This late in the day I stuck with my usual latte and resisted the impulse to get something sweet to eat. Dinner awaited, even if it was leftovers. Besides, on Saturday Cassie had sent me home with some of that delicious shortbread.

At a quarter after five a man wearing horn-rimmed glasses walked into Farley's. His hair was indeed going gray, more salt than pepper. He was probably in his late forties or early fifties, thick through the middle, his belly hanging over the belt of his brown slacks. He looked around and saw me standing near the counter and approached. "Are you Jeri?"

"I am. Thanks for meeting me, Raymond. What can I get you?"

"Black coffee," he said.

I bought the coffee and handed him the mug. We sat down

at a vacant table near the front entrance. He sipped his coffee in silence, still hesitant about talking with me.

I figured I'd better break the ice. "You work nearby?"

"Over at the Ordway Building," he said, naming the tall building that passed for a skyscraper in Oakland.

"Cal and I used to work in this neighborhood," I said. "Around the corner on Broadway. We worked for a private investigator named Errol Seville. That was before Uptown was a trendy address."

Raymond nodded. "Yeah. This area is really changing. Cal told me about working as a private eye. He said he got fired for drinking on the job. We all have stories like that. He still had a lot of respect for the man he worked for, that Mr. Seville. He died a couple of weeks ago and Cal went to the funeral."

"I was at the service, and saw Cal there." I sipped my coffee. "He told me he was sober and had been for several years."

"He was," Raymond said. "Cal had a lapse at first, after he got out of detox. Many of us do. It was right when he started the program. But he climbed back on the horse and got real serious about working the twelve steps. He loved his daughter. He told me he always wanted to be there for her."

"It's his daughter I'm working for," I reminded him. "She came to me because Cal and I had worked together. She is upset about Cal's death, of course, and because one of the people at the work site told the police that Cal had been drinking on the job."

Raymond stared at me, then shook his head emphatically. "No way. Cal was sober, nearly four years. They must have done an autopsy. Did it show any alcohol in his system?"

"I don't have the autopsy results yet. But I suspect they'll show Cal hadn't been drinking. Someone would like people to think that he was, that somehow he was drunk and fell into the water at the job site. Which would conveniently make his death an accident, not murder. I'm not buying that and neither is Madison Brady."

Raymond swallowed another mouthful of coffee. "He did say there was some guy at work that was riding him all the time. It wasn't another security guard. He had everything good to say about that company he worked for. The man who runs it was an old friend of Cal's from the Navy and he had a lot of respect for him. No, Cal's problem was with another guy, working at the construction site. From what he said, it sounded like this guy had just taken a dislike to Cal from the start."

"I think I know which guy," I said. "Did Cal talk about the job?"

"We talked about a lot of things, including his job, and mine." Raymond's glasses were sliding down his nose and he pushed them up. "Cal liked the security guard gig, but he kept saying he wanted to be a private investigator again. He thought maybe he could get some firm to take him on."

"It looks like he was investigating something that happened at the work site."

"He told me about that," Raymond said. "A guy who got hurt on the job. Cal wanted the man to file a workers comp claim, but he wouldn't because he was undocumented, and he was afraid of the guy in charge."

"Did Cal ever mention the name of the man in charge?"

Raymond thought for a moment. "Brice. That was the guy who seemed to have it in for Cal. I'm pretty sure that was the name. Cal thought maybe he could put some pressure on Brice because he was hiring illegals. But whatever Cal was doing, he hit a brick wall. The worker who got hurt disappeared, went back into the woodwork. Or maybe he got paid to go away. Anyway, after Cal talked with him a couple of times, he couldn't find him."

It was the same dead end I'd encountered after reading through the notebook I'd discovered in one of Cal's books. Cal had been investigating the worker's injury, but I had the feeling there was something more, something I was missing.

"What else did you and Cal talk about, besides the program?" I asked.

Raymond smiled. "Our kids. I've got three boys, he had his daughter. I'm still married, thank goodness. My wife really stuck by me while I was getting sober. I've been sober eight years now."

"Congratulations," I said. "It's hard. I'm impressed by those of you who do the work and make it through."

"They're not kidding when they say it's one day at a time."

Raymond sipped his coffee. Then he smiled. "It's also true what they say about alcoholics drinking lots of coffee. I drink gallons of the stuff, all hours of the day."

I laughed. "I drink lots of coffee, too. I've never been an alcoholic. I guess caffeine is my drug of choice. Chocolate might be right up there. Sugar. Never met a pastry I didn't like."

"We all have our addictions," Raymond said. "Some of them more destructive than others. What else did we talk about? The Navy. Cal and I were both in the Navy, so we had that in common. And baseball. I'm a baseball fanatic. Cal liked it, too, but he wasn't as crazy about it as I am."

"Which team do you like?"

"The A's, the Giants, I like them both." A grin transformed his face. "Cal favored the A's. Sometimes he went with me to the games, at the Oakland Coliseum. We had a great time, sitting there in the bleachers on a sunny day, with a bag of salted peanuts, a big frosty Coke and a couple of hot dogs."

Baseball. I remembered what Mack had said when we were out on the boat on Sunday, during our conversation about a waterfront ballpark. I wondered if Cal had heard the same talk that Mack had, about someone buying property near the Fifth Avenue Marina to build a ballpark.

"If you like the Giants," I said, "you must go over to San Francisco to that waterfront baseball park."

"Oh, yeah." He took another sip of coffee. "I love going over there. A great place for baseball. I wish Oakland had one on the water."

"They keep talking about building one over by Jack London Square."

"That's what I hear," Raymond said. "Some location at the Port of Oakland. Makes sense, I suppose, because the city already owns the land." He finished his coffee and set the mug on the table. "Come to think of it, Cal said something about a ballpark the last time I saw him. About how maybe it was going to be more than talk."

That was interesting, I thought, given how much the subject

of a waterfront ballpark in Oakland had come up over the past few days.

"The man who took a dislike to Cal is Brice Cardoza," I said. "It looks like this animosity dates to the time the worker was injured in the accident. Brice is the one who told the police that Cal had been drinking on the job. Evidently something happened one morning when Cal was due to be relieved after working the night shift. Supposedly he was stumbling around and Brice assumed he had been drinking. A coworker of Cal's, another security guard, said he was sick. Did Cal talk to you about this incident?"

"Oh, yeah," Raymond said. "He called me later that day. He was really upset about that. We got together and talked about it. Cal told me this fellow Brice was really nasty about it. He accused Cal of drinking at work and was demanding that his Manville Security boss fire Cal. But it didn't happen that way. Cal told me something made him sick. When he was on the night shift, he always had a big thermos of coffee, a couple of sandwiches, and other snacks to get him through the night. That evening, he bought the sandwiches at a deli. One was roast beef and the other was tuna salad. He told me the tuna must have been off. You know anything with lots of mayo can go bad. Cal figured it could have been food poisoning. But he wasn't sure."

"That's a good assumption. Why wasn't he sure that it was food poisoning?"

"Brice was there that night, when Cal reported to work a little before eleven. Evidently Brice is there at the construction site late at night, a lot. Cal says it's not the first time he's come to work and found Brice there burning the midnight oil."

I wondered just why it was Brice Cardoza found it necessary to work late at night in the construction site trailer.

"Anyway," Raymond continued, "Cal checked in and relieved the swing shift guard and put his sandwich and snacks in the refrigerator inside the trailer they have there at the construction site. When he called me the next day, he said Brice was there, in the trailer, with another man. This other guy was just leaving when Cal showed up. Cal told me he'd seen this guy with Brice before, and he thought the man looked familiar. That night he said something about it to Brice."

My mind was working on scenarios. This was the same shift when Cal got sick and in the morning Brice had accused him of being drunk on the job. What if it wasn't food poisoning that made Cal sick? What if Brice had done something to Cal's sandwich?

Who was the other man? Was it the person I'd seen with Brice on Sunday, leaving the work site in a silver Lexus?

"Someone could have tampered with Cal's food," I said.

Raymond nodded. "Cal had the same thought. Why would anyone do that?"

"To get him fired." Again I was left with the same question. Why?

Before I went home, I had one more stop to make. Earlier in the day I had looked through Cal's books again. This time I found a scrap of paper on which he'd written an address on Twenty-first Avenue, with the name "Manny" scribbled below. I was guessing that Manny was Manuel Álvarez, the one who'd been injured at the Cardoza construction site. I figured if Álvarez was working again, he would be home this late in the day. Did he still live there? I had no way of knowing, other than knocking on his door.

Oakland's San Antonio district is the area between Lake Merritt and Twenty-ninth Avenue. The name comes from the Rancho San Antonio land grant and the settlement that sprang up around San Antonio Creek. This neighborhood was once the town of Brooklyn, formed from Clinton and San Antonio, eventually folded into Oakland in the 1870s.

International Boulevard, formerly Fourteenth Street, is the spine that runs through the district. The population includes Asians, Latinos, African Americans and whites from all over the nation, and world. The Asian population breaks out into significant numbers from China, southwest Asia, Korea, Japan and the Indian subcontinent, while the Latinos are largely from Mexico, as well as Central and South America.

I turned east off International Boulevard, onto Twenty-first.

On one corner was a hole-in-the-wall eatery with a sign advertising *bahn mi*, Vietnamese sandwiches. The opposite corner held a taquería. Just down the block was an auto body shop.

I passed the next intersection and slowed the car, looking at addresses. This part of town was densely packed with houses and apartment buildings, not much space between structures. Not much parking, either. I took the first available parking spot and set out on foot.

I found what I was looking for, six green stucco cottages, three facing three, on either side of a central driveway that led back to a parking area. Each cottage had a small front yard with brown grass. Several yards contained tubs planted with vegetables and flowers. Two little girls, about eight years old, sat on the porch of the first cottage on the right, playing with dolls. They looked at me curiously as I started up the driveway.

According to Cal's note, Álvarez lived in the second cottage on the left. A tarnished brass "B" hung above a peephole in the front door. The mesh screen door was torn on one corner. A container under the front window held a butternut squash plant, its trailing vines tied with twine to a wooden trellis.

I stepped onto the front porch and pushed the doorbell. No answer. I listened and heard music, then a loud voice speaking in Spanish. It sounded like a radio. I could smell something cooking. Was it coming from this cottage, or one of the others?

I rang the bell again. The music volume went down. The door opened and I saw an older woman, gray hair pulled back from her forehead, her worn hand on the collar of her white blouse.

"*¿Por favor, dónde está Manuel Álvarez?*" I said.

She shook her head. Whether she didn't understand me or she didn't know where Alvarez was, I couldn't tell. Somewhere in the back of the cottage I thought I heard a door close.

I took a business card from my bag and held it up, hoping to reassure her that I wasn't from the police or immigration.

"*¿Manuel Álvarez?*" I said again. "*Por favor, dónde—*"

I saw movement to my left as someone rounded the corner, coming from the back of the cottage. A woman rushed at me, pushing into my personal space, her arm raised. She shoved me back. I dropped the business card and struggled to maintain my balance. She came at me again, this time leaning toward me, her face just a few inches from mine. She spat out a question in accented English. "What do you want?"

I stepped back and looked at her. She was in her early twenties, short and slender, with long black hair tied back from her head. She wore blue jeans, a yellow T-shirt, and a pugnacious don't-mess-with-me look.

"Manuel Álvarez," I said. "I just want to talk with him."

Dark brown eyes narrowed in her thin face. "What about?"

"Rosaura," the older woman said. The two conversed in Spanish. I heard the young woman say *Tia*, aunt. Then both of them spoke at once, arguing.

I held up my hands, summoning silence, trying to look as non-threatening as possible. "I'm not a cop. I'm not from Immigration. I'm a private investigator. My name and phone number are on the card."

Eyes wary, Rosaura stooped and picked up my business card. She examined it, then held it out to her aunt. "What do you want with Manny?"

"He was hurt in an accident at a construction site, a couple of months back. I want to ask him some questions about that."

Rosaura translated for her aunt, then she glared at me. "So? What are you going to do about it?"

"I don't know that I can do anything about it."

"Then why are you asking?"

"There was a man who worked at the same place as Manuel. His name was Cal. He was investigating the accident."

Rosaura shrugged. "What about him?"

"He's dead."

Some of the anger went out of Rosaura's face. The door opened wider and a man appeared, standing beside the aunt. I surmised that he and Rosaura were brother and sister. They looked enough alike, with their thin faces and dark eyes. Manuel was older, though, in his late twenties, I guessed.

He, too, spoke with an accent, the words coming slowly. "I'm Manny. Cal is dead?"

"His body was found in the Estuary a week ago," I said. "I think he was murdered."

Manuel crossed himself. "Who would do such a thing?"

"That's what I'd like to find out."

"How can I help?"

"Tell me what happened at the work site, when you were injured, and after."

He nodded. Then he unlatched the screen door and motioned me to come inside.

The living room, like the cottage itself, was small. A square dining table with four chairs took up space in one corner of the living room, along with a sofa, two easy chairs and a stand with a TV. To the right a bathroom was tucked between two bedrooms. A large pot on the stove in the tiny kitchen gave off a mouth-watering smell. The back door that Rosaura had used to exit the cottage stood open.

Manuel gestured toward the chairs and we all sat. "Tell me what happened."

"I got hired to work at the site in August," he said. "I was doing day labor, picking up jobs on Twelfth."

I nodded. I knew the place he was talking about. For several blocks along Twelfth Street, leading toward the Fruitvale BART station, men stood in clusters at the curb, looking for day labor jobs that paid in cash. It was a common sight all over the East Bay.

"The contractors, they pay by the hour, not the whole day. Sometimes I pick up a job that's just for two or three hours. Brice, the boss, he comes along in that white pickup. He hires me, says he will pay good wages. I go to work for him. When it's time to get paid, he pays in cash and gives me less money than he promised." Manuel shook his head. "What am I going to do? Who do I complain to? I don't have a green card. I am afraid he will report me."

"It happens all the time," Rosaura said.

I was sure it did. What Brice had done was wage theft. It was illegal and a big problem all over the state. Practices such as not paying workers for all their work, violating minimum wage laws, not paying overtime, or forcing people to work off the clock were common. As Manuel pointed out, he was undocumented, which made him particularly vulnerable to an unscrupulous employer. There was always the threat that someone might report him to the police or immigration authorities. And I wouldn't put it past Brice to do just that.

"I kept working there, three more weeks," Manuel said. "Because I need the money, to pay the rent on this place and buy food."

"What about the accident? I heard you were excavating a trench and the dirt collapsed on you."

Manuel touched his right arm. "Yes, that's what happened. It was scary. I was covered by dirt. My arm was hurt. The others dug me out. Cal was there that day, and he helped."

"You saw a doctor."

Rosaura chimed in, indignant. "The boss wouldn't call an ambulance. He didn't want anyone to know Manny was hurt, because it might cause him trouble."

"Another man drove me to the hospital," Manuel said. "My arm hurt bad. I thought it was broken. A bad sprain, the doctor said. I couldn't work. Brice owed me money for three days' work that week, but he didn't pay. I called him. He said, don't bother me, you're fired, don't come back."

I shook my head, wondering how many times this story had been repeated at the construction site. Maybe that's what Cal had been after, the bigger picture.

"How did Cal get involved in this?"

"He thought it was bad, what Brice did, when he wouldn't call an ambulance," Manuel said. "He came looking for me. I told him Brice wouldn't pay me for the work I did. Cal was angry. He said it was wrong and he would do something about it. What he thought he could do, I don't know."

"What happened after Cal started looking into your situation?" I asked.

Manuel exchanged glances with Rosaura. "Phone calls. Two

of them. I had a phone where you buy minutes. I got calls on that number. Someone called me, saying not to make trouble."

"Threats? When was this?"

Manuel was hazy on the dates but he'd received both calls before Cal's death. He'd gotten rid of the pay-as-you-go phone and obtained another. There was little else he could tell me. Before I left the cottage, Manuel said, "Cal gave me money, to help with the rent. Ever since I got another job, I have been saving to pay him back. Now he's dead. He was a good man."

"Yes, he was." And he didn't deserve to die the way he had.

Chapter Twenty-two

I HAD A Tuesday morning meeting with a new client, an attorney whose office was near the Federal Building in downtown Oakland. Now that we had discussed the case, I returned to my office and mapped out further investigation into the matter. I glanced at my calendar, where I'd written down my twelve-thirty lunch date with Duc, at The Slanted Door, a Vietnamese restaurant in San Francisco's Ferry Building.

Why not take the ferry? I went to the Internet, where I checked the online schedule for the San Francisco Bay Ferry. I could catch a boat at a quarter to twelve. That gave me plenty of time.

I'd had no response to my phone calls to Grace Portillo concerning Cal's autopsy, and I'd fielded several calls from an anxious Madison Brady wondering about the autopsy results. Madison was calling me instead of the Oakland Police Department. It had been more than a week since his body was found. Either the coroner was overwhelmed, which was entirely possible, and Grace Portillo didn't have any results yet. Or she was dodging me. I called Homicide again. This time Grace was in her office.

"I've been meaning to call you," she said. "But I caught that shooting in West Oakland yesterday. One dead, one in the hospital."

"I heard about that on the news." I leaned back in my chair. "Autopsy results on Cal Brady?"

Grace sighed. "You know my partner doesn't want me talking to you."

I had encountered that feeling many times before. The police didn't want to share information with the nosy private eye, but they were quite happy for any leads I could provide.

"You're talking to me now," I pointed out.

"I suppose it wouldn't do any good to tell you to leave the investigating to us."

"You can tell me."

"But you'll ignore me." She sounded resigned.

"You know if I get any leads I'll share them with you."

"Can we meet somewhere?"

"I'm catching the eleven forty-five ferry to San Francisco," I said.

"I can be at the ferry terminal at eleven-thirty. If I just happen to run into you while I'm on my lunch break, and if you just happen to ask about the autopsy…" Grace's voice trailed off.

"Got it. See you then."

I worked at my desk a while longer, then I walked over to Broadway and caught the shuttle, riding the bright green bus down to Jack London Square. I got off at the Embarcadero and walked two blocks to the ferry terminal at the foot of Clay Street. I was early for my meeting with Grace. I strolled toward the pier where the ferry would dock and stood for a moment at the gate, looking out at the water separating Oakland from Alameda, the town where I'd grown up.

Years ago the Key Route trains had crisscrossed the East Bay, bringing passengers to the bay, where they caught ferries to San Francisco. There had been dozens of ferries per day. The Bay Bridge, which loomed high in the distance, had been built in the mid-thirties, providing a way for auto and train traffic to cross the bay. Gradually ferry traffic dwindled, replaced by buses. In the 1970s the Bay Area Rapid Transit system opened, with its trains running far below the water's surface, in the trans-bay tunnel. The ferries were still here, though, used by commuters and weekend sightseers. There were daily ferries between Oakland, Alameda and San

Francisco. Other ferries plied the waters, bringing commuters from the East Bay cities of Richmond and Vallejo, and from Sausalito, Tiburon and Larkspur in Marin County.

I turned around, the pier at my back, and retraced my steps toward the ferry terminal. Then Grace rounded the corner, coming from Water Street, which led over to Broadway. I quickened my pace, joining her as she sat down on a nearby bench.

"Grace Portillo," I said. "How serendipitous to run into you like this."

She rolled her eyes. "Don't push it. Cal Brady's blood alcohol count was zero."

"No alcohol in his system. So much for the story that he got drunk and fell in the water."

She gave me a sidelong glance. "I didn't buy that story anyway. Neither did you."

"I figured it was murder. Anything else you can tell me?"

"Brady had trauma to the head and torso, just like I told you the other day. He took a nasty blow to the back of the head, and the coroner found glass embedded in the wound."

I winced at the image her words brought up. "He was hit with a bottle."

Grace nodded. "Looks like it. A bottle full of liquid would be heavy, and if it was used like a bat, that would account for the wound with the glass. There was dirt under his fingernails. It hadn't been washed away by the water. He must have fallen forward and clawed the ground. The body was found with some line caught on it. The ME says it looks like he was tied up. There were marks on the torso consistent with something heavy pulling on the body." She paused. "He was alive when he went into the water. He drowned."

I was angry at what had happened to Cal. "Someone hit him over the head with a bottle, enough to incapacitate him, but it didn't kill him. Then the line was attached to the body, with something heavy on the other end, to weight down the body so it wouldn't be found."

"You said it, I didn't."

"What about the attempted break-in at Cal's apartment? If he was murdered, someone has his keys."

"We didn't find a key ring with the body," Grace said. "But that doesn't necessarily mean anything. His keys could be at the bottom of the Estuary. Whoever tried to get in on Tuesday came up empty, because of the neighbor. The video the neighbor shot with her iPhone is so shaky we can't identify whoever it was, much less be sure of the gender. From her description, I'm guessing it was a man. I doubt that he will be back."

"Wouldn't do him any good. Madison and I packed up all her father's stuff and moved it to another location."

"If you find anything of interest while you're going through all that stuff, let me know." Grace stood up. "I told my partner I was going to Cost Plus." She gestured in the direction of the import store, on the other side of the Embarcadero. "I guess I'd better do that, and grab some lunch while I'm at it."

She walked up Clay Street toward the Embarcadero. A blast on a horn made me turn around. The ferry was approaching. I walked toward the gate that led out onto the dock. I could pay my fare onboard. While I waited for the boat to dock, I mulled over what Grace had told me.

Whoever killed Cal didn't intend for the body to be found. When the corpse surfaced and the cops showed up, that's when the story about Cal being drunk on the job also surfaced. And who was telling that story? Brice Cardoza. It kept coming back to Brice.

The ferry crew tied up at the dock and opened the gate. Those of us who were going to the city waited until passengers got off, then we headed down the dock and boarded the boat. As the ferry headed out into the Estuary, I found a seat on the open upper deck. I zipped up my jacket. It was sunny but the breeze off the water was chilly. Along the waterfront, enormous container ships lined up at the Port of Oakland piers, cranes and stacks of containers looming over them.

The ferry made its scheduled stop in Alameda, with a few people getting off and more passengers boarding. From the upper deck I gazed at what remained of the old Naval Air Station at the northwest tip of Alameda. Before World War II, it had been an air-port, the place where the *China Clipper* took off for its trans-Pacific flights. During and after the war, it had been an important base. It closed in 1997 and the city of Alameda had spent the past twenty years trying to figure out what to do with the land. The USS *Hornet* was still berthed there, and a number of small businesses had set up shop. I had been to the huge antiques and collectibles market that took place there the first Sunday of each month. At the very tip of the island, though, the runways that had seen so much air traffic were cracked and pebbled, full of weeds, home now to birds and ground squirrels.

The boat moved into the open water of San Francisco Bay, rocking in the wake left by a tugboat moving ahead of us. The Bay Bridge towered above us, the new cable-stay section that had replaced the old cantilevered section which had been damaged in the 1989 Loma Prieta earthquake. The boat was dwarfed as it went between two of the massive pylons anchoring the bridge to the bedrock below the water.

Ahead of us was the Ferry Building, another Beaux-Arts struc-ture from the last decade of the nineteenth century. As ferries gave way to buses and cars driving across the Bay Bridge, the Ferry Building had gradually become run-down, cut off from the rest of San Francisco by the Embarcadero Freeway.

More freeways had been planned to bisect the city, but the freeway revolt of the early 1960s had stopped construction. As a result, the old Embarcadero Freeway famously went nowhere, ter-minating at the foot of Broadway in San Francisco. The same 1989 earthquake that had damaged the Bay Bridge also left the Embar-cadero Freeway in disrepair. It had not collapsed, like the elevated Cypress structure in West Oakland, but according to engineers, it came close. The need to tear down the Embarcadero Freeway provided San Francisco with the opportunity to reclaim its water-front vista.

I remembered the big debate, which boiled down to two choices—rebuild the freeway or replace it with a widened Embar-cadero. Despite the naysayers who wanted the freeway rebuilt, the structure came down for good. The result was a beautiful broad boulevard, with wide sidewalks crowded with people all the time. San Francisco had reclaimed this section of its waterfront.

The Ferry Building itself got a restorative makeover. The vast interior ground floor, which had once been used for baggage handling back in the heyday of the ferries, had been turned into a huge marketplace with restaurants, shops and food purveyors whose wares ranged from meat to produce, caviar to artisan chocolate, locally made cheese to delectable baked goods. The Saturday farmers' market drew hordes of people to stalls in front of the building and at the back, where several ferry docks were located.

When my ferry docked at twelve-fifteen, I had a quarter of an hour to stroll through the building, tempted by the wares on either side of me. Then I left the building, walking to the bayside entrance to The Slanted Door. The restaurant served modern Vietnamese food, done very well, to the point that the place appeared on many "best restaurant" lists. There was a line of people waiting inside, at the bar and the hostess station. I was glad Duc had made a reservation.

Duc Ngo was at the bar, a wiry Vietnamese American man with close-cropped black hair and a twinkle in his brown eyes. He wore a well-cut gray suit with a red tie. He was about my height and when he saw me, he threw an arm around me for a quick hug. "Jeri Howard. How the hell are you?"

"I'm fine. It's good to see you." I leaned back and surveyed his attire critically. "You look very FBI, with your gray suit and power tie."

He laughed and steered me to the hostess station. "You haven't changed a bit."

The hostess, menus in hand, escorted us past the long rows of tables, all of them full, and seated us at a table for four near the window. Our server appeared at the table and asked what we'd like to drink.

We both ordered iced tea and looked at the menu. "I've got a jones for the shaking beef," Duc said. "I always have it when I'm here."

The server reappeared and wrote down our order for crispy Imperial rolls, green papaya salad and shaking beef. She took the menus and left.

"I was sorry to hear that Errol had died," Duc said. "He was a good man. I really learned a lot working for him. I remember that funky building on Broadway."

"You wouldn't recognize the neighborhood," I said. "There have been a lot of changes. It's called Uptown now, and it's trendy."

"You went to Errol's funeral? I'm sure there were lots of ex–Seville operatives there."

"Yes. Including Cal Brady. He'd sobered up, went through detox and AA. He was working as a security guard in Oakland."

Duc frowned. "You're talking in the past tense. Did something happen to Cal?"

"He's dead. Cal's body was found in the Estuary a week ago Sunday, in a place called Clinton Basin."

Duc gave me a sharp look. "Accident?"

I shook my head. "I talked with the detective on the case right before I caught the ferry. Cal was murdered."

"Why would anyone want to kill him? Cal was a nice guy. He had a drinking problem, of course. Even so, I was sorry when Errol fired him. Clinton Basin, you said. Is that where he worked as a security guard?"

The server delivered our food and we each took an Imperial roll. I spooned a serving of shaking beef onto my plate while Duc helped himself to the papaya salad.

"Clinton Basin is where the tide and current carried the body," I said. "Cal worked at a construction site south of there, on the Oakland Embarcadero. It's called the Cardoza development."

Interest flickered in Duc's eyes as we traded serving dishes. Interest triggered by the name Cardoza, I was sure. Why?

I glanced up, looking past Duc at the next table. The man seated there had lowered his menu and was talking with the server. With his dark hair and thin, long-nosed face, the man looked familiar. Where had I seen him before?

Then I remembered.

Duc dished up some shaking beef, I took papaya salad and set down the dish. I cut off a bite of Imperial roll. As Duc raised chopsticks to his mouth, I fixed him with a look. "This isn't just two old acquaintances meeting for lunch, is it?"

"What makes you say that?" Duc asked.

"Your colleague at the next table," I said. "I saw him outside the Biergarten in Oakland last Thursday night, when I was tailing a man named Brice Cardoza. Was he doing the same thing? Or does he just like the beer in Oakland?"

Duc gave me a wry smile. "You always were good."

"Still am." I forked up another bite of Imperial roll. "What's going on?"

"I can't talk about an ongoing investigation," Duc said.

"But there is one." I waved my hand, drawing my own conclusions. "You might as well ask what's-his-name to join us."

Duc laughed and turned. "Hey, Harvey. You've been made. Take a chair."

The other man, who looked to be in his early thirties, pulled a glum face and got up from his table, indicating to the server that he was joining us. Duc made the introductions. "Jeri Howard, private eye extraordinaire. Harvey Lowenthal, FBI."

"Nice to meet you," Harvey said, looking chagrined and not entirely convinced that he was pleased to make my acquaintance.

I took a bite of the papaya salad. "Okay, you have an ongoing investigation involving either the Cardozas, father and sons, or the development they're putting up on the Oakland waterfront. You would like information from me. But you won't give me any information in return. Seems a bit one-sided, Duc."

He shrugged. "I'm afraid that's the way it has to be. For now."

"You FBI guys." I gave an exasperated sigh.

"Yeah, I know. I really was planning to call you, when I heard that Errol died. I know you were close. Then I had to go out of town. Thursday Harvey saw you at the beer garden. He took a picture of you. When I saw it the next day, you had called and left a message. I decided I'd better return your phone call. You're investigating Cal's death?"

"I certainly am."

"Do you think Cal's death is linked to the Cardozas, or where he worked?" Duc asked.

"Could be."

The server loomed over our table, delivering an order of cellophane noodles. When she had gone, Harvey attacked the noodles with gusto.

I thought about Duc's job with the FBI. "You work with the division that investigates fraud and corruption."

Duc nodded. "Yes. We were busy recently with something here in the city that you may have read about in the *Chronicle*."

"It involved a state senator and a couple of city employees," I said.

The case had been all over the news. It involved pay-for-play politics. The term meant that certain people, in the recent case the city employees, had received money in the form of "campaign contributions" from other people. The purpose of the money changing hands was to gain access to politicians, again in the recent case, the state senator.

If Duc had been involved in that case, I was betting his interest in the Cardozas was along the same lines. That could explain the envelope Brice handed to the blonde Thursday afternoon.

"Okay, I get it," I said. "As far as you're concerned, I'm a civilian and you don't want me messing with your investigation, whatever it is. Though your case appears to have something to do with the Cardozas. Why else would Harvey be tailing Brice to the beer garden?"

Harvey took refuge in his cellophane noodles. "I can neither confirm nor deny."

"What's your involvement?" Duc asked. "Cal?"

I snagged another Imperial roll. "Cal's daughter showed up in my office a week ago. She asked me to look into his death. Cal had worked as a security guard at the construction site since they broke ground last spring. He got crosswise with Brice Cardoza, son of Roland and brother of Stephen. Brice is the construction site manager. After Cal's body was found, Brice told police, and anyone who would listen, that Cal had been drinking on the job. In fact, a few weeks earlier, Brice made the same claim and was pressuring Cal's employer at the security company to fire Cal. From what I can find out, Brice's accusation that Cal was drinking on the job is false. Cal was sober and had been for several years. Brice had a grudge against Cal and that was his way of retaliating."

"You had words with Brice on Thursday at the beer garden," Harvey said. "I was watching from the patio."

"We did indeed have words," I said, remembering the confrontation. "I learned that Cal was doing an investigation on his own, concerning a construction worker who was injured on the job. The man was undocumented and Cal evidently figured Brice was using a lot of undocumented workers and then discarding them if they got hurt. But I'm not sure that's why Brice is so skittish at the mention of Cal's name. Cal must have stumbled on something else."

I turned to Harvey. "You were outside the restaurant and then you went inside. You must have seen Cardoza and the blonde. And the envelope." At the look on Harvey's face, I added, "Right, you won't confirm or deny. By the way, the blonde's name is Zoe Erland and she works for an Oakland City Council member named Audrey DeSousa, who I hear is very pro-development. The Cardozas are developers and they are also big DeSousa supporters." I glanced at Duc. "Let's take a detour, into our past lives as operatives for the Errol Seville Agency. Remember Leo Walker?"

Duc nodded. "He worked for Errol, back in the day when it was you, me, Davina and Cal."

"The very same."

"White guy, blond, full of himself," Duc said. "You and he clashed a few times, as I recall. He was a hustler."

"Interesting that you should put it that way. I had lunch with Davina Roka last Wednesday. She described him the same way."

"I assume you brought this up for a reason. How does Leo fit into the mix?"

"I'm not sure," I said. "But I hadn't seen him or talked with him in years. Until last Friday afternoon. I had just interviewed Cal's employer. Leo just happened to bump into me on the corner.

Except I think bumping into me was his plan. He seemed interested in finding out what I was working on."

"Pumping you for information?"

"That's what it felt like. He told me he was a consultant, gave me a business card with no address, just a phone number and email address."

"Consultant, right. These days everyone's a consultant." Duc sipped his tea. "So what brought Leo out of the woodwork?"

"I'm not completely sure, but I have a theory. On Thursday afternoon, I had my confrontation with Brice Cardoza. On Friday afternoon, I run into Leo, or he runs into me. Perhaps the first encounter led to the second. As to why, I'm not sure. Right now, not all the puzzle pieces fit together."

Duc and Harvey traded looks. "If you figure out how they do go together," Duc said, "I would be very interested in finding out."

"But you're not going to tell me anything other than what I've already guessed," I finished.

He shrugged. "I can't."

I took the last Imperial roll. "Fine. Then you can pay for lunch. I've got to catch the two o'clock ferry back to Oakland."

Chapter Twenty-three

~~~~~~~~~~~~~~~

I WAS A BIT annoyed with Duc, or so I told myself as the ferry crossed back to my side of the bay. Still, he had provided information, whether he intended to do so or not. And since I'd taken a photo of Leo's business card with my phone, I shared that with him.

It appeared Duc and his colleagues in the San Francisco office of the FBI were taking an interest in the Cardozas. Or was their interest focused on Audrey DeSousa, the Oakland City Council member? Given Duc's involvement in the recent political corruption, pay-to-play case, it was easy enough to connect the dots between DeSousa and the Cardozas. Zoe Erland, the woman who'd collected an envelope from Brice Cardoza on Thursday, worked for DeSousa.

How did all this figure into Cal's murder? Had Cal uncovered something else in his quest to help the injured worker? That could explain why he'd kept the news photo showing DeSousa and Erland with the Cardozas.

Had Cal asked the wrong question of the wrong person? And where did Leo Walker fit into this?

When I got back to my office, I switched on my computer. I wanted to do more research on Audrey DeSousa, to augment what I'd found out during my talk with Nyah Stubbins and my earlier Internet searches. I read articles and dug deeper, looking for everything I could find. I clicked link after link and finally I found myself staring at an article speculating about a waterfront ballpark for Oakland.

Speak of the devil, I thought. And the devil is always in the details.

Audrey DeSousa was all for a waterfront ballpark, but she didn't like the idea of locating at Howard Terminal, for all the reasons that Mack, Dan and I had discussed during Sunday morning's boat trip along the Estuary. There were better sites closer to Jack London Square, the council member said. She didn't specifically mention Fifth Avenue. But the dots connecting the ballpark to that location were too big to ignore.

I could look up a lot of things online through the Alameda County website, but the ownership information was not posted there, although property ownership is part of the tax assessment roll, which is of course a public document. But in these Internet days, privacy is a concern and the property roll does list home addresses. I didn't have the option of an online shortcut. However, I could find what I needed by going to the public records section at the County Administration Building on Oak Street, a ten-minute walk from my office.

I had a good idea why someone was purchasing land near Fifth Avenue. Now I needed to find out who.

Several hours later, I emerged from the County Administration Building, carrying a number of photocopies. I had a clearer picture of what was going on, although not a complete one. My research into property transactions for the land around the marina showed me that over the past few months, parcels near Fifth Avenue had been purchased by two companies, Abrantes Limited and Tagus Development. With those two names, I could do more research, using several databases.

I walked back to my Franklin Street building. As I got off the elevator and walked toward my office, the door to the law firm of Alwin, Taylor and Chao opened. Bill Alwin came out, carrying his briefcase. He stopped when he saw me.

"I understand you're going to be our first tenant," he said.

"Yes, and I'm happy about it. Cassie says you'll be signing the papers soon."

"Later this week, I think. Or early part of next week. Then we remodel. So it will be maybe two, three months before we can move in. I'm hoping we can make that happen by January. That gives us time to prepare for the move, though."

"This is one change I'm really looking forward to," I said as I unlocked my office door.

Once inside, I looked around at my long narrow office, the home of Howard Investigations ever since I'd started my own business. Desk, chairs, filing cabinets and their contents, the little refrigerator and the microwave—all of these would have to be moved. Would my new office be the same size as this, or bigger? Would I have a window that looked out on something besides the roof of the building next door?

I was getting ahead of myself, but I could use this time to prepare for the move, as Bill had said. I could begin by purging filing cabinets and moving files to offsite storage.

I set my photocopies on my desk. However, the red light on my phone was blinking. I reached for the receiver with one hand, taking up pen and paper with the other to jot down the messages.

Madison had called. I called her back and told her that I had talked with Detective Portillo about Cal's autopsy. "There was no alcohol in his system. He wasn't drunk."

"I knew it," she said, sounding relieved. "I just knew Dad hadn't started drinking again. When will they release the body? I'd like to schedule a funeral."

"That I can't tell you. Since it's officially a homicide, you'll have to get that information from the police."

We talked a while longer, then ended the call. I returned several other calls and set up another meeting. Then I did some filing, a task I hate, but necessary. At a quarter to five, I decided it was time to go home and get some dinner. I was looking forward to a quiet evening with my feet up and cats snuggled around me.

The phone rang. I picked it up and said, "Howard Investigations."

"This is Charles Vance," a man's voice said. "You called me and left a message, said Mack Kelsey gave you my number. I'm sorry I didn't get back to you sooner. My wife and I were out of town."

"I'd like to talk with you, Mr. Vance. Would it be possible to meet with you and Mrs. Vance sometime tomorrow?"

"Is this about the store?" he asked. "We already talked to that other guy."

I leaned over my desk, suddenly alert. "What other guy?"

"We talked to a guy a few weeks ago. Brady, his name was. Say, what is this all about?"

"I'd like to explain that to you in person," I told him, reaching for my calendar. "I can meet you any time, any place, even tonight. It's that important."

Chapter Twenty-four

W E DIDN'T want to sell," Charles Vance told me. "We were forced into it."

It was just after nine o'clock on Wednesday morning. The Vances lived in a well-maintained one-story stucco bungalow in San Leandro, on Maud Avenue. The house was a mile or so from the downtown BART station. I could hear a rumbling sound every time the trains passed by on the elevated tracks.

We were seated in the living room, me on the sofa and Vance on a battered-looking leather recliner. He was in his late sixties or early seventies, I guessed, with thinning gray hair and a crepey neck above the collar of his plaid shirt. His gray slacks hung on his spare frame.

Mrs. Vance, a pleasant woman wearing jeans and a flowered shirt, had short hair that had once been dark but was now mostly gray. When I arrived she had been on the front porch with a watering can, attending to several pots of chrysanthemums. She had escorted me into the house and headed for the kitchen, where she poured coffee for all three of us. She also brought in a serving plate heaped with dark brown cookies, their tops decorated with sugar and bits of crystallized ginger.

"I baked these this morning," she said. "Chewy ginger cookies."

I took one of the cookies, still warm from the oven. I bit into it, relishing the blast of gingery flavor. "These are wonderful."

"Thanks. They're Charlie's favorite." She offered her husband the plate of cookies. He smiled at her and took two, setting them on a napkin on his knee. Mrs. Vance settled on the sofa next to me.

I looked at Vance. "When I spoke with you on the phone yesterday, you said you'd already talked with someone about this. Was his name Cal Brady?"

Vance nodded. "Yeah, that was the name. He called us and said he wanted to ask some questions about what happened with us and the store. I talked with him on the phone, never met with him. That was—" He stopped and looked at his wife. "When was it, Dolores?"

"Three weeks ago," she said. "It was right before we went up to Eureka to see our son and his family."

Vance fixed me with a speculative look. "Who is this Brady fellow? Somebody you work with?"

"Cal Brady," I said. "He was someone I used to work with, and he died recently. I have reason to believe he was looking into events happening at the Cardoza development site on the Embarcadero."

"Died?" Vance stared at me. "What happened to him?"

"His body was found in the Estuary a week ago Sunday."

Mrs. Vance gasped and her husband's mouth turned down in a frown. "I don't like the sound of that," Vance said. "He seemed like a nice guy when I talked to him. How can we help?"

"I'm assuming Cal took notes when he spoke with you, but I haven't been able to find them. Could we go over what you told him? Mack Kelsey, the man who gave me your phone number, told me you were getting a lot of pressure to sell your store and your land. I assume that pressure came from Cardoza Development."

"The Cardozas." Vance spat out the name as though it left a bad taste in his mouth. He rinsed it away with a swallow of coffee and set the cup on the end table. "I know Roland from way back. So does Dolores. We all went to high school together. I'm still here in San Leandro, and he moved up to the Oakland hills."

It sounded as though Vance resented Roland's success. But he may have had reason.

"Tell me what happened with the store."

"Dolores and I had that store twenty-six years," he said. "We built it up from scratch. Before that, we had a hardware store here in San Leandro. We both like boats. We still have a sailboat, a thirty-six-footer. We've got it berthed at the San Leandro marina. I always wanted to get into the marine business. That stretch of the Embarcadero used to be industrial and retail. Ship repair facilities, marinas, boat supply stores like mine. Now you've got hotels and restaurants. They even put in a Starbucks, in that development just north of where the store was. Changes up there, lots of changes. Putting in condos and apartments right and left. Just like that Brooklyn Basin project and the development the Cardozas are putting up."

"The Cardozas approached you about buying your store," I prompted.

Vance nodded. "They didn't want the store. They wanted the land, and the docks I had out behind the store. Like I told you, we didn't want to sell. We were doing good business at that location. There are a lot of marinas on the Oakland side of the Estuary. Where there's marinas, there's people that need gear for their boats."

He reached for his coffee cup. "Roland Cardoza bought that piece of land just south of the store, maybe ten years back. There was a warehouse on it. He tore it down and it was just bare ground for years, waiting for him to do something with it. Then some people showed up and started poking around, taking pictures, making sketches. I figured they were going to build something. Fine, I thought. That's better than a vacant lot. Then one day Stephen came into the store. That's Roland's oldest son. I guess he heads up the company now, since Roland had his stroke a couple of years ago. Stephen's all business, they say. Chilly, like his father. The younger brother, Brice, he's a piece of work."

I nodded. "I've had some dealings with Brice. None of them pleasant."

"Then you know what I'm talking about. Brice is a hothead, a real loose cannon." Vance broke off another section of his ginger cookie. "I guess it was three years ago, the first time Stephen approached us."

Mrs. Vance nodded. "That's right, three years ago. It was during the summer. I remember."

"Stephen came to the store," her husband continued. "He told me the Cardozas had plans to build a development on that parcel. He said he wanted to buy our land to increase the size of their property. Our land plus their land, the parcel would nearly double. That way they could build a bigger development. More square footage for retail and housing. And Oakland needs housing, he said. Made it sound like he was doing Oakland a favor." He made a disparaging sound. "What he was interested in was more money for the Cardozas."

"He offered to buy us out," Mrs. Vance said. "Offered a fair price, I thought at the time."

"You turned him down." I took a sip of coffee and resisted the impulse to eat another cookie.

"We sure did." Vance glanced at his wife. "Dolores and I discussed it, and neither of us wanted to sell. I called Stephen and said, thanks, but no thanks. Not interested. A few weeks later, he was back at the store. He upped the offer. We turned him down, again."

"Mack Kelsey told me the Cardozas kept putting pressure on you."

"Oh, yes, they did," Mrs. Vance said. "It went on for months."

"They wanted to move ahead with the development," her husband added. "But they weren't at the stage where they were ready to break ground. They had to get permits and all that stuff. I understand they were also going round and round with some environmental groups, about access to the water. But they were planning to go ahead, no matter what. They wanted our land, and access to the two docks in the back of the store."

"They came on our property, without so much as a by-your-leave," Mrs. Vance added.

"That's right. One day I saw several men on our property, out back by the docks, taking pictures and making sketches. I went out to see what was up. It was a couple of architects. They were going ahead like the Cardozas already owned the land." Vance shook his head in disgust. "The nerve of those people. I told them to leave. Then I called Stephen, asked him where the hell he got off acting like it was his property. He started in on me again, wanting to buy the land. I told him no, we are not ready to sell."

"But he wouldn't take no for an answer," I said.

"Hell, no. He kept at it. Like a damn mosquito that won't go away. Stephen would make an offer, we would turn it down. Then we started to get phone calls, telling us I'd better sell, or else. I called Stephen and said, what the hell is going on? How dare you threaten me? He acted very huffy, denied knowing anything about those calls. He said that wasn't the way he did business. The hell it isn't. They pulled the same kind of stunt before, with some property here in San Leandro. That was a long time ago, but I remember hearing about it."

"Any idea who was making the phone calls?"

"I figured it was Brice. He's the type who would do something like that. He came over to my store one afternoon, and I confronted him about it. He denied it, of course. It was like Stephen and Brice were double-teaming me, first one, then the other. The phone calls went on for a while. That was bad enough. Then it was the graffiti."

"It was annoying." Mrs. Vance's pleasant face turned indignant. "We were constantly cleaning spray paint off the building. Then we got vandalism. Broken windows, stuff like that."

"I had a feeling it was the Cardozas," Vance added. "But I wasn't sure. How do you prove something like that, unless you got cameras, which we didn't. There are a lot of homeless people camping out down there on the waterfront. And anchor-outs, using the docks in back of the stores. The vandalism could have been those people. At least that's what I said to myself at first."

"I knew it was the Cardozas all along," his wife said. "Roland was like that in high school. If he didn't get his way, he just badgered people until he did. His sons are no better."

"It got worse," Vance said. "They sent some guy to strong-arm me."

"Can you describe him?"

Vance grimaced over his coffee cup. "Yeah. White guy, blond hair."

The exact words, I thought, that Duc Ngo had used to describe Leo Walker.

"Guy had plenty of attitude. Cocky, really full of himself. He threatened me." Vance sat there in his chair, fuming, anger radiating from his lined face.

"We should have called the police, right then," Mrs. Vance said.

"You were there when this happened?" I asked. She nodded. "Can you describe the man in more detail?"

She thought about it for a moment. "He was cocky, the way Charlie says. And scary. Describe him? I'm guessing he was in his thirties, not a young kid. His hair was what I'd call a dirty blond. What I could see of it, anyway. He was wearing one of those hooded sweatshirts pulled over his head, but I could see his hair. His eyes were light in color. Hazel, I think. He had a little gold stud in one ear. And a tattoo."

"I didn't see a tattoo," her husband said.

"I certainly did. It was on his wrist." Mrs. Vance rubbed her wrist. "The left one. That was the side that was close to me. The sleeves of his sweatshirt weren't down all the way. I saw the tattoo. It was a spider. I remember it had purple legs."

She had just described Leo Walker, I thought, remembering the tattoo I'd seen on his arm when I encountered him on Friday.

Consultant, hell. Leo was a thug.

Considering what I knew about Leo from our days working at the Seville Agency, it wasn't that difficult to imagine him going over to the dark side. He would, if enough money was involved.

"Tell me what happened that day."

"It was spring, two years ago," Mrs. Vance said. "I was back in the office and Charlie was at the cash register. It was late in the afternoon, almost closing time."

"I was helping a customer," her husband added. "When the customer left, this guy in the sweatshirt came in. I asked if I could help him. He came at me, backed me against a fixture. I called out and Dolores came from the office onto the sales floor. He threatened us. He said if we didn't sell, we'd be sorry. I told him to get the hell out or I'd call the police."

Mrs. Vance was nodding, her face bleak. "It was scary. I was rattled, I didn't even think to take a picture of him with my cell phone. We should have called the police right away. Now that I look back on it, I don't know why we didn't."

"We were supposed to have an evening out with our daughter and son-in-law that night, dinner and a play that our granddaughter was performing in at her school." Vance's hand closed on a cookie, crushing it. Then he opened his hand and looked at the crumbs. "I told Dolores I'd call the police in the morning. So we locked up the store and left. When we got back to the house later that night, the phone was ringing. It was the manager of the marina next door, calling to tell us the store was in flames. We got back in the car and drove to Oakland. We could see the flames from the freeway. Gutted. Everything gone."

He dusted the cookie crumbs from his hand and reached for his coffee.

"I'm sorry," I said. "I know it's hard for you, to bring it all up again. But I do appreciate your help with this. It was arson?"

"Of course it was," Mrs. Vance said. "The investigators found accelerant all over the place. We had all sorts of flammable stuff there, it's true. But someone had burned the place deliberately."

Her husband took up the story again. "In the morning the store was nothing but a pile of stinking, smoking rubble. We had investigators from the fire department and the insurance company crawling all over the place, looking at us like we torched our own business. It took months to get things sorted out and get a settlement." He sighed. "We didn't have the heart to rebuild. We took the insurance check and retired."

"The Cardozas got the land after all."

His face clouded again. "Not from us. Not directly. We told our lawyer not to sell it to them under any circumstances. We sold it to some other company. The bastards bought it from them. So now the Cardozas are building their damned development."

"What was the name of the other company?" I asked.

"Started with an A. I'll have to look it up."

"Abrantes?" That was a familiar name.

"I think that's it." Vance got up from his chair and moved through the living room to the back of the house. A moment later, he returned with a thick file folder and sat down again, opening the folder. "Yeah, Abrantes Limited. That's the company that bought the land. They must have turned around and sold it to the Cardozas."

"Or transferred it," I said. "I think the Cardozas own Abrantes Limited. They could just transfer the land from one corporate entity to another."

"That makes sense," Mrs. Vance said. "I should have figured that out when we saw the name of the company."

"How so?" I asked.

"My family is Portuguese," she said. "My grandparents came to this country from Caldas da Rainha in western Portugal. Abrantes is a town in central Portugal, northeast of Lisbon on the Tagus River. That's where the Cardoza family came from."

Abrantes Limited and Tagus Development. Both of those companies were buying up property near the Fifth Avenue Marina in Oakland, land that had the potential to become that waterfront ballpark that was on the fans' wish list.

"They own another company, too," Vance said. "They call it Cherrytown. That's what people used to call San Leandro, back when there were lots of cherry orchards here."

That completed the circle, I thought. Cherrytown was the company that had benefited from Leo's inside knowledge when he was working at New Start East Bay. He had given information on a pending property sale to Cherrytown, which had outbid the nonprofit. After he'd left that job, he had gone to work directly for the Cardozas, from the look of things.

I asked the Vances if they knew anything about Audrey DeSousa, since I'd learned that her family, too, came from the same area of Portugal. Vance shook his head. His wife said the name was familiar, but she didn't know anything except that DeSousa was in politics.

I had enough to link Leo Walker to the Cardozas and to the strong-arm tactics and arson that had resulted in the Vances' loss of their business. But nothing yet to link Leo or the Cardozas to Cal Brady's murder. As I drove away from the Vances' house, a fragment of song danced through my mind.

Lydia, the Tattooed Lady...

Chapter Twenty-five

I'M NOT HOMELESS. Not anymore." Lydia tilted her head up, an expression of pride and defiance on her narrow face. "I used to live by the railroad tracks near the Lake Merritt Channel. But I have a home now. It just happens to be a boat. It's a hell of a lot better than living on the streets."

She ran a proprietary hand over the cream-colored paint on the hull. It was early Wednesday afternoon, the sun high overhead. I was aboard the *Maysie*, Lydia's boat, which was anchored in Brooklyn Basin near the back of the Cardoza construction site.

My journey out here began after my morning interview with the Vances in San Leandro. I had called Tony, the homeless man, on the number he'd given me, hoping that he would respond to the message I left on his pay-as-you-go cell phone. He did, an hour later, telling me that Lydia had agreed to talk with me. She, too, had a burner phone, and he gave me the number. When I called Lydia, she told me she would see me, if I got myself out to her boat. For transportation, I turned to Mack, Dan's friend. I met him at the Fifth Avenue Marina and he brought me out into the Estuary, where I boarded Lydia's boat.

Now I sat on the deck of the cabin cruiser, face-to-face with the woman I thought could be a potential witness. According to Tony, Lydia's boat had been anchored close to the construction site the night Cal was murdered. And Lydia had been on deck.

What, if anything, had Lydia seen? I hoped I was about to find out.

Lydia really did have a tattoo, on her right arm, a big yellow rose. Her lean frame was dressed in an olive green T-shirt and a pair of faded and patched blue jeans. She appeared to be in her fifties, but it was possible she was younger. Her face was lined and tanned, and she looked as though she had lived hard and rough for many years. Her brown hair was threaded with gray, short and uneven, as though she periodically whacked it off with a pair of scissors.

The *Maysie* was a twenty-eight-foot cabin cruiser, Lydia informed me when I came aboard, and the boat was about twenty years old. She gave me a brief tour of her living quarters, which were sparsely furnished. The cabin below deck had a small galley, a main cabin, with a small table and a bench seat, and an aft sleeping cabin where I saw several pillows piled next to a down sleeping bag.

The boat had a tiny head that Lydia did not use. As an anchor-out, she didn't have access to septic services. Instead she had a plastic paint bucket with a lid that she used as a latrine, transporting the waste ashore to dispose of it. She took sink baths or used baby wipes, she added. She bought fresh water and food ashore, and the end result, her trash, was neatly bagged in several white plastic sacks. For power, she used battery-operated lanterns and a portable generator.

The area below deck was kept neat and clean. She didn't have many clothes, and they hung from a rope in the head. Piled on a bench in the main cabin I saw a stack of well-thumbed paperback books.

"Where did you get the boat?" I asked, now that we were back on deck. If she'd been homeless, I wondered how she acquired the cruiser.

"I bought it," Lydia said. "I paid two hundred bucks cash money for this boat. I got a brother lives out in Concord. He gave me the money."

"Who did you buy it from?"

She shrugged. "Some guy. I don't remember his name. He had a bunch of boats up by the Fifth Avenue Marina. Boats are big expensive toys. People decide they want to play sailor, they buy a boat, and then they can't pay for it. They bite off more than they can chew. When that happens, they just walk away and leave the boat at the docks. Sometimes they even sink the boat. Drives the marina people crazy, because they have to figure out how to get rid of the boats. So this guy, he grabbed these boats that were abandoned and sold them to people like me. He must have had five or six of them." Her story jibed with what Mack Kelsey told me about the abandoned boats proliferating in the Estuary.

"Lydia, I need to ask about an incident that took place a week and a half ago." I gestured in the direction of the Cardoza work site. "It happened over there, where that development is being built."

"I saw the cops over there last week," she said, a wary look on her face. "I don't like cops. I got a record. Me, I try to stay out of trouble. Since I bought the boat, I just stay here most of the time. I don't bother people and they don't bother me. Suits me just fine."

"The cops were there because somebody died. I knew him. His name was Cal Brady. He was a security guard at that construction site."

She stared at me in consternation, a stormy look in her light blue eyes. "Cal? The security guard? A tall guy with blue eyes, about forty-five? Damn and double-damn. I heard they found a body up by Clinton Basin. But I didn't know it was him. Son of a bitch." She slammed her fist against the hull.

"You knew him?"

"Not really. I met him a few times." Lydia sighed. "Damn. Cal. I met him last summer. You see, I take my dinghy over to that construction site every now and then." She gestured at the blue dinghy. It bobbed gently in the water, tethered to the cabin cruiser by a length of sturdy line.

"You've been dumping your trash at the site," I said.

She nodded. "Yeah. The trash. And sometimes I empty my latrine into the portable toilets over there. I know a lot of anchor-outs empty their pee buckets into the water, but I don't do that. I try to be responsible."

"I appreciate that you don't dump waste into the Estuary," I said.

"I have a lot of freedom, living out here on my boat. But getting rid of the waste can be a problem. With regular trash, I slip it into the cans at the Starbucks or the beer garden. The pee bucket, I take ashore and flush it, wherever I can find a place to do it. Sometimes I talk one of the marina guys into letting me use the facilities. And there's a guy I know who works in the kitchen of that beer garden restaurant, the one that has the docks out back. If he's on shift that night, he lets me dump the pee bucket in the employee restroom there. I don't want that to get around, though, because he'd lose his job for sure."

She grinned as she pointed at the construction site. "When they started work on that development, that row of portable johns was too good to pass up. So are the trash cans they have for construction debris. I go over there about once a week. I have to dodge the security guards, though."

"One of the other guards told me there were a lot of liquor bottles being dumped at the site."

"Not me," Lydia said. "I don't drink anymore."

"Think it could be the homeless guys?"

She shook her head. "Hell, no. Most homeless people I know would take those bottles to a recycling place for some cash. They wouldn't just throw them away."

That told me the liquor bottles had been discarded for the purpose of making it look like Cal was drinking on the job.

"How did you meet Cal?"

"Cal caught me one night, dumping my pee bucket into one of the portables. He was decent about it, said he understood and he'd cut me some slack. He said not to do it too often. We talked. I told him I was homeless before I got the boat. He said he knew what it was like to be down and out. When I said I like to read, he brought me a bunch of paperbacks." She shook her head. "I'm sorry he's dead. He was nice. Not like the other guards. Usually they'd yell at me, tell me to get the hell out of there. Then there was this other guy. He was a real prick."

"Tell me about the other guy."

"Beefy guy, drives a white pickup. He's the boss, I guess. I've seen him on the construction site during the day, wearing a hard hat and ordering people around." She waved in the direction of the Biergarten. "He drinks his dinner. I see him over at that beer garden restaurant, almost every night. He sits on the patio, drinks several beers and eats a basket of fries."

Brice Cardoza. So Lydia knew him by sight. "You had a run-in with him?"

"I sure as hell did. I took my dinghy over to the site one night. I usually go over there around midnight. Most of the security guards don't see me, or don't care. I didn't figure anyone would be in that trailer. Boss man must have been working late, though why he was there at that hour I can't imagine. He was in the trailer with another guy. They came out just as I was dumping my trash in one of the cans. They threatened me. I don't scare easy," she added, "but the other guy was off the hook. He was really getting in my face. I damn near hit him with an oar."

I glanced down at the dinghy, which had two oars in the oar-locks. The oars looked heavy and they were about five feet long. Wielded with intent, they could do considerable damage.

"What did this other guy look like?"

Lydia shrugged. "Skinnier than the boss. Didn't get that good a look at him. He was wearing a hoodie. Had a tattoo on his left arm, though."

Leo. The hoodie and the tattoo fit.

"Hoodie guy came at me," Lydia continued. "I had the oar up, like a baseball bat, ready to smack the bastard. Boss man pulled him away, told him to cool off. Then boss man told me to get the hell off the site. He said if he ever caught me dumping my trash again, he'd call the cops."

"Cal died a week ago Sunday, early in the morning," I said. "When I talked with Tony, the man who gave me your phone number, he told me he was sleeping in the bushes near the fence around the construction site. Early that morning, he woke up because he heard something. When he got up to take a look, he saw you moving around on deck. So you were awake."

"I don't sleep that well," Lydia said. "Insomnia. Most of the time I read in my bunk for an hour or two. That helps. That night you're talking about, I was anchored pretty close to those docks at the back of the construction site. I just couldn't seem to get to sleep. I read for a while. Then I went up on deck. It was quiet, calm. The moon was full later in the week but that night it wasn't quite there. But it was full enough that things were easy to see. I saw lights on in the trailer, which isn't unusual. Cal told me the security guards used the trailer at night. They'd take breaks, eat, use the bathroom in between rounds. Most of the time it was quiet there. But that night, I saw lights, then I heard voices. It sounded like a couple of guys having an argument."

"Could you tell who they were?"

Lydia nodded. "One of them was boss man, for sure. The guy I saw was big through the shoulders, like he is. The other one, I'm not sure. Could have been hoodie guy. Could have been Cal, I suppose."

"You saw two men, not three?"

She nodded. "Just the two. I heard the voices first, then I saw boss man come around the corner, followed by the other guy. They were dragging something. I couldn't get a good look at what they were toting, but I thought maybe it was a trash bag. I remember thinking, hey, they don't want me dumping my trash on their damn construction site, and now it looks like they're dumping trash in the Estuary. They dragged it down the dock and threw it in the water." She shuddered as though she had just realized something. "Good God. It wasn't trash they were dumping, was it? It was Cal's body. They killed him, the bastards."

"I know you don't like cops, Lydia. But what you saw is really important. Would you give a statement to the police?"

"Sure. I will. If it will help put those bastards away for killing Cal."

"Before I bring in the police, I'd like to get a more positive identification."

"How do we do that?"

"As you say, boss man goes to the Biergarten after work. I'm going to make a phone call to see if I can get hoodie guy to join him. I'll be there tonight, taking pictures. When hoodie guy shows up, I'll call you."

Lydia nodded. "I'll row to the dock behind the beer garden. I can't see the patio very well from the dock, though. On the other side there's a ramp that leads up to the kitchen. There's a sidewalk there, that runs along the side of the building and goes out to the parking lot. You just say the word and I'll be there."

Chapter Twenty-six

I LOOKED AT my watch. It was seven forty-five on Wednesday evening. Now that the sun had gone down, the wind had picked up, and it was cold here by the water.

I was behind the Starbucks on the Embarcadero, standing near the fence that separated this spot from the Cardoza construction site. The overgrown hedge hid the place from the view of the parking lot at the side of the building. This was where Tony, the homeless man, liked to pitch his tent. When I arrived, I had fortified myself with a latte from the coffee shop, which closed at eight. The coffee, while hot, wasn't doing the job. I pulled up the collar of my quilted jacket and stuck my hands in the pockets, looking for my knit watch cap. I pulled it out and put it on my head. My gloves were in the other pocket. I fished them out, put them on and took a sip from the latte.

The moon was long past full. This week it was somewhere between the last quarter and the new moon. It was dark back here, with just a few lights illuminating the marina docks to my right, along the shoreline. I peered through the fence surrounding the construction site, past the vacant dock with lights at the end. More light was visible through the windows of the trailer on the work site. The white pickup with the HASSELTINE CONSTRUCTION logo was parked outside, illuminated by the light from a fixture on a pole in front of the trailer. There was another car parked there. I didn't recognize it and I guessed it belonged to the security guard working the swing shift.

Brice Cardoza was working late tonight. He'd been at the site, in and out of the trailer, ever since I'd taken up this position an hour earlier. All afternoon, in fact, according to Lydia, who had been keeping an eye on him from her boat and reporting to me by phone.

Since Brice usually went to the Biergarten after work, I hoped he wouldn't vary his routine this evening.

After my talk with Lydia earlier this afternoon, I called Mack Kelsey, who obligingly motored down to pluck me off Lydia's boat. I collected my car, which I'd parked outside the Fifth Avenue Marina, and returned to my office. There I set the plan, such as it was, in motion.

I still had the card Leo Walker had given me. I called it and got voice mail, as I thought I would. I left a message implying that I had a witness to Cal's murder. In fact, Lydia was a witness who could place Leo and Brice at the scene. I was betting that my words would propel Leo into a meeting with Brice.

I had set my cell phone to vibrate and now it did. I looked at the readout, recognizing Lydia's number. I hit the talk button.

"He's on the move," Lydia said tersely.

"I see him."

I hung up the call. From my vantage point, I saw Brice come out of the trailer. He got into his pickup. I turned and headed for the parking lot at the side of the Starbucks, where I'd left my Toyota backed into a spot. I started the car and pulled out, heading for the street. As I stopped, waiting for oncoming traffic, the white pickup went by. Brice was at the wheel. He was heading up the Embarcadero. There was another car behind him. When that car passed, I pulled out, following. Brice paused at the stop sign at Tenth Avenue. Then the pickup turned left. Good, he was headed for the restaurant.

I turned left as well, heading up Tenth to the parking lot in front of the Biergarten. Brice had parked at the end of the lot. He didn't get out of the truck immediately, though. I stopped my car and watched. He sat in the cab for a few minutes. I couldn't see him clearly. Was he making a phone call, or waiting for someone? Finally he got out of the truck and headed for the restaurant, hands stuck in the pockets of his tan jacket.

Once he'd gone inside, I reached for my cell phone and hit redial, calling Lydia's phone. "Boss man is at the restaurant. No sign of hoodie guy."

"I'm on my way."

It would take some time for Lydia, in her dinghy, to make her way from her boat near the work site to the docks in back of the restaurant, as we had planned. I circled through the Biergarten's parking lot, as though looking for a space. I was really searching for the silver Lexus I had seen at the work site on Sunday. My guess was that the Lexus was Leo's car. I didn't see it. I circled through the parking lot again. The lot was crowded on this Wednesday night. Overflow parking was available in a larger lot at the side of the nearby hotel. I parked there and walked toward the restaurant, wondering if Brice would sit out on the patio. If he stayed inside the restaurant, my task would be more difficult, though not impossible. The patio would make things easier. It was chilly to be sitting outside tonight, but the patio had heaters. Evidently they were sufficient to stave off the evening chill. Most of the patio tables were occupied.

Sure enough, I spotted Brice at the same table he'd been at a few days earlier, at the back of the patio. He was talking with the server. He looked up as she walked away. I stepped between two parked cars, hoping he wouldn't see me.

He turned his head, looking out at the water. I walked along the public access path near the patio, at the back of the hotel, pausing at the railing as though looking out at the boats tied up at the marina docks. I avoided the light spilling from an overhead lamp and stayed in the shadows. My clothing was dark—black jeans, the navy blue jacket and watch cap, black gloves. I stood there, keeping an eye on Brice. He had put his cell phone on the table in front of him. He glanced at it, poking the screen with his fingers, as though sending or receiving a text message. Then he looked up as the server stepped out onto the patio. She walked the length of the patio to his table, delivering a beer and a basket of fries. He took a swallow from the big glass and doctored the fries with salt and ketchup. Then he dug in his fingers and stuck a handful of fries into his mouth.

I couldn't hear from this distance, but his phone must have rung. He snatched up the phone and held it to his ear, listening, then punctuating the air with his hand. He ended the call and set the phone on the table. After another swallow of beer, he worked on the basket of fries.

A few minutes later a vehicle pulled into the restaurant parking lot. Like me, the driver was unable to find a spot near the restaurant. It moved into the lot at the side of the hotel and took a spot there. It wasn't the Lexus, though. It was the Cadillac Escalade, and it was Stephen Cardoza who got out and walked toward the restaurant, his business suit illuminated by the parking lot lights.

This was a new wrinkle, I thought. I already knew Brice was the man Lydia described as boss man. I really needed Leo to show up, so Lydia could identify him as hoodie guy, the other man she had seen on the docks behind the work site the night Cal was murdered.

Two people came out of the hotel, a man and a woman, strolling down to the water. They stopped at the railing near me. I moved away from them, finding another place in the shadows where I could observe the restaurant patio. By now Stephen Cardoza had walked out onto the patio to join his brother at the table. I raised my cell phone, went to the camera feature and snapped a couple of photos of the Cardoza brothers. Then I glanced at my watch. By now it was after eight. The restaurant closed at nine.

When I looked at the patio again, I saw two women walking out of the restaurant, heading for the table where the Cardoza brothers sat. The one in front was Zoe Erland, the blonde I'd seen there last week. The second woman was older, and I recognized her from her photographs. Audrey DeSousa, the city council member. I raised my phone again, this time going to the video feature, and started the recording. Erland sat down next to Stephen, edging close. Was there something going on between the two of them?

DeSousa sat down opposite Stephen, next to Brice. She looked chilly and formal, as though she didn't want to be there.

Soft laughter sounded to my left. The couple who had come out of the hotel were standing at the railing, looking out at the water. His arm was around her shoulder. Then he pulled her close and they kissed. I glanced away, back at the patio.

The conversation at the table that interested me appeared to be getting heated. Audrey DeSousa was leaning over the table, talking with Stephen Cardoza, who looked as though he was getting dressed down and didn't like it much. Brice attempted to interject a few words. DeSousa silenced him with an impatient wave. Then DeSousa got up from the table and walked toward the restaurant. Erland leaned over and said something to Stephen, then she got up and followed DeSousa. After she had gone, Stephen and Brice put their heads together, talking intently.

I was still recording their actions when the restaurant door opened and someone else came out on the patio. Leo Walker, finally. I hadn't seen his car in the parking lot and I hadn't seen him arrive. It was possible he'd parked somewhere else, in the hotel lot or on the street.

Tonight Leo was wearing a gray hoodie. All the better, I thought. He strode toward the table and sat down. I continued recording the three men at the table as Leo helped himself to a handful of Brice's fries. The server came over and he gave her his order.

The couple who were kissing broke off their embrace and began walking along the railing, heading away from me. I heard a splash out on the water and looked in that direction, hoping to see Lydia and her dinghy. I couldn't see her, though, not just yet.

When I looked back at the restaurant, Leo was no longer sitting at the table. He'd gone back inside the restaurant, I guessed, perhaps to use the rest room. No matter. I had enough footage of him for Lydia to look at when she got to shore.

I heard laughter again and glanced at the man and woman, who were now walking back toward the hotel. Another look at the patio told me that Leo was inside the restaurant. I moved closer to the parking lot, hoping he hadn't left. There was a silver Lexus in the lot, one I hadn't seen before. Leo's car? He must have gotten a space when someone else left the restaurant. I glanced at the restaurant's front door in time to see DeSousa and Erland exit. They got into a white SUV parked nearby, with DeSousa at the wheel. She started the vehicle and backed out of the parking space. I turned and headed back toward the patio. Brice and Stephen were still at the table, but Leo wasn't.

Was he still inside the restaurant? I hadn't seen him leave. I had two choices. I could go inside or work my way around to the back, where large windows looked in on the dining room. The path that led from the parking lot back to the guest docks was to the right of the restaurant's front door. I stopped recording and stuck my cell phone into the front pocket of my jeans. Then I left the area near the patio and walked through the lot. I passed the front door, sidestepping two people who were entering the restaurant. I turned onto the walkway that led along the side of the restaurant. I was hoping that by now Lydia was approaching the docks in back of the Biergarten.

Ahead of me, to the left, was a door leading to the kitchen. Just across from this was a row of large trash and recycling bins, backed up to a tall hedge. As I neared the bins, I smelled grease and rotting food, the odors coming from the garbage area. Voices filtered out from the kitchen, in English and Spanish.

I heard a sound to my right, as though an animal was scrabbling in the bushes. Then something hit me on the head, so hard that I saw stars. I stumbled and fell to my knees. As I scrambled to get up someone shoved me down on the sidewalk. I lay on my stomach, my head throbbing. I struggled and my face scraped against something, pebbles or pavement. Now my cheek felt damp, as though bleeding. I struggled to get up. My assailant planted a knee on my back. Hands clamped my wrists together and wrenched them with a vicious painful twist.

A voice I recognized hissed in my ear. "You thought you were so fucking smart."

My plan to lure Leo Walker to the restaurant had worked,

though he'd turned the tables on me. It seemed he had learned something during his brief tenure at the Seville Agency, namely how to spot me while I was doing surveillance.

Now I heard a one-sided conversation, Leo talking on his cell phone. My guess was that Brice was on the other end of the conversation.

"The bitch was taping us," Leo said. "Yeah. I'm on the other side, over where the sidewalk leads down to the dock. Okay. I'll get it."

Leo's hands shifted and his knee jammed into the small of my back. He held my wrists with his left hand and his right began to move over me, looking for my cell phone, trying to get at the video I had shot from my vantage point outside the patio. The cell phone was in the right front pocket of my jeans, so I was lying on it. A few paces down the sidewalk, where the door led into the restaurant kitchen, I saw light spilling onto the pavement. The door was partly open. I heard a man's voice, speaking Spanish. In my peripheral vision, I saw a figure, one of the kitchen workers silhouetted in a doorway. I tilted my head up, but before I could get out words, Leo slammed my face down on the pavement.

I lay still and considered my next move. When I first trained as a private investigator, I took classes in self-defense. I don't use it all the time, but sometimes those moves come in handy. It helped to be standing up, though, instead of facedown on a sidewalk with a knee in my back. If I could get to my feet I could hold my own against Leo.

I heard the man in the kitchen doorway speaking Spanish again, this time with some urgency. Another voice answered him in the same language. A woman's voice. Another kitchen worker? Or was it Lydia?

The voice got closer. It appeared the kitchen worker was coming outside. The pressure on my back lessened as Leo lifted his knee and released my wrists. He rose to his feet. I quickly rolled to one side and scrambled upright as a figure loomed out of the darkness, holding something long, like a broom.

No, it was one of the five-foot oars from Lydia's dinghy. Lydia swung it at Leo. He backed away from her. Lydia charged at him, swinging the oar again. He caught the end and pulled her off balance, trying to wrestle the oar from her hands. I stepped in and aimed a kick at his legs. He turned and charged toward me, fists striking out. I blocked his blow with my left forearm. Lydia swung the oar again and hit him hard in the back. I stepped toward Leo again and delivered an uppercut that sent him reeling back against the wall. Then I kicked his legs out from under him. He slumped against the wall, looking stunned.

"Nicely done," Lydia said.

"Thanks. I know my way around a punch."

Brice rounded the corner from the parking lot. He advanced toward me. "Give me the damn cell phone or I'll take you apart."

"No way, Brice." He was taller and outweighed me but I wasn't in the mood for his bullshit, especially not after being attacked by Leo. I stood my ground, ready to fight. He took another step in my direction.

Lydia moved up beside me. She propped the oar against one of the trash bins. Then she bent down and grabbed a bucket with her right hand, raising it. Her left hand was on the lid, ready to pull it off.

"I got a bucket full of pee right here," she said in a matter-of-fact voice. "I would just love to throw it in your face, asshole."

"Better listen to the lady, Brice," I said. "She's not kidding."

The prospect of a faceful of urine stopped him in his tracks. By that time two of the restaurant's kitchen workers had come through the doorway to join us, everyone talking all at once in Spanish. I took out my cell phone and called 911.

Chapter Twenty-seven

THE REST of the night was a chaotic jumble of images. The Oakland police responded to my 911 call, then Grace Portillo and her partner, Mike Fisker, showed up at the scene. I made a statement at Homicide Section. So did Lydia and the two restaurant workers who'd witnessed part of the confrontation.

Before the evening was over, I had made three additional phone calls. One was to Madison Brady, telling her that the two men responsible for her father's murder were in custody. We arranged to meet at my office the next morning so I could give her more details. The second call was to Charles Vance, who agreed to come to the Oakland Police Department to identify Leo Walker as the man who had threatened and intimidated him shortly before his store burned in the arson fire. The last call was to Duc Ngo at the San Francisco office of the FBI. I told him I had some video he should see. I would let the FBI sort out the pay-to-play business surrounding the ballpark and a certain Oakland city council member and her aide.

It was late by the time I got home. I stripped off my clothes, took a hot shower and fell into bed.

When I got to my office the next morning, Madison Brady was waiting in the hallway when I stepped off the elevator, bearing a pink bakery box full of pastries from La Farine. She started asking questions before I could get my keys out of my bag.

I raised a restraining hand. "Coffee first."

I unlocked the door and we went inside. I started the coffee and sat down, offering Madison one of the pastries first. Her hand hovered over a brioche, then she chose a morning bun and lifted it onto a napkin. She scooted her chair closer to my desk and bit into the pastry. I took the chocolate croissant.

When the coffee was ready, I poured a mug for each of us. We consumed coffee and pastries while I gave her an overview of what had happened, and why.

"While your father was looking into the workplace accident," I said, "he stumbled onto the fact that the Cardozas had used intimidation against the Vances when they wouldn't sell their property. The tactics escalated to the point of threats and ultimately arson. Mr. and Mrs. Vance have both identified Leo as the man who threatened them, so he'll be charged with that. I'm not sure if there's enough evidence to get him on the arson charge, though. Of course, Detective Portillo and her partner are hoping to get him on the murder charge."

"How did Dad get from the workplace accident to all this?" Madison asked.

"I'm not sure. Maybe we'll never know. He connected the dots from the Cardozas buying the Vance property to the Cardozas buying up the property around the Fifth Avenue Marina, to use for a proposed waterfront ballpark. Then he realized that somehow Audrey DeSousa, the city council member, was connected to all this. At some point Leo and Brice realized what he was doing. It was Brice who decided to make it look like Cal was drinking on the job. Brice admits that he and Leo were leaving the empty liquor bottles at the work site. The whole idea was to get Gary Manville to fire him. Brice also says he put some mayo that had gone bad in your father's food to make him sick. That way it looked like he was hung over the next morning. Again he made accusations that Cal was drinking on the job."

Their plans to get Manville to fire Cal hadn't worked, though. At that point Brice and Leo had confronted Cal at the work site. When he resisted, things got physical.

"Brice says it was Leo who hit Cal in the head and Leo who suggested throwing Cal into the water. The two of them dragged him to the dock, weighted him down and threw him in the water."

I didn't say what I was thinking, that Cal was still alive at that point.

Madison must have been thinking the same thing. She'd gotten the details of the autopsy results from the police. Now she shuddered. "The bastards."

"Got that right. They were seen, though. Lydia, the woman who lives on the boat, saw what happened. She'd had run-ins with both Brice and Leo before. She saw them that night, and she identified them. Brice is talking, blaming Leo for what happened. He says Leo is the killer and he just went along. Leo's not saying much. He's playing the part of the tough hustler."

We talked a while longer. I told her what she might expect from the police as events played out over the next few weeks. She said she would let me know the date and time of her father's funeral service.

Then I brushed crumbs from my hands and brought up a subject that had been on my mind. "Are you tired of sharing that apartment near campus with four other people? Sleeping in a walk-in closet?"

"Of course I am," Madison said. "Why do you ask?"

"I have a studio apartment above my garage," I said. "It's about the size of the apartment your dad rented in Oakland. My tenant is moving out sometime before Thanksgiving. Are you interested?"

Madison's eyes widened. "Am I? Of course I am. Where is it? How much is the rent?"

"I live on Chabot Road, a couple of blocks above College Avenue. Easy enough to catch the number 51 bus to campus. If you decide to keep your father's car, you can park in the driveway. As for the rent, we'll talk about that. One question. Will you take care of my cats if I go out of town?"

"I would love to take care of your cats."

I jotted my address on the back of one of my business cards. "You should come over and take a look at the place before you decide. During daylight hours, of course."

"Decide? What's to decide? A place all to myself where I don't have to share the bathroom or kitchen? I'm already sold."

I looked at my calendar. "Today isn't good, but tomorrow would work. I can meet you at the house around four."

Madison smiled. "I'll see you then."

My birthday rolled around a couple of days later. My mother sent flowers, which were delivered to my office during the day. I received several birthday cards from various friends and relatives, and a snarky, laugh-out-loud card from my brother. It included notes from Brian and Sheila, his wife, and from his two kids, Todd and Amy.

Dad was taking Dan and me out to dinner. I asked Dan to come over early, so we could talk.

I went downstairs to my bedroom and pulled a favorite CD from a stack by the player on the nightstand. It was Alberta Hunter's *Amtrak Blues*. I put it in the player, listening to the Memphis-born jazz and blues singer as I went to the closet and selected what I was going to wear that evening. As I dressed, I sang along on one of the cuts, "A Good Man is Hard to Find."

"You got that right," I told the cats, who were curled up in the middle of my bed. "I think I've found a good one. I guess I'd better keep him."

Abigail was asleep and did not share her opinion. Black Bart yawned and stretched, then shut his eyes. I laughed and put on my shoes. Then I leaned over my dressing table and selected a pair of silver earrings.

The doorbell sounded a few minutes later. I went upstairs and opened the front door. Dan's face was hidden behind a large bouquet containing roses, carnations and chrysanthemums. He handed over the flowers and leaned in for a kiss.

"Hey, you clean up pretty good," I said. He was usually casual in his dress, a khakis-and-hiking-boots guy. Tonight he had spruced up a bit, in olive green slacks and a rust-colored sweater that set off his dark coloring.

"So do you." He looked me up and down, approving of my gauzy blue-and-green blouse with beads and sequins, worn over a pair of tailored black pants.

I shifted the flowers to one arm and led the way to the living room. "Let me put these in water. I've got a bottle of Chardonnay in the fridge. Let's have some while we wait for Dad."

I took a vase from the sideboard and carried it to the kitchen, filling it with water. I clipped stems and arranged the flowers while Dan took the wine from the refrigerator and opened it, pouring two glasses. When I was finished with the flowers I put them in the middle of the dining table. We sat down on the sofa and sipped wine. Dan talked about his book and I brought him up to date on the case, revealing as much as I could without breaching client confidentiality.

Abigail and Black Bart appeared, climbing the stairs from the bedroom. They went into the kitchen for water and a nosh, then they came back to the living room as Dan got up and went to the kitchen, returning with the wine bottle. He replenished our glasses. Abigail climbed into my lap and Black Bart jumped on the sofa and inspected Dan's hand, then snuggled between us.

My father was due in half an hour or so. I decided I'd better get to the conversation I wanted to have with Dan.

"Last week when you came over for dinner, you asked if I'd ever thought about getting married again."

He nodded. "I wondered when we were going to get around to talking about that."

"You took me by surprise," I said. "I didn't know what to say."

"You looked as though I'd knocked you for a loop." He smiled. "Have you thought about it, in between solving crimes?"

I took a sip of my wine. "I have."

"Come to any conclusions?"

"Not quite. I would say the case is still under investigation."

He nodded, still smiling. "I understand. At least you're thinking about it. So tell me what you've been thinking."

I drank more wine and launched into my spiel. "My first marriage didn't work out. The divorce hurt. Having gone through that once, I'm not sure I want to do it again."

"Once burned, twice shy," Dan said. "I get that. My divorce was more amicable than yours, though it was difficult at the time. Splitting up is never easy."

"No, it isn't. Look at my parents. They got divorced after years of marriage, when my mother went off to Monterey to find herself. On the other hand, your parents have been happily married for ages."

"They've had their ups and downs, believe me," Dan said. "Listen, Jeri, getting married doesn't always lead to divorce. I think we'd be happy in each other's company. We're happy now."

I was happy in his company, I thought, admitting it to myself. I was still resisting, though. "We've known each other a short time. We only met in June. That's five months. Is that long enough to know that we want to get married?"

"It is for me," Dan said. "I always figured I'd marry again, and when I met you, it seemed that I'd found a soul mate."

I smiled at him. "I don't think I've ever been anyone's soul mate before. That's a nice feeling."

Dan took another sip of wine and set the glass on the end table. "If you're not ready to make a commitment…"

"I didn't say that." In my head, I was hearing the lyrics to "A Good Man is Hard to Find." Commitment, huh. "I could do commitment. Marriage ceremony, all that legal stuff, I'm not so sure. Where would we live? How would we balance our careers?"

"We'd figure it out," Dan said. "That's what people do when they're happy in each other's company. I like cats and chocolate. I think your dad's a great guy. Your mother…well, I like her, too."

By now I was laughing. My mother could be intense.

"I'm a good catch, really," Dan pointed out. "And I make you laugh. You should definitely marry a guy who makes you laugh."

"I'm not laughing." But I was. "Okay, you make me laugh."

"I also love you." He pulled me into his arms. As I opened my mouth to speak, he put a finger on my lips. "You don't have to tell me you love me or say anything, not right now. Now that you've thought about it, think about it some more."

"I will." And I meant it.

He kissed me. I returned his embrace, thinking, I could get used to this. We snuggled closer. My hair and my gauzy blouse got mussed.

Then the doorbell rang and we separated like a couple of guilty teenagers. Dad was here and it was time to go out to dinner.

About the Author

Janet Dawson is the author of the Jeri Howard PI series, which includes *Kindred Crimes*, winner of the St. Martin's Press/Private Eye Writers of America contest for Best First Private Eye Novel, and *Bit Player*, which was nominated for a Golden Nugget award for Best California Mystery. The most recent series entry is *Cold Trail*. Two of Dawson's short stories were nominated for a Shamus and won a Macavity.

In addition to a suspense novel, *What You Wish For*, she has written two mysteries set aboard the *California Zephyr*. A past president of NorCal MWA, Dawson lives in the East Bay region. She welcomes visitors at www.janetdawson.com.

More Traditional Mysteries from Perseverance Press
For the New Golden Age

K.K. Beck
Tipping the Valet
ISBN 978-1-56474-563-7

Albert A. Bell, Jr.
PLINY THE YOUNGER SERIES
Death in the Ashes
ISBN 978-1-56474-532-3

The Eyes of Aurora
ISBN 978-1-56474-549-1

Fortune's Fool
ISBN 978-1-56474-587-3

Taffy Cannon
ROXANNE PRESCOTT SERIES
Guns and Roses
Agatha and Macavity awards nominee, Best Novel
ISBN 978-1-880284-34-6

Blood Matters
ISBN 978-1-880284-86-5

Open Season on Lawyers
ISBN 978-1-880284-51-3

Paradise Lost
ISBN 978-1-880284-80-3

Laura Crum
GAIL MCCARTHY SERIES
Moonblind
ISBN 978-1-880284-90-2

Chasing Cans
ISBN 978-1-880284-94-0

Going, Gone
ISBN 978-1-880284-98-8

Barnstorming
ISBN 978-1-56474-508-8

Jeanne M. Dams
HILDA JOHANSSON SERIES
Crimson Snow
ISBN 978-1-880284-79-7

Indigo Christmas
ISBN 978-1-880284-95-7

Murder in Burnt Orange
ISBN 978-1-56474-503-3

Janet Dawson
JERI HOWARD SERIES
Bit Player
Golden Nugget Award nominee
ISBN 978-1-56474-494-4

Cold Trail
ISBN 978-1-56474-555-2

Water Signs
ISBN 978-1-56474-586-6

What You Wish For
ISBN 978-1-56474-518-7

TRAIN SERIES
Death Rides the Zephyr
ISBN 978-1-56474-530-9

Death Deals a Hand
ISBN 978-1-56474-569-9

Kathy Lynn Emerson
LADY APPLETON SERIES
Face Down Below the Banqueting House
ISBN 978-1-880284-71-1

Face Down Beside St. Anne's Well
ISBN 978-1-880284-82-7

Face Down O'er the Border
ISBN 978-1-880284-91-9

Sara Hoskinson Frommer
JOAN SPENCER SERIES
Her Brother's Keeper
ISBN 978-1-56474-525-5

Hal Glatzer
KATY GREEN SERIES
Too Dead To Swing
ISBN 978-1-880284-53-7

A Fugue in Hell's Kitchen
ISBN 978-1-880284-70-4

The Last Full Measure
ISBN 978-1-880284-84-1

Margaret Grace
MINIATURE SERIES
Mix-up in Miniature
ISBN 978-1-56474-510-1

Madness in Miniature
ISBN 978-1-56474-543-9

Manhattan in Miniature
ISBN 978-1-56474-562-0

Matrimony in Miniature
ISBN 978-1-56474-575-0

Tony Hays
Shakespeare No More
ISBN 978-1-56474-566-8

Wendy Hornsby
MAGGIE MACGOWEN SERIES
In the Guise of Mercy
ISBN 978-1-56474-482-1

The Paramour's Daughter
ISBN 978-1-56474-496-8

The Hanging
ISBN 978-1-56474-526-2

The Color of Light
ISBN 978-1-56474-542-2

Disturbing the Dark
ISBN 978-1-56474-576-7

Janet LaPierre
PORT SILVA SERIES
Baby Mine
ISBN 978-1-880284-32-2

Keepers
Shamus Award nominee, Best Paperback Original
ISBN 978-1-880284-44-5

Death Duties
ISBN 978-1-880284-74-2

Family Business
ISBN 978-1-880284-85-8

Run a Crooked Mile
ISBN 978-1-880284-88-9

Hailey Lind
ART LOVER'S SERIES
Arsenic and Old Paint
ISBN 978-1-56474-490-6

Lev Raphael
NICK HOFFMAN SERIES
Tropic of Murder
ISBN 978-1-880284-68-1

Hot Rocks
ISBN 978-1-880284-83-4

Lora Roberts
BRIDGET MONTROSE SERIES
Another Fine Mess
ISBN 978-1-880284-54-4

SHERLOCK HOLMES SERIES
The Affair of the Incognito Tenant
ISBN 978-1-880284-67-4

Rebecca Rothenberg
BOTANICAL SERIES
The Tumbleweed Murders
(completed by Taffy Cannon)
ISBN 978-1-880284-43-8

Sheila Simonson
LATOUCHE COUNTY SERIES
Buffalo Bill's Defunct
WILLA Award, Best Softcover Fiction
ISBN 978-1-880284-96-4

An Old Chaos
ISBN 978-1-880284-99-5

Beyond Confusion
ISBN 978-1-56474-519-4

Call Down the Hawk (forthcoming)
ISBN 978-1-56474-597-2

Lea Wait
SHADOWS ANTIQUES SERIES
Shadows of a Down East Summer
ISBN 978-1-56474-497-5

Shadows on a Cape Cod Wedding
ISBN 1-978-56474-531-6

Shadows on a Maine Christmas
ISBN 978-1-56474-531-6

Shadows on a Morning in Maine
ISBN 978-1-56474-577-4

Eric Wright
JOE BARLEY SERIES
The Kidnapping of Rosie Dawn
Barry Award, Best Paperback Original. Edgar,
Ellis, and Anthony awards nominee
ISBN 978-1-880284-40-7

Nancy Means Wright
MARY WOLLSTONECRAFT SERIES
Midnight Fires
ISBN 978-1-56474-488-3

The Nightmare
ISBN 978-1-56474-509-5

REFERENCE/MYSTERY WRITING

Kathy Lynn Emerson
How To Write Killer Historical Mysteries: The Art and Adventure of Sleuthing Through the Past
Agatha Award, Best Nonfiction. Anthony and
Macavity awards nominee
ISBN 978-1-880284-92-6

Carolyn Wheat
How To Write Killer Fiction: The Funhouse of Mystery & the Roller Coaster of Suspense
ISBN 978-1-880284-62-9

**Available from your local bookstore
or from Perseverance Press/John Daniel & Company
(800) 662–8351 or www.danielpublishing.com/perseverance**